MJ Miller

The Christoph Curse

Port Washington Public Library
One Library Drive
Port Washington, NY 11050
(516) 883-4400

© Copyright 2019 MJ Miller

All rights reserved. This book or any portion thereof may not be reproduced or used in any manner whatsoever without the express written permission of the publisher except for the use of brief quotations in a book review. Thank you for respecting the work of this author.

This is a work of fiction. Names, characters, places, and incidents either are the products of the author's imagination or are used fictitiously. Any resemblance to actual persons, living or dead, businesses, companies, events, or locales is entirely coincidental.

ISBN: 9781085972604

Acknowledgements

As always, a big thank you to everyone who made this possible; Emily, for being my fabulous editor, Doug, my fabulous rock, Melissa for letting me vent, Maria for being the most awesome sounding board and to Val for cheering me on.

For Eric. 2 down, 98 to go.

Chapter 1

The young woman paused momentarily before grasping the large brass knocker. Taking a deep breath, she rapped the knocker against the massive oak entry door, several times, and waited, holding her breath.

She could hear slow, methodical footsteps approaching the door, and as she quickly tried to brush the stray curls off her face, the door slowly opened. It was silent, none of the expected creaks most of these old Victorian manors exhibited. She felt herself take a quick breath as she stared at the man holding the door, a quizzical look crossing his face.

He was tall, really tall, with broad shoulders and a trim waist. But it was his eyes that seemed to shoot beams right through her. Piercing blue, with long black curled lashes. His sun streaked brown hair was curly and long, almost shoulder length. Truthfully? He was by far the most stunning man she had ever seen.

"Yes?" he showed no expression as he waited for her to speak.

She stammered briefly. "I'm, um, I'm looking for Greg?" It really wasn't meant as a question but she was still somewhat stunned by this magnificent creature.

"Greg's gone. Something I can do for you?" The man replied impatiently.

"When will he be back?" she pressed on.

"He won't." The reply was terse.

It didn't deter her. "Well then tell me how I might reach him please," her voice became professional, business-like.

"I'm afraid that's not possible." The man's facial muscles were obviously tensing.

"Look, it's very important." She looked directly at the imposing figure and straightened to her full height of 5'2" which barely reached his shoulders.

"Why don't you come in and tell me what's so important." The man stepped back and waved an arm in the direction of the foyer.

Her eyes widened, and for just a moment, the man thought he sensed fear in them.

"I don't bite you know," he actually smiled as he said it. Something about her struck a chord within him, and he kind of wanted to see her relax, whoever she was.

Her reply was swift and came out in a rapid flurry of words.

"I don't know that. I don't even know who you are. If you'll just tell me how I can reach Greg, I'll be on my way."

The man tensed again. "You can't. Like I said, come in and we'll discuss whatever it is." He tried rather unsuccessfully to relax his posture.

"Look. Let's start over." He held out his hand. "I'm Greg's brother, Sam. And you are?" He waited, watching her expression. She was electrifying. Her long mass of red curls framed a delicate but lively face. Natural color blushed her cheeks, with just a hint of makeup around her bright green eyes to highlight them, but nothing more. She was like an ethereal creature standing there. And he felt there was more. Something inexplicable.

"Well?" Sam's eyebrows lifted in anticipation and a bit of exasperation.

"Sarah," she barely choked out the name as she stared back. Then looked down to see his outstretched hand. She knew she was supposed to do something. Take his hand. Yes. Shake hands. But she was frozen. Like that time in third grade when Mrs. Hammerschmidt told her to hold hands with Buddy Tramer, aka the spitter, on the class field trip. Everyone knew Buddy liked to pretend he was a baseball player and spit in his hands. Yeah, that's about how she felt right now. Logically she knew this perfect specimen did NOT spit in his hands, but still her hand simply would not move.

"Sarah. Would that be Sarah Smith? Sarah Jones?"

She looked back up at him, saw his mouth quirk and swore under her breath.

"Bennett," she breathed out on the name, trying to control her nerves. Whether it was because of his overwhelming presence or the sheer masculinity that seemed to ooze from this man, she didn't know. All she knew was that he took her breath away. And nobody took Sarah Bennett's breath away.

"There. That wasn't so hard, was it?" He withdrew his hand, realizing she'd never take it. "Why don't you come in," he said as he moved aside so she could step through the door.

Sarah hesitated only briefly, but seeing the firm determination on his face, she stepped into the foyer of the large house. He motioned her into the room off the entry, which appeared to be a study. It was beautifully appointed, she admitted silently. The built-in library casings, the cherry wood desk, antique globe, the large overstuffed leather chair and sofa set were all inviting and sophisticated. Not what she'd imagined would suit Greg, that was certain. She always thought his style was more The Jetsons meet the Kardashians.

Sam strode past her and headed to the wet bar on the other side of the room. Turning, he smiled briefly.

"What can I fix for you, Sarah Bennett?" he said her name with a slight mocking tone, which did the trick. Annoyed her enough to help her relax.

"Nothing. Or...water is fine."

"Water it is. Have a seat," he said, waving her toward the sofa. She walked over and nervously perched on the end of the sofa, as if ready to flee at any moment. Sam observed her with some amusement. She was very skittish, and he meant to find out why.

"So," Sam said lightly, handing her the water. "What's this all about?"

"It's a private matter," Sarah replied, "between Greg and me. Look, I'm sorry, I can't say anymore. It wouldn't be right." She tried for an apologetic tone.

"Well, I'm afraid whatever you have to say you'll have to say to me. You won't be speaking to Greg anytime soon." Sam's voice was firm, with a trace of anger, and Sarah wondered if maybe she should just bolt now. No. Stick it out, she thought.

"I have something for him." Sarah spoke quietly. It wasn't a lie. It was a form of the truth. She was becoming increasingly aware that this had been a monumentally bad idea. Possibly bordering on downright stupid she realized. She should have gone through an attorney.

"Well, then just give it to me." Sam smiled, but it seemed not to reach his eyes.

Sarah took a deep breath. She needed to get a grip and handle this with some measure of discretion.

"I'm afraid it's not that simple," her voice trailed off as she glanced away. Focusing on a paperweight on the desk, she tried to compose herself. OMG, she thought. There's a freaking spider in that paperweight. A tarantula. Who has a paperweight with a tarantula in it? She could feel her face flush, and knew she was beginning to panic. Her heart raced as she waited for him to say something. Why didn't he just laugh and tell her to come back when Greg was here? Why was he acting so weird? Creepy. What if those panels on the wall concealed more surprises? Hatchets or medieval swords.

"And why not?" he asked.

Even his voice sounded odd, dangerous even, she thought.

She glanced back at him and noticed the frustrated look on his face. Sarah realized this was going nowhere and quite possibly she was chatting away with a serial killer. She'd just leave the note for Greg she'd written in case he wasn't home and get the heck out of dodge. She'd go home, call an attorney and go from there. She jumped up suddenly.

"Tell you what. Since this doesn't involve you, I'll leave now, if you'd just give him this." She reached into her purse, pulled out an envelope and quickly handed it to Sam.

"Tell him to please call me." She turned quickly and hurriedly strode out, making a beeline for the front door. She raced down the steps and practically jumped into her car. Now all she had to do was pray it started. Not that it shouldn't, but she'd read enough novels and seen enough thrillers to know this is how it ends for the naive young woman who didn't plan ahead. Back in the real world, of course, her car did start and she raced out the long drive as fast as she could, not exhaling until she was safely back on the highway into town.

He didn't go after her. Instead, he twirled the envelope slowly around in his hand, as his gaze followed her through the window. A curious smile played on his lips as he watched her peal out the drive. Bundle of energy, that one was, he thought. Not his usual type of course. Sam was usually drawn to tall, elegant women. Patrician features, high cheekbones. Not fairy like creatures with fiery tempers. But damned if he wasn't drawn to her. Of course, obviously she was after Greg, not him, so it was pointless. He'd never wanted Greg's leftovers. Especially now. There was a time when he might have gone after her anyway. Before. But not ever again. All that was past. No more competition. No more rivalries. He shook his head, still amazed at himself for even opening the door to this creature. But the minute he'd seen her face pop up on one of the 12 monitors in the hall security bay, he had to. It was a mistake though. He knew better.

Looking down at the envelope, he shrugged and tore it open. Opening up the letter, he read through it, his face tensing as he did. He braced his shoulders, and lifted his head, looking into space. The letter drifted out of his hands, falling slowly to the floor. He stood there frozen. Of all the things Sam expected, this didn't come close. How he didn't see it coming he hadn't a clue. He'd assumed she was one of Greg's flighty ex-girlfriends and he was enjoying tormenting her. Partly out of some childhood jealousy he'd never gotten over. Greg had always been the girl magnet. Always. While Sam had a long history of one-hit wonders. Women always seemed eager to go out with him, but only once or twice. He couldn't seem to hold their interest. He was the guy women would crawl out the bathroom window to escape. Greg on the other hand had them eating out of his hands after 5 minutes. But that was then. And this was now.

He moved slowly, laboriously, over to the chair and sat, closing his eyes for just a moment. He read the letter over again. None of this could be true. It couldn't be happening. First losing Greg. That was unbearable. As different as they were, as much as they grated on each other, they loved each other. They were brothers after all. But this? He hung his head down and felt the wet tears as they flowed down his face.

Chapter 2

Sarah had barely made it into her apartment when her phone rang. Dropping the bag of groceries on the counter she grabbed it and spoke hurriedly.

"Yes? Hello?" Her greeting was breathless, and slightly nervous.

"Sarah?"

"Yes? Who's this?"

"Sam. Sam Livingston."

She swore softly.

"What was that? Never mind, we need to talk." His voice sounded gruff.

"No, actually, we don't. This doesn't concern you." She held her breath, nervous, hoping he hadn't opened that envelope, but of course knowing he did.

"Actually, it does. Very much," Sam replied.

Ignoring it she tried to switch gears. "How did you get my number, anyway?" She held her breath, still hoping that he hadn't read the letter.

"Not important," he said impatiently. "Look, let's not do this over the phone. Meet me for dinner, say 7 at O'Rourke's." It came out as an order, not a question and it set Sarah off. She was used to giving orders, not taking them.

"No can do, sorry. I mean, not tonight, at least not on such short notice." She meant it to come out firm and direct, but instead she felt like a rambling fool. What was wrong with her? Nerves. Just nerves. She couldn't mention Addy. If Sam hadn't opened the letter, he wouldn't know, and she'd just as well leave it at that. Though he must have. He had her phone number.

"Find a way. 7. In fact I'll pick you up." Sam's tone was becoming slightly dictatorial.

"No!" she yelled involuntarily and cringed at her mistake. That was not the right approach. Time for a change in tactics. She tried for a polite tone.

"What I mean is no thanks, I'll meet you there." Without waiting for a reply, she disconnected, and took a deep breath. That s.o.b! Who the hell did he think he was? Sam Livingston, that's who. Billionaire, gazillionaire, whatever. The man was infamous in Rockdale. Owned most of it. She'd only been back a few months, and even she'd heard about his exploits. Of course her sister Megan had told her plenty about the notorious Livingston brothers anyway. She smacked her forehead and rolled her eyes. How could she not have realized who Sam was? Who else would have answered the door? She was so flustered it hadn't even occurred to her. She must have come off looking like nothing but an idiot. Even so, if he thought he could push her around because of it he was dead wrong.

She took a deep breath and placed both hands on the counter to steady herself. She needed to be calm, cool, relaxed. She needed to be strong, for Addy. Oh geez she thought, Addy. She was already late picking her up. Grabbing her keys, she ran out the door and down the block to Mrs. Shaunnesy's house. Grace Shaunnesy was her lifesaver! Maybe she'd be free tonight and save her again.

*****

"Sweetie what's wrong? You look positively shaken." Grace's calming voice enveloped her as she drew her into her living room.

Sarah sighed. "Nothing. Everything, oh Grace I'm a mess."

"Well sit down, and I'll fetch you a drink. Then you can tell me what's happening, and we'll let Addy nap a while longer." Grace's voice was soothing, just the effect Sarah needed.

"Thanks, Grace. You're a peach." When Grace returned, she sat down next to her and patted her knee gently.

"OK. What's happened to put you in such a tizzy?" Grace smiled warmly, helping her to relax. Sarah gazed at her longingly. It was as if Grace had been brought into her life, not for Addy, but for herself. Sarah relayed her attempt to see Greg. By the time she finished, Grace had a strange look on her face.

"This brother of his. You like him." Grace smiled then. "It seems you'll have to go through him to get to Greg so maybe you need to use your business savvy, eh? Treat him as you would a potential takeover target. Isn't that what you call them?"

Sarah smiled. "Yes. That's right. And you are right as usual. Not about my liking him, just the way I should deal with him." Grace nodded but didn't comment further. Which unnerved Sarah.

"Grace, I do not like that man. He's arrogant, smug, condescending, pig-headed, rude and well, I think you get the picture."

"How about tall, dark, handsome, electrifying? Wouldn't that describe him as well?"

"Grace, really! Where do you get this stuff? He's nothing special, trust me."

"Mm hmm."

Sarah sighed in exasperation. There was no arguing with the woman. Admittedly, if she did she'd be lying anyway. Sam Livingston was all those things and more. And that was the real kicker.

*****

Sarah drew a deep breath as she paused outside the front of the restaurant. A well-known haunt for the upper crust, this was one of the few restaurants she hadn't been to yet, and she wished he'd chosen one of her regular spots. She could have had a little more control being on familiar turf. But even with little time to get ready, she knew the appropriate attire. She'd ended up choosing a black pencil skirt and an emerald silk blouse, classy enough for any venue or anyone with taste. Though right now she didn't care about impressing anyone, particularly Sam. What an arrogant bastard, she thought, as she shook her head in dismay. This was not going as planned.

All she wanted was to talk to Greg about Addy and see what he wanted to do. If he didn't want to raise her, he could give up any rights to clear the way for Sarah to adopt. It would be hard, financially, but Addy was her flesh and blood. Greg would help. Unless he refused for some reason to acknowledge Addy. But she knew he wouldn't. And he'd want to be a part of her life even if he wasn't cut out for parenthood.

Exhaling slowly, she headed up the few steps and pulled the heavy door open. It was dimly lit inside, and she blinked as she tried to adjust her eyes from the bright setting sun outside. The hostess approached her immediately and murmured quietly.

"Mr. Livingston is expecting you, if you want to follow me?"

So, Sarah thought, he'd either described her to the woman perfectly or was watching the door. She could just picture him sitting in a far corner, signaling as she entered.

She tried to relax as she headed towards the back, yup, just as she thought. A back-corner table neatly tucked out of view from the other dining patrons. Sam stood quickly and pulled out her chair. She sat down and placed her purse on the window ledge next to her. Always a smart move when you need a quick escape. A trick she'd mastered through her endless rounds of business lunches, something that was all in the past now, she thought ruefully.

She looked directly at Sam, her eyes challenging him to speak first.

"So, Sarah, let's cut to the chase." His voice was gruff and terse. "How much?"

Her eyes narrowed, and he could see fire in them. But she didn't speak.

"Well, how much?" Sam repeated the question.

Tilting her head, she bit back a nasty retort.

"How much?" she repeated quietly, her temper rising.

"Yes. How much?" Sam didn't blink, just stared at her stone-faced.

"I heard you the first time," Sarah replied bitingly. "But I haven't the foggiest idea what you're asking." They both knew she understood perfectly well what he was asking, what he was thinking.

"Perhaps you've made a mistake?" she asked, hoping to give him some benefit of a doubt. He couldn't be this much of a jerk.

"No mistake. I read your little letter." Sam waited, tapping his fingers on the table. Clearly he had a temper as well.

"Mr. Livingston," Sarah paused on the name for emphasis, "if you read the letter as you say, then you clearly understand what I want. Or should."

"Exactly right. I just don't know how much." His voice was dangerously low now, and Sarah was getting impatient.

"Look, Mr. Livingston," again she bit off the name for emphasis, "I don't feel like going around in circles with you. What I want," and she looked directly at him without flinching, "is for Greg to meet his daughter."

"Well that's just not going to happen," Sam replied angrily.

"It isn't your decision, it's Greg's."

Sarah's temper was full blown now, and her voice was raised.

"I don't care if you have more money than Midas, this is a child we're talking about, and how you try and control your brother's life is your business but Addy is mine."

"Look lady, I know this game." Sam smiled sardonically. "Just name the price, and then we'll get the blood drawn, and determine just how far you're willing to carry this little scheme of yours."

Enough. Without a word, Sarah stood abruptly, grabbing her purse as she slid her chair back. Her eyes blazed as she looked pointedly at him.

"If you'll excuse me, I have other things to do, which are slightly more important than being insulted by you." Sarah was back in control. Her voice was now dangerously quiet, not intending to make a scene, but definitely needing to make a point. "Addy is a living breathing beautiful baby girl who deserves every ounce of love Greg and I have to give her. I know Greg's feelings on kids. I know he'll gladly get involved as best he can. Personally, Mr. Livingston, not financially." She paused and took a calming breath before continuing. She was far from finished with her speech.

"It's not money Addy needs, it's her father. If I have to work three jobs to see she's cared for, you can bet I will. And it still wouldn't stop me from having Greg be a part of her life. I feel sorry for you, you know. Because she's your niece and you've just made it clear you don't want and will never know the joy of that relationship. But I will find Greg with or without your help. You can't keep this from him forever nor should you. He deserves to know. What kind of brother are you anyway? You should be ashamed."

With that, she swung around and walked toward the exit, thankful she'd worn flats and wasn't going to trip and do a face-plant, afraid to look back, afraid to let him see how much he'd rattled her. The nerve of that bastard. Suddenly she felt a hand on her shoulder, stopping her in her tracks.

"Wait. Please. I'm sorry."

She didn't turn around, though his voice was husky now, not brittle or harsh.

"Sarah?" It was a plea now, and she couldn't resist. She looked over her shoulder and up at his face. His muscles were taut, strained. Oh no, she thought. He'd get no sympathy from her. She knew if she didn't leave now, there would be a scene in the restaurant. And Sarah was never one that cared

14

for that, so she slowly raised her arm, and taking his hand removed it from her shoulder gently.

"I'm sorry too, Mr. Livingston, more than you'll ever know."

And with that she walked out the door, down the steps and handed the ticket to the valet for her car. She didn't look back. Her eyes had welled with tears, but she wasn't going to let him see that. She knew he was standing there watching her. When I find Greg, if he doesn't want her, she'll be mine and Mr. Sam Livingston will be out of the picture, she thought. Good God, he was Addy's uncle and all he cared about was money. No matter what, Sarah vowed, that man would never be involved in Addy's life. Never.

Chapter 3

Sam paced back and forth behind his desk, periodically glancing over at his attorney.

"Well? What did you find out?" Sam asked gruffly. It had been a week since that fateful meeting with Sarah.

Bill Abbott looked over at his client, shaking his head slowly.

"Sam, you're going to have to calm down. Now sit." Sam didn't move. "I said sit, Sam, now." Sam grudgingly obeyed. Bill was about the only person he knew who would speak to him like that and get away with it.

"First off, here's the birth certificate." Bill laid it on the desk and waited while Sam looked it over.

"Adelaide." Sam paused. "Our mother would have loved that."

He crinkled his brows in confusion then.

"Wait, this says the mother's name is Megan Wiley. This woman's name was Sarah Bennett." Sam looked up at Bill and narrowed his eyes triumphantly.

"I told you it was money, didn't I? All we have to do is find this Megan Wiley." Sam looked smug, though his eyes betrayed a tinge of disappointment. He really hadn't wanted Sarah to be a schemer. A part of him wanted for it all to be true. Yet not true because he didn't want to feel anything for one of Greg's women.

"Not so fast Sam. Megan's gone too."

"What do you mean gone. She took off and left the baby? What kind of woman was Greg hooked up with anyway?" Sam shook his head in disbelief. Bill crossed over to the desk and handed Sam another paper.

"A remarkable one, Sam," Bill's voice was subdued, and filled with emotion. "But by gone, I mean she died too." Sam took a sharp breath as he looked down and saw the evidence for himself. Greg's baby daughter was now an orphan.

"Dear lord," he whispered. "What happened to her?"

"Died during childbirth, hemorrhaged out. It happens, even today."

"Why didn't Sarah's note to Greg mention that? Why didn't she say it was Megan's baby? She made it sound like it was hers. What was I supposed to think?"

"Christ Sam, you don't tell a man his pregnant girlfriend died giving birth in a letter!" Bill was shocked that his longtime client could be so insensitive.

"I guess you're right," Sam replied, genuine remorse in his voice. "Sorry. I suppose she wanted to let him know in person. That's why she was so adamant about speaking to him. Who is she in all this anyway?"

"Megan's sister."

"Different last names?" Sam was curious. Greg didn't usually go for married women, or maybe Sarah was the married one.

"Megan was an actress. Wiley was her professional name."

Bill continued on. "Here's a copy of the will, bestowing guardianship onto Greg in case of Megan's death."

"But Greg died 3 months before Adelaide, Addy, was born."

"She didn't know Greg was dead, Sam. She must have figured he'd taken off for good, that's my best guess. I didn't know where Megan was. Didn't even know she was pregnant. We saw her with Greg quite a bit but didn't know how to locate her."

"Shit." Sam didn't usually swear, but sometimes the occasion called for it. Sam looked up at Bill....the hurt evident in his eyes.

"Do you think he knew, Bill? Would she have told him?"

"I don't know. I would think so. Sarah might know, if you can get her to talk to you again." Bill shook his head, wondering how Sam was going to handle all this.

"What now?" Sam spoke quietly.

"She's your niece Sam, but she's Sarah's niece too. You'll have to work this out."

Sam drew in a deep breath and looked at Bill with raw emotion on his face. "I'll raise her. I can give her everything. She'll have anything she needs. I owe Greg that much. She needs me."

Bill waited a moment before answering. "I'm no family law expert, Sam, and we'll need one for this. It's a tricky business. You just can't go take the baby from her aunt."

"I'm her uncle."

"Look, your brother seemingly abandoned his pregnant girlfriend and the will is also quite specific as to what should happen in the event that both parents are deceased. The mother's wishes are clear, her sister gets guardianship. If you want Addy, you'll probably have to prove Sarah is unfit. Are you willing to do that?"

"I don't know." He really wasn't so sure how far he'd go. There was something about Sarah that pricked at his conscience. Sam Livingston was considered by most who knew him as a cold, calculating businessman. It's a perception he'd fostered over the years. He'd needed to in order to keep everyone at arm's length. And though Bill in fact had an inkling of the real Sam, he never let on. He knew Sam had good reasons for it, and accepted it. Played along with it.

Sam cleared his throat. "What's to prove, Bill?" He continued. "I already know enough. She lives in a cramped, one-bedroom apartment in a low-income area, works all day and can't care for Addy herself. Whereas I can provide all Addy needs right here."

Bill looked curiously at Sam. "Where did you find all this out? I thought I was looking into this for you?" Bill knew however that Sam would never fully delegate anything. He always had to be involved.

"I did some checking myself. Went by her apartment, chatted with neighbors, I have my ways, Bill." Sam's voice held a tinge of sarcasm.

"Wouldn't it be better for all concerned if you shared custody?" Bill looked pointedly at Sam. Hoping he'd take the hint.

"Ha!" Sam laughed ruefully. "She'll never agree since she thinks I'm the devil incarnate. And it would involve Sarah too much in my life. It's out of the question."

"What you're suggesting would certainly involve Addy in your life as well, can you handle that? Maybe it would be better just to go for visitation. See if there isn't a peaceful way to ensure Addy's welfare is put first, eh?" Bill pressed on, hoping to get Sam to see reason.

"Sorry Bill. You're right. You're a father, so you know these things. I have no experience there. But she's my niece and I'll do everything for her I can. Understood?" Sam made it clear his statement was not to be questioned.

"Understood, Sam. But first I want you to try and make amends with Sarah. I'll set up a meeting for tomorrow morning. 9am, my office. So try and act more human this time, eh? Relax!" Bill shook his head and smiled. The last thing Sam Livingston would do is relax.

"Easy for you to say. And what makes you think I didn't act human?" Sam's voice was petulant.

"Because you went over the scene in great detail and you obviously not only insulted her but probably did irreparable harm." Bill was chastising him and he knew it.

"OK Bill. Be human. Relax. I can do that." Sam looked at his old friend, his eyes betraying his emotion, knowing full well everything in his life was about to be turned upside down.

Chapter 4

Sarah heard the phone just as she turned the key to unlock her door. Baby carrier with Addy sleeping peacefully in one hand, grocery bag in the other, her fingers struggled to remove the key quickly. It was a precarious balancing act but one she was slowly becoming used to. Pulling the key out, she leaned her head down and grabbed it between her teeth while she turned the knob and pushed the door open. Depositing the groceries and the baby on the table, in the middle where there was no danger of the carrier falling off, she grabbed her phone from her purse.

"Hello?"

"Is this Sarah Jane Bennett?" Oh lord, not again. Since they had to ask and used her middle name, obviously a telemarketer.

"No, it's the psychic hotline and I sense you're about to be disconnected." She hung up and turned to release Addy from the carrier.

"Gotta start blocking those calls," she muttered quietly. She lifted Addy gently so as not to wake her.

Laying the sleeping infant against her shoulder, she strode into the bedroom and placed her in the crib next to her bed. She paused to watch her for a moment. She was precious and beautiful and all that was left of her sister. And she was determined to be the best mother to her she could be. She may not have been ready for it, or wished for it, but it was so. And at 27, she was surely able to take this on. It had meant giving up her career, at least for now, but sometimes life has other plans for you, and you play the hand you're dealt.

She heard her phone ring again. Checking one last time to make sure the rails of the crib were locked in the up position; she went to answer it.

"Listen, buddy" this time she was more abrupt, as it was the same number on the caller ID.

"Ms. Bennett this is Bill Abbott, I'm Greg Livingston's Attorney. Do you have a minute?"

"Oh! Mr. Abbott! I sense I've made an error, eh?" Sarah laughed, hoping to break any tension. "I didn't recognize the number and seems lately all I get are telemarketers and robocalls!"

"Totally get it," Bill chuckled, "no harm done."

"Have you spoken to Greg, Mr. Abbott? I'm assuming that's why you're calling. Though I can't understand why he hasn't called me himself." She kept talking, not waiting for a response. "He has my number and I can't believe he hasn't tried to contact Megan in all this time. Sorry, I guess that's really not your concern, is it? I take it you've seen my letter?" Sarah had been so glad to get the call, she was rambling. "Sorry, I guess we should start again. I'm just so relieved you called."

"Quite all right," Bill replied, thinking he was out of breath just listening to her. "Yes, I have seen the letter. And, as any good lawyer does, I did a little checking of my own, I hope you don't mind. Megan, Megan Wiley, was your sister, is that right?"

"Yes."

"Well, there are some things we need to talk about then. I wonder if you could come by my office tomorrow, say 9am?"

"Oh, I'm afraid not, Mr. Abbott," Sarah replied regretfully.

"Bill"

"OK Bill. I have to work at 7 am and I don't finish till 3, can we do it then?"

"I really don't think we should wait that long, so how about I come by your place and we can talk tonight. It's really quite important."

"I suppose, we'll have to be quiet though, as the baby's asleep, hopefully for the night." Sarah sighed. She didn't know if this was a good idea or not, she could only hope that if Greg trusted him, she could too. Greg must still be overseas, she thought.

"I've got four of my own, Sarah, I understand."

Sarah breathed a sigh of relief. "Good...maybe you can give me some advice? I'm kind of at a loss right now." Keep it friendly she thought.

"No problem. I'll bring some reinforcements with me."

"Reinforcements?" The worry in her voice gave her away.

"Don't worry, not Sam, my wife. She's the poster girl for maternity!"

Sarah chuckled.

"You must have spoken to Sam, huh? Don't believe a word he says. But definitely bring your wife. It would be a godsend Bill; shall we say in an hour?" That would give her plenty of time to straighten things up and compose herself.

"Sounds great." He read off the address to make sure he had it right, and she hung up feeling a little better. Bill Abbott had a relaxed manner about him, and she was sure he would be easier to deal with than that idiot brother of Greg's. Not that she really thought he was an idiot, maybe just an arrogant authoritarian wanna be king. And in her previous life she turned guys like that into shark bait. She still didn't understand what the deal was with Greg. This wasn't like him at all. He may have been a carefree sort, not the settling down type. But he wasn't heartless. He loved Megan, that much Sarah knew. Why he had stayed away was just a mystery. Even if he didn't know Megan was pregnant when he left, which he did, he would have called when he got back. She'd certainly left enough messages for him.

She checked on Addy once more, before heading into the bathroom to freshen up. She didn't want to look frazzled or worn out. She knew she needed to have an image of confidence about her. Sarah was determined to ensure Addy was taken care of. One way or another.

When the doorbell rang, Sarah jumped. She'd become so lost in thought while putting on a pot of coffee she'd almost forgotten why she was doing it. She was startled even more when she opened the door and saw the couple standing there. They looked almost like a matched set. Barbie and Ken. Both mid-forties, attractive, almost the same height, and both wore a warm, genuine smile. Could have walked straight off the cover of a magazine.

Sarah smiled back, reflexively. "Hi. I'm Sarah. Come in, won't you?"

They stepped inside, as Bill introduced himself and his wife, Carol.

"Please, sit." Sarah motioned to the chairs at the kitchen table. "Can I get you some coffee?"

Carol smiled softly. "That would be lovely, thank you."

"I'm sorry about the accommodations. I don't have a living room per se, so the kitchen is really the only place to sit." Sarah sighed, looking about, thinking of her old place. The third floor of a Victorian manor house just outside New York City. It had been an elegant, rather expensive home she'd moved into only a year and a half ago. Much like the Livingston brothers' home she mused. Her dream apartment. She'd been on the fast-track once upon a time. But that was then, and this is now.

She took the chair on the opposite end of the table. Slowly sipping her coffee, she looked up at the pair.

"I don't mean to be blunt, and I appreciate your being here, but I have to know. Where is Greg? Have you spoken to him?" Carol leaned across the table and gently laid her hand over Sarah's.

"Sarah, how well did you know Greg?"

"Not as well as Megan did," Sarah smiled softly, "but well enough. We often did things together. I love to cook, Megan didn't. So they came over for dinner quite often. But I'm pretty sure Greg knows his way around a kitchen as well. I think I was being taken advantage of!" Sarah actually laughed at that. She paused and looked at Bill curiously. "I don't understand what's happened, he was due back long before Addy was born and I'm positive Megan told him about the baby before he left. She swore she did, and he said he'd be back."

THE CHRISTOPH CURSE

She swung her glance from Bill to Carol and stiffened suddenly. It was plain to see that something was terribly, awfully wrong. She closed her eyes, and when she opened them, she felt tears forming.

"Please. You asked if I knew him, didn't you? Not if I know him. Something awful has happened. I can see it on your faces."

Bill spoke first. "There was an avalanche...." he paused. "Greg didn't make it, Sarah. I'm sorry, we both are."

The tears were streaming down her face, unchecked. First Megan, now Greg. A man so full of life and love he actually captured Megan's heart, and hers, and he was gone. Addy's father was dead.

"We loved him dearly and I can see that in your own way you cared for him too," Carol said softly.

Sarah was stunned, but something was nagging at her. Something wasn't adding up.

"I'm sorry," she said quietly. "But I feel like I would have read about that or at least heard about it. A man like that doesn't just, well, die young, with no news? He was a Livingston after all. Again, not meaning to be rude, but it simply doesn't make sense."

Bill and Carol looked at each other, then back at Sarah.

"You're right of course, normally it would have been big news," Bill replied. "The family chose to keep it private, however. For a variety of reasons."

Sarah nodded, accepting their excuse for the time being, but not totally buying it.

"What now?" she whispered softly. "What do I do now?"

"You take care of Addy." Bill's voice was soft, but firm.

"And we'll be here to help." Carol's voice was just as firm. "Greg was like a brother to us and Addy will be like our niece as well." Her words gave Sarah a bit of comfort. Suddenly Sarah's eyes widened, as the realization that there was someone else involved dawned on her.

"And what about Sam?" Sarah almost choked on his name.

Bill chuckled softly. "I'm sorry about that Sarah. I can't even begin to imagine how he reacted to you. But knowing Sam, you'll not easily forget. He can be, well, let's just say he can be tactless. But he means well."

"He treated me like some money hungry scheming bitch, Bill." Sarah almost smiled at that.

"Yes, well, he had no idea about your sister."

"I'm sorry but seriously, Megan and Greg were together for 3 years, how could he not know? And again, not to be rude, but how did you not know?" There was no malice in her question, just curiosity. "I can't believe Greg never mentioned Megan."

"Actually, Carol and I did know your sister. But Greg and Sam shared a house, Sarah, not their lives. Greg was always off on an adventure. Sam had wanted Greg to settle down for years. After a while, they just stopped sharing their personal lives." Bill's tone was apologetic.

Carol interjected. "Greg made us promise not to tell Sam. He was afraid that Sam would try and buy her off. Ridiculous of course. Sam wanted nothing more than to see Greg happy with someone special. But we kept our word."

"We didn't know how to reach Megan," Bill added. "Her phone number was unlisted and we had no way of finding her. We checked with the Actors Guild and they wouldn't release the information. Seems many of her records were under Megan Bennett, so we simply couldn't locate her. Sam didn't learn about Megan till I met with him this morning. He called me last week about the situation and asked me to look into it. Since the letter you wrote didn't mention Megan's name, it took me awhile to get the facts straight. Especially since Greg and Megan had been together for so long. I was a little startled myself thinking there was another woman." Bill smiled ruefully at that. "When I realized it was Megan, and that she'd died, it nearly broke my heart. We'd gotten together quite a few times, you know."

"So I guess it's my fault Sam assumed the worst," Sarah realized aloud. "I didn't think to put Megan's name in the letter. I assumed Greg would know who I was talking about."

"Of course he would, it's not your fault. Sam just jumped to conclusions," Bill smiled curiously as he spoke. "Actually that's quite uncharacteristic of him. He's usually much more cautious than that."

"I liked your sister," Carol interrupted, wanting to redirect the conversation. "She was so full of life! Like Greg, she seemed to radiate sunshine. I see a lot of her in you, you know."

"Thank you for saying that," Sarah replied with a sad smile. "I adored her. She was everything I'm not, but mostly just a fabulous sister, and the only family I had left."

"Until now." Carol spoke with a warning in her voice. Not sinister, just a reminder.

"Addy."

"Yes. Addy."

"So, are there papers I need to sign? What happens now?" Sarah was trying to summon up strength and barely succeeding. She had prepared herself for every eventuality. Except this one. She needed to take a firm hold on everything or she'd fall apart, that was clear.

"There's only one thing I can think of. I'm sure Bill will agree and that's to please let us see that darling baby." Carol smiled warmly at Sarah, hoping to get one in return. She wasn't disappointed.

Sarah hopped up. "Oh I'm sorry, of course you want to see her. Follow me." She led them down the hall, tiptoeing on her approach.

She stopped at the open doorway, pausing to gaze over at Addy, sleeping like an angel, she thought as she smiled. She turned and nodded to Bill and Carol to enter the room. They were quiet as mice, she noticed, not uttering a sound. But as she followed them to the crib and stood beside them, she noticed their faces held expressions of tenderness, awe, and complete joy. She liked these people, she thought, very much. They would be good in Addy's life. And lord knows she needed a helping hand right now.

They watched Addy for several minutes, then quietly exited the room. Back in the kitchen, Bill turned to Sarah and smiled. "Don't worry, it'll work out. Remember, Carol and I are here to help. That's one special little person in there, and you can bet we'll be here to see you both make it."

"Thanks." Sarah smiled back.

"Bill, I think it's time we let Sarah get some sleep." Turning to Sarah, she spoke warmly. "I understand you have to be up early for work, so we don't want to keep you." They both gave Sarah a quick hug before leaving. Suddenly the small apartment felt warmer, and somehow cheerier. As if Sarah were no longer alone in the world, caring for a new life that hadn't been intended for her. Or maybe in the big scheme of things, it had.

*****

Sam had been pacing back and forth in his study for what seemed like an eternity. Ever since Bill called to tell him he was going over to see Sarah. When the phone finally rang around 10pm, he glanced at the caller ID and grabbed it on the first ring, launching in without saying hello.

"Did you see her?" His impatience was evident.

"Yes, we did. Carol came along too. She's an absolute angel, Sam. I think I'm in love."

"That's great, but I'm talking about Addy, my niece? Remember her?"

Bill laughed out loud. "I was talking about Addy, Sam."

"Oh. Well of course. So fill me in." Sam's tone was brusque, mostly because he'd never been so embarrassed. If he knew Bill, he'd never hear the end of it. Bill relayed the conversation, or most of it, leaving out Sarah's comments about Sam.

"Look Sam, I think you need to get together with Sarah and smooth things over." Bill tried to sound business-like, but secretly he was thinking that he'd like to be there to watch the sparks fly, and fly they would.

"OK, I'll find some time, I'll take care of it." Sam's voice held his usual air of authority, so Bill was quick to snuff it out.

"Sam, Sarah isn't what you're used to. And she's grieving just like you are. So tread carefully." He hung up, not waiting for Sam to reply. This was going to be a dicey situation; professionally, personally and legally. Establishing some boundaries for Sam now would be critical.

Chapter 5

The morning rush had finally subsided, and Sarah took a moment to relax behind the counter, leaning against the large, cold beverage case. She closed her eyes for a moment, savoring the aromas floating around. They ground their coffees fresh daily, and the blend of the different varieties helped to create, in Sarah's mind, the perfect atmosphere. They served coffee, cold drinks and baked goods delivered daily by a nearby bakery. It wasn't a difficult job to handle the morning crowd, as they grabbed their coffee and danish on the way to work. It wasn't that long ago she had been one of them. Ambitious, young, racing through life trying to climb an invisible ladder that seemed precariously slippery most of the time. Rockdale wasn't a large city, but just 20 miles from New York, it had seen a surge in population with the influx of tech businesses looking to relocate out of New York. Her eyes still closed, she took a deep breath and tried to relax. The shop was empty except for the owner, Karen, in the back. There was a bell on the door to signal a customer, so Sarah could relax until she heard it. She enjoyed these quiet moments. It seemed lately they were few and far between.

"Tempting."

Oh no! Sarah cringed. She knew that mocking voice. It sent shivers through her. Opening one eye confirmed her suspicion. And her worst nightmare come true. She closed her eye and slumped slightly. She was wearing one of the new t-shirts Karen had ordered thinking it could bring some extra sales. A simple white t-shirt, but across the chest, in big letters, it read 'ENJOY'. Of course the back featured a steaming mug of coffee. But the front was quite clear, positioning the word just across her breasts. It was supposed to be funny. And most of the customers treated it that way. But with Sam Livingston standing there on the other side of the counter staring at her chest, it was mortifying.

Taking a breath, she opened her eyes and straightened up. Looking him in the eye, she set her chin firmly upward.

"What do you want?"

"You." It slipped out before he could catch himself. "What I mean is your time." He tried, and failed to regroup. "I… I need to talk... to you." He stammered a bit, and Sam Livingston never stammered. Absolutely never.

"So talk," she tried to keep her tone civil, but it was hard. He stood there, legs apart, hands on his hips, glaring at her with a fierceness that unnerved her. She tried to stare him back down but something about his stance was making it difficult. She'd gone head to head with some of the toughest business adversaries in the country. But Sam Livingston made them seem like rookies.

"Not here." His tone was terse, and firm.

"Then it'll have to wait. If you'll excuse me I've got things to do." She tried to act nonchalant.

"Fine. What time do you finish here?" He in turn tried to put a friendly spin on it, but it wasn't working.

"3, but I've got things to do then," she replied with the same forced friendliness.

"I'll be back then. I'll tag along" Sam bantered back.

"I don't think so."

"I do."

"Tough"

"Yeah, it is."

They glared at each other silently. Suddenly Sam turned and briskly walked out. Sarah stared at his retreating back, dumbfounded. Nice butt. The thought just popped into her head. She shook her head and her eyes widened. It was just beginning to dawn on her why she couldn't control herself around Sam Livingston. He was so rugged. And so damn good looking. And she was experiencing a sensation she hadn't had in a long time. Well she'd have to get over that real fast she thought. He was an arrogant s.o.b and she had no intention of letting her defenses down. She had to think of Addy first. And last. No room for anything else right now.

"Who was that?" Karen's voice interrupted her thoughts, and Sarah could sense immediately that Sam had affected her friend as well.

"That, Karen, is Sam Livingston."

"Oh shit, the brother? That's the brother from hell?" Karen shook her head, chuckling. She was a few years older than Sarah, and opposite in every way. Karen was tall and striking with a personality to match. Brash, loud, no nonsense and with a heart of gold.

Sarah had kept Karen in the loop as to what had been happening. And Karen had empathized with her, while helping her keep perspective as well. No pity from that corner.

"Yep. The monster himself." Sarah grimaced.

"Well lordy lordy, he is something, isn't he? Maybe you don't dislike him as much as you think. You know what they say? A thin line between..."

"Don't go there, Karen, don't even think it. He's evil and arrogant and mean and I hate him!"

"Uh huh."

"I mean it!" Sarah knew she sounded unconvincing.

"Sure ya do, sweetie but you could have a little fun and still hate him. I mean can you imagine him in bed?"

"I said don't go there. I don't want to imagine that man within 10 feet of me, let alone in my bed!"

"Uh huh." Karen smiled and started to whistle as she walked toward the counter. Sarah frowned, frustrated. Karen had hit a nerve. She was most definitely attracted to Sam and that was a seriously bad thing. She just had to keep reminding herself of that. But now that Karen had planted that seed in her brain, the idea of Sam, and her, she couldn't shake it. It probably would be spectacular. Sarah knew she was headed for trouble this time and had no idea how to prevent it.

The day seemed to drag on after that. She kept eyeing the clock, dreading the 3 o'clock hour when she was sure he'd show up again. Her stomach was doing somersaults and she couldn't concentrate.

At 3 o'clock there was no sign of him, and breathing a sigh of relief, or was it disappointment, she grabbed her purse and called out goodbye to Karen and practically ran out the door. If he was running late, she could escape before he arrived. If she wanted to.

She hit the sidewalk at a light jog and headed for Grace's. It was just around the corner and up the block which made everything easier. She'd pick up Addy and head over to the apartment, again just a few blocks from Grace. Megan had been anticipating needing a sitter and had interviewed her beforehand. She'd wanted everything set up in advance. When Sarah had brought Addy home she'd immediately contacted Grace and made sure she would be available.

When Megan died, everything was in such chaos. Sarah had Grace take care of Addy while she worked, but the commute was too much so she moved to Megan's place. When her job became too much, she downsized her life. Instead of 16-hour days power-brokering and networking, she had 8-hour days pouring coffee and the rest taking care of Addy. The work wasn't challenging, and certainly not lucrative, but she actually enjoyed it. They had a regular midday crowd, and Sarah was naturally social and friendly. She chatted with them, played chess with them, even doled out advice. She wouldn't get rich this way, but life actually had a more pleasant aspect now. She'd put a pretty good portfolio together over the last few years, so money wasn't a huge issue for her. She would have to be careful, but there was plenty to provide for Addy.

As she rounded the corner, a private limo pulled up slowly by the curb. It made her nervous, and she glanced over trying to look casual as she picked up her pace. It seemed to be following her, but the windows were tinted so a brief glance didn't help her identify the occupants. She turned back to look several times, trying to discern what she could. She realized it must be Sam. *Coward.* Approaching Grace's building, she took the steps up two at a time and yanked open the outer door. Grace had given her the key, so she didn't have to buzz. Sarah glanced behind her to make sure no one followed. No one meaning Sam of course. Coast clear, she breathed easier and went inside.

Grace opened the door on the first knock, almost as if she sensed Sarah's arrival. Grace had a habit of doing that. Sarah didn't really believe in things like a sixth sense, but Grace definitely had something. That's what Megan really loved about her. Megan was the creative one in the family. Well, at least she was the one who pursued her creative side. After their parents died, Megan had been 18, Sarah 14, Megan had taken care of her. Foregoing college, which she said was a waste, she went into modeling, and slowly got into acting with bit parts in local off off Broadway plays. With a few commercials, she made a decent living. Enough to support them both. She didn't touch any of the life insurance money from their folks. Instead, Megan used it to help Sarah with her expenses at Harvard. She had what was called a free ride, but there were still expenses… books, transportation, a little pocket money as well. Megan took care of Sarah, and she would now take care of Addy. Pay it forward. Though Sarah recognized from the beginning that Addy was a gift, not an obligation. Perhaps Megan had felt that too.

"Hi Grace" Sarah was breathless from running.

"Sit down, child, and rest here." Her voice sounded concerned.

"What's wrong?" Sarah eyed her curiously.

"I don't know. I just know you need to stay right here for a moment." She frowned and wrinkled her brow, as if trying to remember something.

"Grace, what is it? Do you see something?" She was uncomfortable talking about Grace's unique ability, to sense things, and this only piled on the anxiety since it appeared to involve her. Especially since she was already nervous about the limo. She wouldn't say anything to Grace though, she really didn't want confirmation that it was following her.

"No, Sarah, it's not like that. I just have a feeling, that's all."

"All right. I'll stay for a little while but only if I can have one of those cookies I smell. And don't try to tell me I don't smell cookies." Sarah smiled, hoping to get Grace to relax and forget about whatever she sensed.

"Cookies and milk coming up." Grace crossed the room to where Addy lay in the portable crib, looking snug and content. Picking her up, she let Addy fuss for a moment, then placed her in Sarah's arms, where she quieted down and snuggled her little head against Sarah's chest.

In a flash, Sarah's eyes were closed.

She felt a gentle tap on her shoulder, and suddenly realized she'd fallen asleep. She shook her head, trying to wake up, and upon opening her eyes, realized she was still holding Addy. Carefully shifting her position so Addy could lay comfortably on her shoulder, she smiled softly at Grace, somewhat melancholy. She realized she had to tell her about Greg.

"Grace, I have news about Addy's father. It isn't good." Sarah paused and took a deep breath. She hadn't yet come to terms with it, so it was hard to say out loud.

Sarah's voice shook and the words seem to fall out of her mouth in a rush.

"He was killed in an Avalanche before she was even born."

"Oh my goodness!" Grace placed her hand over her heart as if to steady herself. "I can't tell you how sorry I am to hear that. Such a shame for the little one. And you as well. How are you holding up? Quite a shock I imagine."

"I don't think it's quite sunk in I suppose. I sometimes wonder though, how much do you think one person is supposed to bear in this life? I'm not complaining Grace, but I think I'm done taking my share of misfortune. Perhaps I'm cursed."

"Hush now, there's no such thing. You know we're taught that we only get as much as we can handle, though I do agree you've had more than your share for now." Grace smiled gently at Sarah, knowing somehow that there was probably a whole lot more for her to face.

"I suppose I better get Addy home now, and I'm sure you've things to do. I'm sorry for falling asleep like that. I don't usually do that you know," she smiled sheepishly.

"It's fine dear, you've had some upheavals and your body is just reacting. Go get some sleep and I'll see you tomorrow." With that she took Addy and placed her in the carrier, ushered the two of them to the door and watched as they headed down the hall. Turning back inside, she frowned again.

Something was wrong. Something was going to happen. It wasn't clear. She'd have to work on it.

Chapter 6

It was getting dark out, so Sarah walked home quickly with Addy. She knew the neighborhood well and was on a wave-as-you-passed-by level with many of the residents who sat on porch stoops around dinnertime. Though she felt pretty safe, she knew better than to relax her guard. As she rounded the corner, she saw him, sitting awkwardly on her front steps. Even in the dusk she could sense he was out of place. He sat with his back straight, almost uncomfortably, instead of the relaxed slouch typical of her neighbors. She paused for a moment, debating whether or not to turn back around and wait until he'd left. But she had a hunch he'd sit there all night if need be. Sighing, she continued toward her building, her strides becoming brisk as she tensed up, awaiting the inevitable battle ahead.

He stood as she approached, staring at her intently. Damn him! She suddenly felt naked, as if he were reading her thoughts and knew her next move before she made it. This was how her clients' targets must feel when she faced them off during a major deal. She always felt a sense of guilt when she'd successfully targeted a company for acquisition. This time the shoe was on the other foot and she wasn't sure she could handle it.

"Evening," his voice was husky and sensual, though definitely a trace of sarcasm in it.

"Sam," she nodded as she tried to head past him toward the door. He was quick to block her, his eyes flashing as he stared at the carrier. Sarah suddenly realized she was out of options now. She also felt a pang of sympathy. Looking back and forth between Addy and Sam, she knew how selfish and petty she was being, and that simply wasn't her nature. He was her uncle, and hadn't even seen her. So, taking a deep breath, she gently touched his arm to get his attention which had been locked onto Addy.

"Come in," she said softly, "and meet your niece." He stepped aside awkwardly to let her pass then followed close behind. Neither spoke as they headed into her apartment. But she knew he was right there on her heels. As she unlocked the door to go inside, he practically stepped in on top of her, making her jump.

"Sorry," he murmured. She quickly moved forward and placed the carrier on the table and paused for a moment. Sam stopped at the doorway and hadn't moved further. She turned to look at him and saw for the first time the raw emotion on his face. Lord he was terrified. She smiled at him, meaning to comfort him. "Don't worry, she doesn't bite!" He smiled back.

"Unlike her uncle," his retort broadened her smile. So there was a sense of humor in there somewhere, maybe there was hope for him yet.

"Come over here," she whispered quietly. "And try not to wake her."

Sam walked over to the table and tilted his head to the side as he gazed at the sleeping baby. She was perfect. Gentle blond curls wisped off her head, and her long black lashes were definitely Livingston genes through and through. Her soft features looked angelic as she dozed, a small smile playing on her face.

"Look, she's smiling." He sounded amazed. Sarah chuckled and shook her head.

"Gas."

"Gas?" Sam wrinkled his forehead in confusion.

"Yes, gas. They don't actually smile till they're about 10 weeks or so. She's only 8 weeks old."

Sam grinned. "Yeah, well she's a Livingston and that makes her an overachiever. That's a smile."

Sarah sighed. "OK Uncle Sam, she's smiling, just for you. Feel better?"

"Yep. Can I, um..." damn he was stammering again. "Can I hold her?"

Sarah paused to consider, looking at Sam.

"Can you handle it?"

"I'm sure I'll manage," he said with a slight smirk.

"Alright then, hang on." She gently reached in and lifted Addy up as smoothly as she could, careful not to wake her. "OK," she whispered. "Now hold out your arms in front of you."

Sam held his arms straight out in front of himself.

"No, bend your elbows a bit," she said with just a hint of exasperation. "Haven't you ever held a baby?"

"Well, um no..."

"Hold them out like someone is handing you a big box, yes…that's it," she grinned as he awkwardly kept his arms at a slight bend. She laid Addy in his arms.

"Now put your hand behind her neck to support it. Babies can't hold their necks up. Yes. That's it." Sarah breathed out slowly and watched as Sam drew his arms up towards his body and gently cradled his niece. His eyes never left her face. He looked like a man in love, totally and completely lost in love.

Which is exactly how he felt. Sam knew this moment would be burned into his memory forever. Addy smelled like talcum powder and something else. He supposed it was some natural baby scent. Suddenly she opened her eyes and whimpered a bit as she looked right at him.

They stared at one another, sizing each other up, Sarah mused, for what seemed like hours though it was only a few minutes. But she knew immediately those few minutes had done precisely what she'd been dreading. They'd bonded completely. Sam Livingston would be a part of Addy's life. And as much as Sarah resented it, she knew it was right. He had as much right to be in her life as Sarah. Sighing, she mumbled something about coffee and moved towards the counter.

"Is it alright if I sit with her?" Sam's voice was curiously gentle. And it sent an unwanted tingle up her entire body.

"Yes but she's most comfortable in the rocker. It's in our room down the hall."

As Sam headed out of the kitchen Sarah suddenly realized what she'd done. She'd sent him into the bedroom, HER room, where all her things were. Talk about embarrassing. She blushed as she realized there were bras hanging on the bed post that she'd left to dry. Maybe he wouldn't notice. Maybe. But if he missed those he couldn't miss the clean underwear she'd laid on the seat of the rocker this morning. Not the plain jane ordinary ones, oh no, she'd been finally cleaning out Megan's dresser, something she'd avoided for a while. Megan wasn't into ordinary underwear. Nope. Red silk panties. Black silk thongs, the super intimate stuff. Things she probably wouldn't have worn in her lifetime but her sister wore every day. Megan always said they made her feel sexy and adult. Just thinking about it made her blush harder. She set her mouth in a determined fashion. If Sam Livingston was any kind of gentleman he wouldn't mention it. He'd act naturally and have the grace not to embarrass her.

She sat down, waiting for the coffee to brew. Trying to relax, she reminded herself, almost like a mantra, he's her uncle, he's her uncle, how bad could it be? Bad. That she knew.

When the coffee finished, she poured each of them a mug and brought them back to her room. She paused in the doorway. He was leaning back in the rocker, eyes closed with Addy on his shoulder. They looked somehow right. Peaceful. She cleared her throat quietly. His eyes flashed open and a sheepish smile appeared.

"Guess I dozed off."

"Guess so." She strode over and placed his mug on the night table next to him. Let him figure out how to hold a baby AND drink coffee she mused.

He looked at her curiously for a moment.

"Um, you had, well...I found some ah things, here on the chair, I hope you don't mind I, ah, I moved them."

He nodded towards her bed. The flush crept up her neck into her face quickly. She looked over and felt herself get very warm. She looked everywhere but at him. She had never felt so embarrassed.

"So," Sam's voice was tinged with humor, "what did you do before the coffee shop gig. I mean, from the ah, the clothing, I could probably guess." She whipped her head around and glared at him.

"Guess? OK take your best shot!"

"Well, judging from the ah, well, lingerie," he didn't go on, just chuckled to himself.

Sarah shook her head, and decided he was anything but a gentleman. Suddenly she was in motion. Her eyes almost ablaze as she strode over, and swiftly but carefully grabbed Addy from his arms.

"Not funny. Time to go Uncle Sam!" She abruptly turned on her heels and walked out of the room, calling over her shoulder "now!"

She heard him approach the kitchen and busied herself getting a bottle from the fridge. "Sorry. Not funny. OK?"

"No. Not ok. Go."

"Come on Sarah, this is ridiculous," Sam's voice took on a paternal sound, as if he was talking to a small child, and that really irked her.

"What part of now don't you get?" She spoke quietly, but there was no mistaking the hostility.

"Fine, but we still need to talk. Why don't we try dinner again, tomorrow night," he spoke quickly, his voice still carrying a bit of amusement. Though he knew he desperately needed to get back on solid footing.

"Sarah, come on, I said I'm sorry." Maybe it was the contriteness in his tone, or maybe she was just too tired to keep it up any longer. Or, maybe she realized that it actually was funny. But no way she'd let him know.

"Fine." She shrugged her shoulders as she spoke.

"Good. I'll pick you up at 7. We'll go to Renaissance."

"Renaissance?" Her voice was tight and controlled, with just a hint of questioning.

"Yes. Well. If that's OK. I mean if you're not comfortable with that, we can go somewhere else."

"Why wouldn't I be comfortable? Renaissance is fine." Actually, it was perfect, she thought.

"I just thought maybe it, well, wasn't your style." Sam was flustered. He'd never felt so confused about anyone in his life. And he was definitely not controlling this situation at all.

She swung around and glared. "And you would know my style because?"

"OK. OK. I get it. Renaissance it is. I'll see you tomorrow." He couldn't help but smile. Sparring with a woman wasn't something he often did and he was kind of enjoying himself.

She turned her back to him and started to sit down and feed Addy. "Aren't you gone yet?" She couldn't keep the sarcasm out of her voice.

"I just want to say good night to my niece. If that's OK?"

"Fine. Say good night, Addy."

"Good night Addy," Sam couldn't help but smirk as he parroted her. He turned and was out the door before Sarah could think of a retort. She leaned back and closed her eyes as Addy sucked at the bottle. She could feel herself trembling. Then the laughter took over. It was all really and truly mortifying and funny all at the same time and she had to learn to lighten up. She really had no reason to be embarrassed, she could have just said hey it was Megan's. So why didn't she? But she also knew there was no end to Sam's judgmental opinions and he needed to be taken down a peg or two. She had a plan now. She would show him. And show him in no uncertain terms that Sarah Bennett was just as "worthy" as the next. More worthy than him, of that she had no doubt. She'd out-fox him and beat him at his own game, which seemed to consist mostly of humiliation so far. She'd show him humiliation all right! She sighed, wondering what it was about that man that made her crazy. If only he weren't so damn sexy. One minute she wanted to string him up, and the next jump his bones.

Sam wore a grin on his face most of the way home. He didn't need the results of the complete background check he'd initiated to know there was far more to Sarah than he had imagined. Though he was being careless, letting his guard down, and he knew that could lead to big trouble. Everything depended upon his ability to always outsmart his opponent. Anticipating their every move. Every reaction. He just couldn't decide whether or not she was the opponent here.

Chapter 7

Sarah couldn't wait to give Karen the dirt the next morning after the rush had cleared out. "That man sure deserves a kick in the ass," said Karen after hearing all the details.

"Well he's in for it. Guess where dinner is tonight?" Sarah grinned.

"Where?" Karen knew it must be good by the look on Sarah's face.

"Renaissance." She winked at her friend.

"Oooh did you call Antonio yet?"

"Nope, I will if he doesn't pop in this morning. I spoke to him yesterday, just to let him know about Greg. He said he'd be by today."

Karen smiled as she looked over at the door.

"Speak of the devil."

"Antonio!" they both chimed as he came in. Antonio Donofrio. The epitome of Italian elegance, strode in and greeted his two friends with European flair, a kiss on both cheeks. Somewhere in his mid-forties, Antonio was tall, dark and handsome in the classic sense.

"How are my two darlings today? Such terrible news about Greg. Still can't believe it." Antonio paused and shook his head as if to shake off the news. "But enough sadness. Any more juicy gossip for your friend? Have you stomped over that droll brother of his yet?" It was an abrupt change of mood, but they were used to his quick change of temperament.

"No," Sarah answered, "but we will. Tonight. And you my friend, get to play a starring role." Antonio Donofrio was more than a friend to Sarah and Karen. He had been a close friend of Megan's and had helped Sarah get the job with Karen. He was also the owner of Renaissance and would be playing an integral role in her plans.

"So tell me more, I'm all ears."

"We're dining with you tonight. Oh wait. Long story short, the jerk seems to think he can judge a woman by her lingerie which I'd left out in full view in my apartment when he appeared on my doorstep unannounced. He did NOT have the decency not to mention it. And it wasn't even mine. It was Megan's." Sarah breathed a sigh. That had certainly been a mouthful. She hadn't even realized how ludicrous it all sounded until now.

"I already don't like this man. OK, actually I used to before all this, you know he dines with us frequently, but no more. He is no longer on my A list." Antonio flicked his hand in the air as if swatting a fly.

"Thanks Antonio." Sarah smiled. "Here's what I'm thinking. I want you to make sure the whole staff treats me like someone way more important than him. Simple."

"What are you planning?" Antonio was more than curious. He knew this would be good. Sarah's reputation in the business world was ruthless. She could play hardball with the best of them, and often did it at his establishment.

"Oh we'll put him in his place. I want to give him enough rope to hang himself with. That's all. So in the beginning while he thinks I'm a nobody if you could respond to any of my requests as if I were a queen that would work wonders. Just treat him like a jester!" Sarah laughed as she said this, knowing how infuriating it would be to Sam.

"Your wish is my command, Sarah" Antonio smiled as he stood and patted her shoulder in a brotherly manner. "Anything for you and Addy. You know that." His voice was gentle, but very serious now.

"Thanks Antonio. We'll see you tonight." Sarah brushed a kiss across his cheek and smiled.

"Caio, dahlings. Until tonight." And swirling on his heels for dramatic emphasis, he breezed out. Karen sighed. "Ya know if I weren't such good friends with that man."

"Yeah," Sarah laughed, "and if he wasn't gay."

"Yes. That too." They looked at each other knowingly and laughed.

"You good for a few, Karen?" Sarah asked. She wanted to get ready for phase II of her plan. "I got it covered," Karen replied with a grin. "Do your thing girl!"

Sarah spent the next few minutes calling in favors. Making sure the right people were in place. Her fellow diners that evening would be a hand-selected cast of characters. Movers and shakers. Sam Livingston would find out just who he was dealing with and maybe learn a lesson about underestimating his adversaries. At least one in particular.

*****

Sarah studied her reflection in the full-length mirror behind the closet door. It was one of Megan's little extravagances, but a necessary one for a model. And at this moment, for Sarah. She smiled at the image in front of her. She'd pulled out her killer black sheath dress. Low cut enough to tease but conservative enough to meet anyone's standards. And the mid-thigh length was perfect on her. The diamond dangling earrings sparkled against the bright red curls floating around her head like a halo. The simple diamond and ruby sapphire necklace hung delicately against her ivory skin. The sheer black stockings and modest black leather pumps completed a look which basically screamed "Hey jerk, take a good long look because you aren't touching this!" Sarah was pleased. But this was just the beginning. She had much, much more in store.

Her buzzer rang promptly at 7. Sarah was ready. She'd dropped Addy at Grace's before getting dressed, and even though she could answer the door quickly, chose not to. Let him buzz a few times, she thought spitefully. Serves him right. On the third buzz, she casually approached the door and called out.

"Yes, who is it?"

"It's Sam." She heard him pause. "Are you ready?"

"Sure," she called out.

"Are you going to open the door?"

"Sure." Sarah smiled to herself. This was too fun.

"Sarah?" Now she could hear a little exasperation. Good. She unlocked the door and opened it slowly, for effect more than anything. She watched his face as he looked her over, his eyes traveling over the length of her body, back up, stopping at her face. His jaw hung open, and his eyelids appeared heavy. She usually didn't enjoy being ogled, but in this case she would make an exception. All part of a plan.

Sam was poleaxed. She had to be the most beautiful creature he'd ever seen. Before him stood a vision. One he needed to contend with. Damn this wasn't how it was supposed to go. He was so sure she'd be dressed somewhat inappropriately, which would embarrass her and then he'd be in complete control. This was a power play, and he knew it. But he couldn't decide which was worse. The fact that she was a knockout and wouldn't be in the least self-conscious, or the fact that she was heart-stoppingly gorgeous and he couldn't control his reactions. He never had this problem. He was always able to rein in his lust. Total control was essential. Right now he didn't have any control.

"You look, um, well, you look...." his voice trailed off. He was blowing this. She already had the upper hand. And something in her eyes told him she knew it.

"What?" she replied sweetly. "Don't look so surprised Sam, it doesn't work well for you. Shall we?" She stepped out into the hall, turned and locked the door, then lifted her arm for him to take. Like it was a date. He didn't move to take it. He was frozen in place.

"Sam?"

"What?" he practically barked at her.

"Are we ready?" She kept her voice neutral but raised her eyebrows for effect.

"Yes. I mean, yes, let's go." He took her arm and escorted her out to the curb where his private car was waiting. It was a silver Mercedes, complete with tinted windows and a driver holding open the door.

"Is this yours or a service?" Sarah asked, wondering what happened to his black limo that she'd seen following her. She was sure it had been Sam.

"Mine." His reply was terse as he guided her into the back seat, sliding in next to her.

She'd have to ask about the limo later. For now she sat back and smiled to herself as she looked out the window, pretending a nonchalance she didn't really feel. She was wired so tightly she felt like jumping out of her skin. Glancing over at Sam discreetly, she took in the broad shoulders accentuated by the deep charcoal gray suit jacket. Perfectly tailored she noted. He was incredibly male, incredibly potent and if he'd been anyone but Sam Livingston she'd be asking to turn the damn car around and go back to his place and make love till dawn. But he was her enemy for now and all thoughts of jumping his bones had to move aside until Addy's situation was cleared up.

As they pulled up in front of the restaurant, Sarah looked over at Sam and smiled. Not a friendly smile either, he noted, more like a Panther ready to strike. What was she up to? he wondered to himself. He had an uneasy feeling he was about to be outmaneuvered. But that was next to impossible. Getting out of the car, he reached in for her hand to guide her out. The minute flesh hit flesh he felt like a lightning bolt was traveling through his body. Quickly looking at her face, he saw she felt it too. Well, he thought, at least it's mutual. Maybe I don't have such a disadvantage here after all.

As they walked in through the finely etched glass doors, Sarah immediately saw Antonio approach from the rear of the main dining room. He had his 'oh so charming' smile plastered on his face, and immediately zoomed in on them.

"Ah, Mr. Livingston, so good to see you. I have a special table reserved just for you." As they followed Antonio, Sarah walked just behind Sam and grinned broadly. Antonio was leading them to the worst table in the house, right by the kitchen. The table set aside for those who were unknowns, or out of favor with Antonio.

"Here we are," Antonio said as he stepped back to let the Maître d' pull out the chair for Sarah. She put on her most naive look, and pouting, turned to Antonio.

"Oh, I was so hoping we could sit over there, by the wood stove? It looks so romantic." Sarah tilted her head and smiled coyly at Antonio.

Antonio bowed slightly and smiled as he answered. "As you wish."

Sam looked over at Antonio with a frown. This was totally absurd, putting him back here and now one request from Sarah and he was putty in her hands.

"I would be delighted to seat you there. Such a beautiful woman should be shown off not hidden away. Forgive me."

Sarah smiled at him again, and noticing Sam looking the other way, winked.

As they were handed their menus, Sam finally relaxed. He smiled softly as he watched her review the selections. Time for a little set down he thought. The cuisine here was international, and all the entrees printed in their native languages. She'd have to give in and ask for help, the first step in giving him the edge. And a virtual lock-in he thought smugly.

She looked up from the menu, and he could sense the confusion in her. But then she smiled in a way that once again had him confounded. She wasn't confused, she was up to something. He knew it. But damn, she was so, what, stunning? Adorable? He had no appetite and he could feel his body betraying him. This was going to be a long night. He smiled back at her, trying to put an edginess to it. The intimidating look he'd perfected. Only on her it seemed to have no impact. She wasn't reacting!

Their server, Marie, approached, and turned first to Sam.

"May I get you a drink to start? Perhaps a glass of wine?"

"Gin & Tonic for me, thanks." Sam turned on the charm. Marie was young, and blond, and was giving Sam a look that Sarah thought said, 'can I serve myself?' And here she'd expected Marie to be an ally. Humph! Go ahead and flirt, jerk. I'll get even, she thought as she glared at them.

Marie knew she didn't usually drink, so Sarah was surprised when she asked her anyway. But Marie's knowing smile made her relax. Sarah smiled back, realizing the flirting was all for show. So things were going just perfectly.

"No thanks, just a water with a twist of lime for me."

She caught Sam watching her and noticed the slight frown. Good, she thought, he's realized his second mistake. Never drink alone if you want the upper hand. And Sarah, whose parents had died at the hands of a drunk driver, reserved her drinking for special events and the occasional girls' night out.

When Marie returned with the drinks, Sarah couldn't help but let out a soft chuckle. This was going so well.

"So have you decided?" Marie glanced first at Sam, flashing him the flirt look again, and then over at Sarah using her conspiratorial look this time.

Sam proceeded to order a Bavarian Stew, rattling it off in German. When he was through, he looked over pointedly at Sarah and smiled.

"And what will you have, Sarah?" His voice practically oozed with sarcasm.

She hadn't asked for help yet and she'd either break now or starve. He continued to watch her, looking for the first signs of discomfort.

Sarah tilted her head and looked up at Marie. With a small grin, she looked down, then back up and ordered.

"Le Poisson du Jour, s'il vous plaît," Sarah smiled as she handed the menu to Marie.

"Very good choice today," replied Marie as she took their menus, then turned away. Sarah looked over at Sam, and was delighted to see him frowning severely, his forehead creasing as his eyes narrowed.

"Something wrong?" She couldn't help egging him on.

"No. Quite a good accent you have there."

"I minored in modern languages. You look a little peeved, is it something I said?" She pushed a little farther.

"No." He sounded really ticked off, and Sarah couldn't resist smiling. Her smile broadened as she looked up and toward the entrance.

"Oh look who's here. Isn't that something? It's Senator Howmen." She began waving one hand in the air, as if trying to get his attention.

"Sarah, put your hand down." Sam whispered, looking totally mortified.

Good, thought Sarah. She played it up more.

"Senator? Over here!"

"Come on Sarah, a little decorum," Sam now spoke through clenched lips.

Sam turned to see the senator heading their way and mentally prepared for the worst.

"Sarah, sweetheart," the senator's voice boomed as he hurried over and swept Sarah out of her chair and into his arms. The senator, old enough to be Sarah's father, was a big burly man, and he was practically suffocating her, Sam thought. But he obviously was delighted to see her, and they were far more than passing acquaintances.

The senator turned to look at Sam, and though they'd met several times, gave him a cool once over, then nodded briefly.

"Livingston..."

Sam stood, holding out his hand to greet him.

"Senator, good to see you."

Ignoring his hand, the senator replied "Humph" as he turned his attention back to Sarah.

"So Sarah, everything ok? Anything you need, you know you just have to ask."

Sarah gave him genuine smile.

"I know Uncle Dick...and I appreciate that. But I think everything is under control. Or will be." She gave Sam a pointed look and turned back to her godfather.

"I'd like to bring Addy by on Sunday, if that's ok? Aunt Shirley will be back, won't she?"

"You bet. I can't wait to see that little angel. It's been almost two weeks. She's probably walking by now."

Sarah laughed. "Not quite, but soon."

"Well I'll let you get back to business here," he spoke almost in a whisper. Giving Sarah one more quick hug and a kiss on the cheek, he turned and gave Sam one more pointed look and left them.

Sam knew when he was being played. "So he's your uncle, eh?" Sam didn't quite know whether to believe it.

"Not by blood, just by friendship. He's my godfather. My dad and he were roommates in college."

"Your dad went to Harvard?" Sam was on the alert now. He was familiar with the senator's background and knew any friend of Howmen's was important. He made a mental note to look up a Harvard alum named Bennett, from Howmen's class.

"Yes. In fact he did. As did I." There, she thought. That ought to do it.

"Then I guess you and I do have something in common." Sam tried not smile. She was proving to be a worthy opponent.

"All right Sarah. Start talking. I get the point ok? I underestimated you and I apologize. But since you know I've got a background check underway, which obviously I haven't read yet, and that's on me, you might as well fess up now. Why don't you tell me about you, then I won't jump to conclusions." Sam smiled, somewhat sheepishly, and Sarah felt flutters in her stomach. She really wanted to maintain her aloofness, but it was getting just a bit more difficult in the face of the devastating charm oozing off him.

"You never should have in the first place," she retorted somewhat affably, "and now I'm really curious about what those conclusions were!"

"You don't want to know. Oh, great, what now?" Sam braced himself for more humiliation as his eyes focused on the entrance. Sarah looked at Sam as innocently as she could.

"What?"

"Looks like you have a few more surprises in store for me, huh?" Sarah bit back a grin as she turned to see her former boss, Lou Grisham, approaching. Perfect, she thought. Just perfect. The timing couldn't be better.

She stood gracefully, smiling broadly, and waited for Lou to approach. He was in perfect form tonight. Dressed to the nines in his Armani, Lou could be on the cover of GQ. He was in his late thirties, extremely successful, and absolutely gorgeous. He was also very much attached to his work, but no need for Sam to know that. She had once thought about dating Lou, but they'd both agreed it was a bad idea and moved on to become close friends and colleagues. He was incredibly supportive when she decided to take a leave of absence for Addy. He still called her on occasion for assistance on major deals and their friendship remained solid.

He smiled that 100,000-watt smile and tenderly brought her into his arms. Not the bear hug the senator doled out. This was different, and Sam was startled by his reaction. Damn if he wasn't jealous!

"Hey Sarah," Lou whispered in her ear, for effect. Then he stepped back as if to look at her. "How are you, you look wonderful. Things good?"

"Yes, Lou, they're fine. And you? I really have missed you!" Sarah made it sound almost nostalgic. Like he was an old flame. Sam began to seethe.

"Me too, it's been awhile. So who's your friend?" Lou glanced over at Sam as if noticing him for the first time. Sam didn't know if he was angry or actually impressed with Sarah's ruse. He knew who Lou was, and Lou certainly recognized him. He stood and turned to Lou.

"Sam Livingston. We've met before I believe." Sam had his cold business tone back, for once.

"Oh yes. Livingston. Just acquired your media property up in Connecticut, right?"

"Yes. And as I recall you made a tidy sum on that deal, thanks to my generosity."

"Your generosity? Or Sarah's skills?"

Sam swung around to look at Sarah.

"You? Oh no, I'd remember you if you'd been involved."

Lou chuckled. "Actually, she wasn't in attendance. She's been operating on a remote basis for a while."

Sam looked utterly confused. And Sarah loved it.

"That was your deal? I wondered who the target was." Sarah's voice held a glib tone.

"Don't know much about our Sarah, do you Livingston?" Lou's voice held humor as well.

"No, but I was just about to find out." Sam was definitely annoyed now. Lou turned to Sarah, and gave her a kiss on the cheek, and pulled her in close to whisper in her ear, this time out of Sam's hearing.

"You go girl, go for the jugular and don't let go." Sarah smiled as she stepped out of Lou's embrace. "Ah, look, our food's here. Call me Lou, we'll get together soon, OK?"

"You got it Sarah."

Sarah smiled to herself as she sat back down. She hadn't realized that last consult on the media acquisition was a Livingston deal. Lou had provided her with enough information without divulging any details that might be considered a breach, as she wasn't on the official payroll nor assigned to the deal. This was too good to be true.

Looking up at Sam, she realized he'd been not just stunned, but completely overwhelmed. Things had almost worked too well. She almost felt guilty, almost.

They ate in silence. When they finished, Sam paid the check, and then rose to leave, Sarah rising as well. They gathered their coats at the coat check and headed to the street.

"If you don't mind, I'll just grab a rideshare. I need to pick up Addy. I'm sure you have things to do."

"We're not through here, Sarah, we still need to talk."

"You know, you're beginning to sound like a broken record. You keep saying that."

"That's because we can't seem to get it right." Sam let out a frustrated sigh. "Tell you what, I'll give you a ride, we'll collect Addy, go back to your place and this time we're going to talk. No more games."

Sarah sighed. "Fine Sam. Whatever you want." That bit about getting it right somehow struck her as if, well, oh no. There it was again. That pit in her stomach. Damn him. He's talking about Addy, and Sarah couldn't seem to get past her own reaction to him. Misinterpreting everything. Sarah suddenly looked across the street and narrowed her eyes.

"Say, is that your limo? Where's the Mercedes?" Sam looked across the street, following her gaze. "Nope. Not mine. Don't have one. Why?"

"You don't?"

"No, I don't. Isn't that what I just said?"

"Sorry, it's just, oh never mind. I'm sure it was just my imagination," Sarah replied somewhat distractedly. Sam suddenly felt a foreboding tingle up his spine.

"Tell me."

"Look, Sam, it's nothing. Drop it. Whistle for your driver, or whatever it is you do, and let's go."

Grasping her arm in a firm grip he turned her to face him. His face actually wore a look of concern, mused Sarah.

"Why did you think that was my limo?" She looked across the street as it pulled away. Turning back to face him, she suddenly noticed how close he was to her and she caught her breath.

"Because when I went to pick up Addy after work yesterday, I thought it was following me, Okay? I figured it was you, that's all. I guess I'm a little suspicious of you, go figure!" She chuckled softly. But Sam didn't laugh. Or return her smile. He looked more worried than before.

"Sarah, did they follow you all the way?"

"No, just to the corner and when I got to Grace's they disappeared."

"Who's Grace?"

"The babysitter. When I came out, I figured you'd be there, but then when I got home there you were on the steps. I figured you'd just turned around, came back and had them drop you off."

"Look. Change of plans Sarah. I can't explain now." Sam's voice was low, and tense. "But we need to get Addy. Then we're going to my place."

"Sam, I have to be at work at 7am. Your house is miles out of town. Going out there is going to make that too hard for me."

Sam gripped her arm tighter, almost painfully.

"Sorry Sarah, call in sick. We've got to go. Now. I'll explain later. I don't suppose you caught the limo's license plate, did you?"

Sarah looked curiously at him. "I might have. But what's this about Sam. You think I was followed, don't you?" She stiffened suddenly and felt a nervous tingle.

"Why would anyone follow me? I really don't have any enemies that I can think of," her voice held a note of fear.

"No, but I do."

"Oh God, Sam. Addy?" Sarah's voice was raised at least an octave. "You think someone's after her?"

He didn't answer, as the Mercedes pulled up he grabbed the door handle, not waiting for his driver. "Get in," he said quickly as he practically shoved her in the car, sliding in next to her and slamming the door.

"Tell Tom where to go. The address, now."

Sarah rattled off Grace's address quickly, her eyes never leaving Sam. He was still holding her arm. She watched his face, trying to figure out what was happening, scared now beyond belief. She realized something far more dangerous than Sam had invaded her life and it terrified her.

CHAPTER 8

As the Mercedes pulled out into traffic, Sam glanced over at Sarah, and saw genuine fear in her face. His features gentled as he tried to calm her.

"It'll be okay, Sarah. Don't worry. Just relax. Nothing's going to happen. If I can help it," he muttered the last comment under his breath as he turned away. Just seeing that look in her eyes felt like a punch in the gut. Bill had been right. Involving them in his life was a mistake, he was putting them in danger. They pulled up in front of Grace's building, and Sam leapt out the door, pulling Sarah with him. He finally let go of her arm, let her unlock the door and lead the way inside. She ran down the hall and stopped short when the door suddenly opened, and Grace appeared.

"Sarah. What is it, what's happened?"

"Grace, you're okay? I just, I'm sorry, I mean is Addy okay?"

"Of course, she's fine. What's all this about?" Grace didn't seem nervous or worried, which instantly made Sarah feel better.

"I have no idea," Sarah sighed as she looked over at Sam, who came to a quick stop next to her.

"Care to explain now?" She tried to sound light, but the anger was evident. He'd just scared the daylights out of her, and she was just as confused about it as Grace was.

"I'll explain in the car. Grace?" Sam held out his hand to her. "Sam Livingston, Addy's uncle, I need you to get Addy and gather some things for yourself and come with us. We don't have time to discuss it, I'm sorry."

Grace eyed Sam closely, and with a brief nod, turned and went in to do as he bade her. Sarah stood wide eyed and mouth open.

"Close your mouth before the flies get in." Sam couldn't resist.

"How could you order her around like that?" Sarah huffed out in a breath.

"You don't see her arguing, do you?" Sam smiled and winked, as Sarah glared. She couldn't help but notice that whenever Sam Livingston smiled, her knees turned to jelly and her stomach flipped over. It was unacceptable. And it really pissed her off. He terrorizes her with his neurotic behavior about the limo, and then turns on the charm, as if that is going to work.

As Grace returned and handed Addy over to Sarah, she looked at Sam one more time. "I'll get my things. Sarah, don't argue with him."

"I hate when she does that," Sarah huffed out.

"Does what?" Sam was still smiling, but a hint of caution had flickered back in his eyes.

"She's a bit on the psychic side, did I mention that?"

"No you didn't. But I'd prefer to think perhaps she just has good instincts and probably knows you too well."

"She's only known me a few months. You'll see. Not that I believe in this stuff but she's got this sixth sense or something, and it's a bit creepy," Sarah replied.

"Hmm. Well, I guess we'll wait and see."

Grace returned with an overnight bag, stepped out and locked the door behind her. Sam took her bag for her, then took her arm to lead her down the hall, leaving Sarah behind, holding Addy, frozen in place. This was getting way too weird for her, and she didn't like being ordered around anyway. Sam was good at ordering people around. Sarah wasn't good at taking orders. This was going to be difficult.

Sam stopped suddenly and turned. "Come on we're wasting time," he said to Sarah rather sternly. He turned to continue out the door, and Sarah, on an impulse, stuck her tongue out at him. She smiled, then, thinking how much better she felt having done it.

"I saw that," she heard him call out and her eyes widened. Seriously this man was infuriating.

She hurried to catch up and followed them out to the car. She buckled Addy's car seat in place, which would normally only take a minute but with Sam's 'help' took more like fifteen. He wanted to make sure if need be, he could handle it himself. Annoyed, Sarah took the seat next to Addy, while Sam helped Grace into the front passenger seat, and then took his place on the other side of Addy in the back.

As they drove away, Sam watched Grace discreetly. He had to admit she was exactly the kind of person he'd have chosen to care for his niece. Somewhere in her sixties, her face was smooth, very few wrinkles, except for the laugh lines around her eyes. When Grace smiled, she lit up and spread a warmth around her. That was a good sign. And she was competent. He could see that too. Grace turned to look back at Sam and smiled.

"You approve, do you? Well I'm glad of that." Sam laughed, and figuring she'd caught him studying her, replied with good humor.

"As a matter of fact, I do."

Grace nodded. "This is about that limo, isn't it?"

Sam's eyes narrowed as he glanced over at Sarah then back at Grace.

"You saw it." It was more of a statement than a question and Grace continued without confirming it.

"There's danger there. You two will have to work together you know, or they'll be trouble." She turned back in her seat, and Sam looked over at Sarah, trying to gauge her reaction. Sarah's eyes were wide, and her hands were clenched. She returned Sam's look, and he could see the fear in her eyes. She may not want to admit it, but she really bought into this psychic stuff, and that wasn't good. Though he did wonder because Grace was right. The limo did represent danger, he wasn't sure what it was yet, but he felt the same way.

He'd have to tread lightly on this, and keep Sarah in the dark. He'd have to speak with Grace about her 'sensing' things. Convince her to keep it to herself. If Sarah knew the half of it, she'd be out of the car and out of town before he could blink an eye.

"Sarah," he spoke quietly, trying not to rattle her any further.

"Start talking Sam," she replied, through clenched teeth. She didn't know if she was scared or angry, maybe a little of both. But she knew she needed answers.

"Look. Sarah. It's a bit complicated."

"You're a crook, aren't you? What? Gun running? Drug smuggling? Why do you have enemies Sam, but more importantly why was someone following me?" Sarah folded her arms across her chest and leaned back, exhaling slowly. A small effort to calm herself which definitely wasn't working.

"I'm not a criminal," Sam replied hotly.

"No? Then what?"

"What I do is important, Sarah, but sometimes dangerous, and I can't involve you or Addy or Grace. You'll have to trust me."

"Trust you? Can't involve us?" Sarah leaned over and around the car seat to look directly at Sam. Without thinking, she pointed a finger at him and started poking him in the chest. "Listen, Sam Livingston, if you're going to do stuff that puts Addy and me in danger, you're damn well going to tell us why. Understood? Or better yet, I'll guess. How's that?" She was still stabbing with her finger.

"First, if you're not a criminal, then you're government," she gave him a jab. "Because they are the only other 'employer' that keeps secrets. Second," she jabbed him again, "it's gotta be pretty high-level stuff. Which makes it dangerous. How'm I doing so far?" One more jab. "I think I'm right. And whatever it is you're up to is affecting others now, not just you. So if I'm going to protect Addy and myself, I'm going to need to know what's going on. Are we clear?" One final jab and she swung around and returned to her side, leaned back and crossed her arms again.

Sam said nothing. She peeked over without turning and saw he was just staring at her. Good. Let him. Then one side of his mouth started to quirk up and she could see him struggling not to smile. The nerve!

"This is not funny." Sarah huffed out. By now Sam was outright laughing.

"Don't you dare laugh at me. I'm serious Sam, stop it! How could you laugh at this?"

"Not this, Sarah, you. Did you know when you get mad your face turns red, and your ears too! And that finger poking thing. Was that supposed to make some sort of point?" By now Sarah was getting so mad her eyes were practically shooting darts, so Sam decided to quit while he was ahead.

Composing himself, Sam went on. "When we get home, we'll talk about all this, okay? For now why don't you sit back and relax, take a nap or something."

"Relax. Right. I found out I was being followed by some stranger in a limo when I'm headed to pick up Addy no less, and then I'm practically kidnapped by you and I should relax." She was totally frustrated.

"That pretty much sums it up. Yep." Sam looked smug as he leaned back and closed his eyes.

"Besides, you promised to spill it in the car, remember? Well we're in the car so spill! What if they're following us right now? Or what if they're waiting for us at your house? Hmmm?" Sarah wasn't about to leave it alone.

"Sarah. You're letting your imagination run wild. We're safe now." Sam tried to sound confident, but he really wasn't all that sure how safe they were. That they weren't being followed he was sure of, his driver was one of the best, and was highly trained in evasion. And the house was as secure as Fort Knox. He himself had seen to that. But the danger was there lurking somewhere. He had to find out more about the limo and who was tailing Sarah. And why. And he sensed he didn't have much time.

Hopefully, Sarah could remember the license plate. Damn he let her distract him, she'd probably forgotten whatever she'd seen by now, he'd waited too long. What was it about her that made him lose his focus!

"Sarah?" Sam kept his voice gentle and firm. "What can you remember about the limo. I need you to think. Okay? It's really important. I shouldn't have waited this long to ask, I'm sorry. Just try to remember." He reverted to his interrogation techniques. Keep her calm.

Sarah shot a look. "I may be scared and pissed off, but I'm not suffering from memory loss quite yet." She responded with an obvious tone of disdain.

"OK. I wasn't trying to imply anything, sorry." He tried to keep his voice calm, though she really was getting under his skin.

"Apology accepted." Sarah replied haughtily.

"Well?" Sam pressed on.

"Do you have something to write with?" she asked.

"It's not necessary." Sam's reply was smug.

"Wanna bet?" Sarah retorted.

"No." He leaned forward and reached into a pocket built into the back of the driver's seat and pulled out a small tablet. Opening it, he picked up the stylus pen and waited. Making sure he was ready, she gave him a telling look, and began.

"OK. Late model black limo, sedan not stretch, tinted windows, about an 8 on a scale of 10, New York license plate 459gx2c, no license holder frame. Front right corner had a dent about 6 inches, paint chipping off in the perimeter. Door handles pull up not out. Couple of dings on the trunk lid. Looked like hail damage maybe." Sarah paused and took a breath.

"You have a photographic memory," Sam nodded as he spoke. "Should have known." We'll be able to trace this no problem, he thought, with relief.

"I'm not through," Sarah continued.

"There's more?" He sounded doubtful.

"Of course," Sarah replied.

"OK, what else?" Sam tried to imagine what other possible details could come out of that little head.

"The driver was bald, couldn't see any passenger in the back but I thought it was you so I didn't look very closely."

"What else about the driver?"

"Nothing."

"How about facial features?" Sam was excited by the information she could pull out.

"I didn't see." Sarah shrugged.

"But you saw he was bald, you must have noticed something else." Sam narrowed his eyes, as if not believing her.

"I saw light reflected off his head which tells me he's bald. I never saw his face."

"You've got quite the head for details Sarah." Sam was impressed as hell, but he didn't want to make too much of it.

"As you say, photographic memory." She shrugged again nonchalantly, though inside she was overjoyed at his reaction.

"You're just full of surprises, aren't you." Sam came back dryly.

"Yep." She replied with a grin, imitating his previous behavior with a little cheekiness of her own.

Sam pulled out a strange gadget then, one she'd never seen before. Looked almost like a portable scanner with a mini keyboard and screen. Sarah watched him as he typed, hit the enter key and then watched the tiny screen as he waited for some sort of response.

The handheld device suddenly beeped, and Sam studied the scrolling data. Nodding his head, he turned it off and glanced at Sarah, expecting her to grill him. When she didn't, he was surprised. She looked curious, yes, but more as if waiting for an explanation. But of course, having some weird desire to push his luck, he grinned at her and turned back to the screen. That'll set her off, he thought. Just why he enjoyed seeing her riled was a mystery to him. He'd analyze the data later, and maybe get some answers.

She remained quiet after that, and Sam turned to study Addy, still sound asleep. She reminded him of an angel and his heart seemed to lurch whenever he looked at her. He had so carefully orchestrated his life. Kept his emotions in check, and never ever got too close to anyone. It would be too risky. But one look at Addy and he was hooked. And he knew, somewhere deep in his gut, that if it came down to it, he'd give it all up for her. Everything. He just hoped it wouldn't come to that.

They pulled up in front of the house and within seconds the driver was out and had Grace's door open. Sam got out and came around to open Sarah's door, but she'd already beat him to it. He reached to help her out, but she ignored him while she unhooked the carrier, lifted it up and handed it to him. He held it awkwardly as she got out, then reluctantly handed it back to her when she reached for it. She still hadn't said another word to him.

As they approached the door, Sam began pushing buttons on a panel outside. A green light flashed on, and Sam spoke directly into the small speaker below.

"Livingston," he said in a clear tone. A buzz sounded and he opened the door quickly. Sarah glanced up at him curiously. Sam shrugged.

"Security system," was all he said.

"Voice recognition? Isn't that a bit much for a residential alarm?" Sarah's tone was somewhat sarcastic. She was getting a nagging feeling that there was far more to this man than anyone knew.

"I'm testing it out," he replied with another shrug.

She followed him inside and once again was awestruck at the absolute perfection of his home. It was classy, imposing, and somewhat surreal. The truth was, she was totally jealous. She'd had to give up her beautiful apartment and here Sam had this whole amazing house! She sighed and shook her head.

"Something wrong?" Sam asked. Startled, she realized he'd been watching her.

"No. Nothing. I like your house. That's all."

"You like it, eh?" His response was teasing.

She bit back a nasty retort. "No, I love it, OK? It's perfect. Aren't you lucky." Why is it she couldn't control her reactions around him? This was not typical behavior for her and it was driving her nuts.

"Look. Just point me in the right direction. I need to change her, feed her, and settle in."

"Tell you what, I'll come with you and you can show me the routine. I'll need to know anyway."

"Fine." Sarah's voice sounded almost snippy.

"Fine." Sam replied in the same tone.

Sam swung around and headed towards the main staircase. It was wide, and curved around to an upper landing. Sarah followed him up and into the first bedroom. Her eyes widened in surprise, before they narrowed and her face reflected anger. The room was all set up as a nursery, down to the wallpaper with nursery rhyme characters. The crib was decked out with pink bumper guards and matching sheets. A giant teddy bear in the corner. It was the perfect baby room.

"What's all this, Sam?" Sarah blurted out quickly.

"Something wrong?" He sounded genuinely confused. "I thought it looked perfect."

"Perfect if you intended all along to have Addy live here, you mean. This was obviously done before tonight. Which means you planned to take her, didn't you?" Sarah was infuriated. "From the looks of it you must have had someone come in as soon as you knew about Addy."

Sam felt cornered. "I just thought she'd stay here once in a while, if you agreed," he drawled out the last word. "I never thought you'd keep her from me," he continued. "Or was that your intent all along?"

Sarah breathed deeply, exhaled, and relaxed her stance.

"Sorry. You're right. It's beautiful and I'm not angry that you wanted her here. I'm just afraid. I don't know what you want. And this certainly is far more than she has now and it just ticks me off, that's all." She actually felt better being honest about it.

"Sarah, I'd never take her away from you." Sam was surprised to realize it was true. Which raised a whole new set of issues. But right now they needed to talk. There were things Sarah needed to understand, and she wasn't going to be happy about any of it. And for the first time in a long time, Sam felt badly about interfering in someone else's life. His facade was crumbling, just when he needed it most.

CHAPTER 9

Sarah looked around the room once more in amazement. Turning to Sam, she asked him to go retrieve the diaper bag from downstairs, which she'd forgotten.

"No need. Just get what you need from here," he smiled as he walked over and opened up a small door in the wall revealing a linen closet fully stocked.

Sarah's eyes widened as she took it all in. There were at least a dozen hooded bath towels, cases of diapers in various sizes, several full crib sets, washcloths, baby shampoo, a baby tub, powder. Everything you could imagine.

She chuckled softly, shaking her head, as he turned and grinned.

"Sam, what the hell were you thinking? You're not opening up a daycare here! And don't tell me you did this yourself; I won't believe you!"

"Well, no, I made a deal with my housekeeper. I pretty much gave her carte blanche to set up the nursery," he smirked as he spoke. "I told her I wanted it to be perfect."

"Does the word excess mean anything to you?"

"Actually, I kind of told her that whatever she did for Addy, she could do the same for her own granddaughter, whose arrival is anytime now," Sam laughed. Sarah laughed too. It actually felt good to share a moment like this with Sam. She wondered how often he relaxed like this.

"OK. Let's get started." She placed the carrier down and lifted Addy up and onto the changing table. "Diaper please?" She held out her hand as a surgeon would, waiting for a tool. Sam looked at the various packages on the shelf, utterly confused.

"The number 2 will work," Sarah supplied helpfully. Sam took out the package, and after some difficulty, managed to retrieve a diaper and held it out for Sarah.

"Oh no, you're doing this." She chuckled a bit as his face paled.

She watched Sam as he approached the changing table with a certain trepidation in his step. She stepped back to give him room, hovering though, just in case. She held back a grin as he reached to unfasten the Velcro with his thumb and finger as if afraid it would jump up at him. He lifted Addy's legs, one in each hand, and looked to Sarah questioningly.

"Want to grab that out of the way?" he asked.

"Uh uh," she replied as she gave up trying not to grin. "Try holding both feet with one hand and remove the diaper with the other."

Sam sighed. "OK. Should have thought of that myself."

Sarah opened her mouth to speak, then suddenly closed it, smirking.

Sam tossed the old diaper in the pail next to the table, then placed a clean one under her bottom.

"Hey!" he yelled.

"Something wrong?" Sarah mused.

"She just, well, you know. She wet again. I just put the clean one there, and now it's already wet," he complained, though humorously.

"Cold air," Sarah laughed. "Next time, wait a moment before removing the old one."

"Cold air?" Sam looked over at her with a quizzical glance.

"Yep. Remember when you were a kid, the trick about sticking someone's hand in cold water when they're sleeping?"

Sam chuckled. "Yeah. I remember. I did it to Greg all the time."

"Same principle." Sarah made no move to get a new diaper.

"You want to hand me another one?" Sam waited. "Please?"

Sarah sighed and went over to retrieve it.

Sam grunted, took the diaper and went back to work.

"How did you get to be such an expert so fast?" Sam really was curious.

"I read all of Megan's books. Watched endless YouTube videos and of course, Grace," Sarah laughed softly. "Mostly Grace."

It took a few more tries to get it right, but he eventually caught on. He had an easier time feeding her. He positioned his large frame in the rocker, and settled in with Addy while Sarah went down to fetch her bottle. Once satisfied that Sam had things under control, Sarah left him alone then, with only a final mention about burping her when she finished. Sam was too engrossed in feeding Addy to pay attention, though. He heard something about a cloth and his shoulder, but he'd seen it on TV enough to know you just place the baby against your shoulder and pat her on the back. How hard could it be!

Sarah stood in Sam's study, gazing at the portrait above the fireplace. It was of an older man, who bore a remarkable resemblance to Sam. The hair was grayer, but the same piercing blue eyes and bold features were there. From the outfit he was dressed in, Sarah guessed it was done sometime in the mid 1800's. She knew a little of the family background, after all the Livingston's were one of Rockdale's oldest families. They made their fortune in shipbuilding, and some of the finest cruising ships today still bore the Livingston name. Hearing sounds from the foyer, she turned to see Grace and Sam entering the study.

Sam's face looked slightly pale, and at first Sarah became worried that something was wrong with Addy. Until she saw Grace biting back a grin.

"Something wrong, Sam?" Sarah smiled instinctively. Whatever it was wasn't serious in Grace's mind.

"Seems Addy gave him a little fright with her burping," Grace interjected.

"I thought she was sick. You could have told me she'd spit up!" Sam was beginning to think Sarah deliberately set him up. Again.

"I did. I distinctly remember telling you to make sure you put a cloth diaper over your shoulder in case she spit up," Sarah replied.

"Yes, well, no harm done, I suppose." Sam's voice was gruff.

Sarah took a deep breath and looked directly at Sam.

"OK, Sam, it's time to have a talk. I think Grace and I deserve an explanation. And while you're at it I could also use a large t-shirt or something to sleep in, perhaps a clean toothbrush and a comb would help as well."

"Ah… of course." Sam looked a little embarrassed. And a little flushed. The image of Sarah in nothing but a t-shirt was vivid in his mind.

"Since you let Grace get her stuff together, but not me, I'm guessing you can help me out, right?" Sarah knew she sounded a bit snarky, but suddenly realizing she was still in her silk dress and had nothing with her pissed her off.

"There are some things in the room next to Addy's. Go help yourself. You'll be staying there anyway. I'll go change myself, and we'll all meet back down here for that talk." Sam sounded conciliatory, and Sarah could do nothing but go along.

Sam watched as she turned and left the study, trying to clamp down the lust he felt when he thought of her headed upstairs to change. He shook his head slowly and mentally chastised himself. There was no room for Sarah in his life and he needed to keep it all in check. He couldn't even allow himself a brief fling, not that she'd go for it anyway. He'd have to just ride this one out. Though it made him angry in a way. Why should he have to give up everything? Why couldn't he just for once, live for today. Greg managed it. But Sam saw to it that Greg could. He made sure his younger brother didn't have to suffer the trappings he did. But in the end, it didn't matter. He failed to protect him. And he couldn't afford to fail Sarah and Addy.

Sarah turned to Grace as they reached the top of the stairs.

"Are you all settled in? Where are you sleeping?"

Grace smiled and pointed down the hallway.

"Right past your room there's another," Grace replied. "Quite lovely actually, I can't remember the last time I stayed in such a lovely home. It's like staying at the Ritz. Even has its own bathroom," Grace chuckled.

"You're really enjoying all this, aren't you?" Sarah queried.

"I'm an old lady, Sarah, and this is more excitement than I've had in years. So I guess I'm going to make the most of it." Grace laughed aloud, seeing the horrified expression on Sarah's face.

"Don't worry, love, it'll be just fine." she said soothingly.

"Maybe, but doesn't it frighten you? We don't know Sam from Adam and quite frankly he bugs me. We've got someone following us, he's got enemies we don't know about, and we're stuck here 'til who knows when. I'm sorry I can't get up the enthusiasm you seem to have for adventure." Sarah stalked off to the room Sam had indicated and entering quickly she shut the door and leaned against it. And then looked around, and sighed.

And sighed again. Grace was right. It was pretty much perfect. There was a canopied double bed, with sheer white fabric draped over the top. A large easy chair in the corner, and a beautiful small vanity desk under a large arched window. There was a walk-in closet and a full attached bath. It was a wonderful guest suite, and there was an adjoining door to Addy's room. Sarah hated to admit it to herself, but the accommodations were pretty much 5 star and light years away from Megan's tiny apartment. Hell they were far better than her old place just outside the city. She could definitely live here, she thought. Though that was NOT going to happen. Not in a million years.

Suddenly it dawned on her that maybe that was Sam's intention. He'd just have her and Addy live here. Maybe Grace too, and then the legal problems surrounding the guardianship wouldn't be an issue. She shook her head and tried to clear her thoughts. No use drumming up problems, she had enough already. She'd wait to hear him out. Then she could make some decisions.

Stepping into the closet, she saw it had a fairly complete women's wardrobe hanging. Curious, she began probing the clothes. There were several pairs of jeans and slacks, a few dresses, a robe, a variety of tops and opening the top drawer of a small dresser revealed panties, bras and several nightgowns. She wondered who it all belonged to, then her eyes widened as she realized everything still had the tags on them. Everything. They didn't belong to anyone. Instinctively she knew that when she checked the sizes, they'd be her size. She sighed as she reached for a pair of jeans and a sweatshirt. He'd had his housekeeper do it. Of course he did. Just like Addy's nursery furnishings. It was all planned. Damn. It wouldn't be so irritating if it hadn't been for that limo. There were all kinds of things going on, and Sarah was determined to get some answers. She couldn't help but smile though when she put the clothes on and saw how well they fit. Sam was a hell of a judge of women's proportions. She frowned then, suddenly, realizing he must be some sort of womanizer. Probably had a dozen different women he dated at any one time. What was it Bill had said? That Sam resented Greg's lifestyle? Huh! At least Greg was a one-woman man!

She finished dressing and went to check her reflection in the bathroom mirror. She noticed a basket on a small bench next to the vanity, with a comb, brush, and gift sized bottles of shower gel and shampoo. She took the comb and ran it through her curls, which were tangled up and putting up too much resistance. Giving up she went out to see if Grace was ready.

She tapped lightly on the door to Grace's room.

"Grace? You ready?"

"One minute, dear, and I will be," Grace replied softly. The door opened, and Sarah had to smile. Grace was in her flannel nightgown and wrapped in a terry robe. But it was the slippers that made the picture complete. Bunny slippers. Sarah hadn't seen those in years. Though truth be told, she had her own pair tucked away in a trunk of old stuff in the apartment building's basement.

They headed downstairs, and as they reached the bottom Sarah could see Sam through the open French doors that led to the study. He was standing in front of the fireplace, one arm leaning on the mantle. He'd changed into more casual clothes, but he still didn't appear relaxed. His expression seemed tense, and worried. Which automatically signaled trouble to Sarah.

The nagging fear was back.

They stepped into the study, and Sam turned and smiled at them.

"Ladies," he said. "Please, take a seat." He waved one hand over toward the leather sofa.

Sarah looked at him suspiciously but said nothing. She and Grace took their seats and waited for Sam to speak. No sense attempting to ask questions until she heard him out.

Not wanting to look directly at him, her eyes were again drawn to the portrait. Sam noticed the direction of her gaze and smiled.

"My great great great grandfather."

"I thought as much," said Sarah, smiling back. "I can see the resemblance."

"Well supposedly I'm just like him. I hope so. You know he started out as a deckhand on a cargo ship. Learned everything he could and then started building his own ships. He started small of course, sloops and sailing boats for the well to do who lived in the Hudson Valley. Eventually he got a commission for a full-size ship and the rest is history." Sam shrugged. "The American Dream fulfilled."

"As I recall, Livingston Shipping LTD built quite a few ships for the slave trade," Sarah mused.

"Yes, that's right. But that's not the whole story," Sam replied smugly.

"What he had slaves to build them too?"

"Not quite. He was an abolitionist. His ships, while it's true they were commissioned by slave traders, were uniquely designed. Into each slave-trading ship he built several secret compartments inside the holding cells where these poor souls were usually crammed into. The rooms were small, designed to hold maybe 50 men and women. But the traders usually overfilled the rooms, perhaps with over 100. By the time they were out to sea, there would only be 50 left. There was an escape hatch built right in. Those who weren't afraid to swim were able to drop down a chute and right into the water, swim to shore."

"You're making that up!" Sarah blurted out.

"Nope," Sam grinned. "I can hold my head up way high when I talk about him. He was a great man!" And Sam meant it. He'd grown up on stories about his ancestors, and with all their wealth and standing in society, they were all good decent people.

"What other deep dark secrets should we know about?" Sarah asked, amused at Sam's obvious pride.

"Oh there's lots to tell but it can wait. Right now I'm going to explain what I think is happening. I can't be too specific, and I need you to understand that. I have the information on the limo so we'll start with that," Sam went on. "It belongs to the Chamandian Embassy."

"Chamandia?" Sarah probed. "The tiny little principality in the Indian Ocean?"

"That's it." Sam continued, impressed she knew of it. "Now as to why they were following you," Sam cleared his throat. This would be tricky.

"I've had some dealings with the government there and they haven't always gone their way. Some of the Chamandian officials would like to see me out of the way."

"So why follow me?" Sarah pushed.

"Because of Addy, I suppose." Sam sounded vague, and Sarah wasn't biting.

"Come on Sam, not good enough," Sarah responded angrily. "Explain what you mean by 'out of the way'!"

Sam looked directly at Sarah; his face taut.

"Out of the way, Sarah, as in dead. They want me dead."

"And Addy?" Sarah gasped. "You think they'll use her to get to you? Will they hurt her? Why don't you call the cops or the FBI?"

"I can't explain it all to you, I wish I could." Sam was brusque. "You'll have to trust me to protect us. All of us."

Sarah took a deep breath.

"I don't know if I can do that, Sam. I need to know more than you're telling, I need to protect Addy, and myself as well. I can't do that if I don't know what I'm facing."

"I know and I'm sorry," Sam replied honestly. "But the more you know the more danger you're in. Can you trust me on this? Please?" Sam's voice trailed off as he turned to Grace.

"Grace, I'm not sure about all this intuition of yours, but I could use some back up right about now and I think she'll listen to you."

Grace nodded and turned to Sarah, placing one hand on Sarah's and squeezing gently.

"I know it's a lot to ask of you, but even if you don't fully trust Sam, you can trust me when I tell you he has your best interest at heart." Grace looked pointedly at Sam. "But you'll have to justify my faith, you understand?"

Sam smiled warmly at Grace, before replying.

"I do." He changed tack quickly. "So should I check on Addy? Do you think she's okay up there by herself?"

"Relax Sam," sighed Sarah. "Our little princess is sleeping I'm sure."

"What did you say?" Sam looked over at Sarah as if she'd grown horns.

"I said she's sleeping. What's with you? Are you okay?" asked Sarah.

"I'm fine, it's nothing," he said brusquely.

"Well you look a little funny, that's all," Sarah remarked dryly.

"Sorry," Sam said quickly. "Anyway, the good news is I don't believe that the limo posed any danger. In fact I think it was just the opposite. I believe the ambassador had information that you might be in danger and was simply protecting you. At least that's what I'm told." Sam knew it was true, but there was such a thing as too much information. He had to reveal as little as possible. And he wanted to ease their fears at the same time. He was waiting on more information. He'd received some very disturbing news when he checked out the limo tailing Sarah. And he had some decisions to make.

"Look, why don't we all turn in, and we can talk further in the morning. We're all safe and sound here, so there's nothing to prevent a good night's sleep," Sam kept his voice neutral, and light.

"OK, Sam, sleep it is. But we will talk more about this. Or we're out of here. Clear?" Sarah looked directly at Sam now, steeling herself against the wave of emotion that hit her every time she did.

"Absolutely clear," Sam replied with a small smile. He was really beginning to enjoy the little bits of sparring with her. It made him feel alive. He'd spent years mastering his emotions, existing on some cold plane of existence. And suddenly it was as if it was all for nothing. The minute Sarah and Addy came into his life, everything changed. Although if he wasn't careful, it might completely shatter everything.

After heading up to her suite and readying herself for bed, Sarah suddenly felt that restlessness that had been haunting her creep back up. Quietly, she went over to Grace's door and knocked gently.

"Grace, are you up?" she asked softly.

"Yes, Sarah, come in," Grace replied in the same hushed tone.

"I'm sorry to disturb you, but I don't think I can sleep," Sarah apologized.

"Me either, child," Grace smiled knowingly. "Too much excitement and mystery, eh?"

"Oh, Grace," Sarah moaned. "I just don't think I'm up to all this. What on earth is going on? Can you tell?"

"No, dear, I can't. I'm sorry, I only get feelings, you know, hunches. And my hunch tells me there is an awful lot going on, but that it will all work out. I'm sure of that. But I do feel like you have to trust Sam, completely. He means you no harm. He'll need your help."

"Then he needs to tell me more. I can't help him if I don't know what's happening," Sarah complained.

"I know, and I'm sure he'll tell us more when he himself knows. Right now I feel as if he's sorting through things, trying to come up with answers." Grace sounded so wise Sarah could do nothing but nod her head.

"Ok, then, I'll let you get some sleep. And I'll do the same." Sarah smiled softly at Grace and went back to her suite feeling only a bit more relaxed. Pulling back the plush down comforter, she slipped in between the cotton sheets, closed her eyes and tried to sleep. It was no use, though. What little sleep she got was fitful, filled with half-waking dreams of her and Addy running through dark tunnels trying to get towards safety. It was the same scene over and over. The tunnel was dark, made of stone, and eerily damp. She could actually feel the chill in her skin. When dawn broke, she was awake. Safe in the bed. And terrified.

Chapter 10

Sam fared no better than Sarah in his quest for sleep. He had peeked in on Addy before heading to his room, and ended up just rocking in the chair watching her sleep. Things were escalating now. He'd prepared most of his life for this. Yet now that it seemed so inevitable, he didn't quite know how to handle it. The unexpected birth of Addy complicated things. And then there was Sarah. It seemed she was the one. Smart, strong-willed, independent with a heart of gold. Pretty much perfect. And while she was evidently scared out of her wits right now, she managed to keep herself together. She was everything Sam wanted and more. But too many obstacles were in their way. Too many secrets. He thought about what he could tell her. And what he couldn't. If he gave her enough information for her to be comfortable with the situation, she could be very useful. But there were very few people Sam could trust. One mistake and it would all be over. Could he trust her? How far would she go to protect Addy? He knew he'd have to make up his mind by morning. One false step and it could all end in a flash.

When the sun finally rose, Sarah threw on a robe she'd found hanging in the closet, not even bothering to remove the tags. In fact, the nightgown she'd found still had the tags on as well. Stepping into the hallway she heard a door open and turned her head towards the sound.

"You look like hell," Sam mused as he strode down the hall.

"Right back at ya," Sarah grinned spontaneously. "At least your clothing doesn't come with the tags still on."

Sam chuckled. Grace appeared like magic right at that moment. Sam shook his head.

"Grace looks like she's the only one who got any sleep!"

Grace smiled. "And good morning to you two, I'm going to get Addy up and going, maybe one of you could scrounge some coffee?"

"Not a problem. That much I can handle. Sarah? Why don't you come down with me and give me a hand? We can finish our talk." Sam's voice was suddenly stiff... and neutral, and Sarah sensed he was struggling with something.

"Fine by me. Can you talk while cooking breakfast too?" Sarah smiled, trying to lighten Sam's mood.

"No. And I can't cook when I'm not talking. Sorry." But Sam didn't look very sorry. His eyes were bright and she knew what was coming. "But you can, I bet."

"Cook?" asked Sarah innocently.

"Talk and cook breakfast. At the same time." Sam added the second part for emphasis. "Sorry, Emma, the housekeeper with the excess decorating skills, is off this morning, so we're on our own."

"Okay, lead the way," Sarah sighed. She definitely set her own trap this time.

Sarah followed Sam down the stairs to the foyer and around the stairwell to a narrow corridor that led to a swinging shuttered doorway. Sam pushed the shutters open and walked through, and as Sarah followed him she gasped in amazement. What was more than likely the original kitchen and dining room had been completely renovated. Transformed into a great room, the kitchen was off to the left and a wraparound peninsula with bar stools separated the cooking area from what appeared to be a living room/dining area. Everything was done in Charcoal, White and Chrome. Recessed and drop-down pendant lights had replaced the original wall sconces, and where you would expect a chandelier might have been originally, there was now a ceiling fan with tropical palm fan blades. The whole thing was just a little out of sync with the rest of the house. The back wall was entirely glass, providing a spectacular view of the lawn and gardens behind the home. It was a stark contrast to the remainder of the house, which while certainly having some renovations over the years, the Victorian flavor and essence still existed. But here in this room it was like walking into a new century.

"Like it?" Sam asked as he saw her expression.

"Yes. No, I mean I do like it, but it's not my style. It just doesn't seem to belong, that's all." Sarah shrugged her shoulders apologetically. She really wasn't trying to insult his taste.

"You're right. It was Greg's idea." Sam laughed as he waved a hand over towards the kitchen.

"He's the one who cooked, so he ruled the day when we tackled this part of the house. If I didn't give in to his demands, he'd stop cooking, and I'd starve. Well, in all fairness, Emma does feed me. But then he started traveling more and more, and cooking for me less and less anyway. I got suckered," he smiled sadly, "but I didn't mind."

"No, I don't suppose you did. Now it makes sense. Funny, Greg always let me do the cooking since Megan couldn't boil water. He never mentioned he had serious culinary skills." Understanding the sudden melancholy Sam was experiencing she tried to lighten the mood. She headed to the fridge and began pulling out what she'd need for a nice healthy omelet. Eggs, milk, butter, bread, some cheese and whatever vegetables were available. As she gathered everything on the counter and began rummaging for utensils and a pan, she decided to kick off the necessary discussion.

"Alright, Sam, I can cook and talk so let's get this started. Tell me about Chamandia, and why the government there would care less about me or my niece."

"My niece too," Sam replied, as if that answered her question.

"Granted. Your niece too," Sarah shot back.

"OK. Sorry," Sam apologized, again. It seemed he was constantly doing that. He looked over and watched her as she prepared the omelet. She was really beautiful, he thought. Even all rumpled up with tags hanging off her, nothing distracted from her vibrance. He thought about just walking over and pulling her into his arms. But he couldn't. Shouldn't. Anything on that score would have to wait. Instead he pulled out a pair of scissors from the utility drawer, deciding the tags needed removal.

"What the hell are you doing Sam?" Sarah almost jumped out of her skin. "I'm trying to cook here."

"Tags," he replied as if that made perfect sense.

"It's a fashion statement. Ever hear of Minnie Pearl?"

Sam ignored her hands batting away the scissors as he went to work looking for the little plastic pieces to cut.

"Let's start with Chamandia, okay?" Sam began. "How much do you know about it?"

"As much as the next person, I suppose," Sarah replied. "Ouch, quit poking me."

"Oops," Sam chuckled.

"Playground for the rich and famous, beautiful setting, beautiful people, low crime," Sarah paused. "They've had some weird stuff in the royal family though, if I recall," Sarah began chopping quickly as if thinking made her work faster. And helped distract her from Sam's hands and the scissors. If he didn't finish soon she might actually smack him.

"Weird how?" Sam asked her calmly, though his mind was racing. Don't let her know too much, he silently pleaded.

"Well, the ruling prince." She continued without waiting for a reply. "He's got no heirs. I remember a few years ago reading how his wife and maybe his child were killed in a car crash, and supposedly he's the only royal left." Sarah straightened suddenly. "I remember now, in the article it talked about the unexpected, or was it untimely deaths of practically the entire royal family! Some sort of curse."

"The Christoph Curse. I suppose it's true. Mostly." Sam spoke quietly.

"I'm going to take a stab in the dark here," Sarah stopped working as she spoke. "Here is a wealthy principality, with a dying monarchy. Whoever takes power there will be controlling vast wealth. You indicated there are those who want you out of the way, which tells me you're probably assisting the Prince in some fashion. And you probably have great influence there. How am I doing so far?"

"Right on target," Sam chuckled softly.

"So who stands to benefit if you're out of the way? Who's first in line, so to speak?" Sarah still hadn't gone back to preparing breakfast. She stood with knife in one hand and onion in the other, her eyes staring unseeing out the glass window wall.

"That's the tricky part. The political situation has been volatile for the past 60 years. But the problems go all the way back to the late 18th century." With all the tags removed, Sam began rummaging in the kitchen then, realizing that nobody was making coffee which he desperately needed. As he got the beans from the freezer and ground them, he thought about how to best bring her into the picture without revealing anything too dangerous.

"Sam?" Sarah looked over and smiled at him. He felt like a fist was squeezing his heart when she did.

"What?" He was taken off guard for a minute.

"You were saying?" Sarah said impatiently.

"Yes, right. Well, it goes back to the founding of Chamandia. Back in 1770, a British ship wrecked on the coast of an island in the Indian Ocean. The crew and passengers disembarked and set up camp. They were marooned there, and after several months, they'd basically colonized the place. Well the ship's captain, a man by the name of John de Guerre, proclaimed himself King of the Island. Which he duly named Isle de Guerre." Sam smirked and waved his arms for effect. "Now, he was a fairly decent man, a bit of a pompous ass, but all in all took good care of his charges. He put everyone to work including himself, and formed a fairly decent society. They built housing, mostly huts I assume, gathered food, fished and traded with the native population. It wasn't a deserted island after all, there were indigenous groups there. After a decade or so, another ship on the same route docked and sent a scouting team to the island. Upon discovering the survivors of the wreck, they realized they stumbled upon something important. As soon as they returned to England some 6 months later, they delivered the news to old King George that his ship had been found or rather the survivors and their village. They also relayed that furthermore, the captain was laying claim to the throne of his newly founded kingdom."

Sam paused for a moment, grabbing 3 mugs from the cupboard and filling each one with much needed coffee. He handed one to Sarah, and one to Grace, who'd silently entered the kitchen during his little speech. Grace had Addy snuggled in one arm, and deftly took the cup, and Addy, over to the counter and sat herself on the stool.

"Sam, I hate to interrupt, but do you have a small mat or rug I can lay her down on?"

"Actually, I think Emma had put some things in the hall closet. I'll check." Sam returned quickly with a little play mat, complete with plastic teething rings and sound makers attached along with a portable crib.

"Perfect." Grace smiled. "I take it Emma is the housekeeper?"

"That's her," replied Sam. "Housekeeper and baby planner extraordinaire!" He chuckled and realized suddenly how much he was enjoying this. Talking about Chamandia was actually pretty cathartic. And being here with Sarah, Addy and Grace made him feel more like he was home than ever before. After helping Grace set things up for Addy, Sam took his coffee and sat on the stool next to Grace. Sipping slowly, since he'd over-poured, he continued.

"Where was I? Oh yes. King George was not happy to hear about this new found kingdom in paradise, mostly because of course it wasn't his. And since de Guerre was commissioned by the Royal Navy and was acting on behalf of the Crown when he wrecked, old George decided to put his own man down there. So George decreed that Isle de Guerre was to be under the charge of His Majesty and would be dubbed a principality. George Christopher was bestowed the title of Prince. Nobody really knew where he had come from. Rumor has it he was a bastard son of George, but that's yet to be proven. In any case, Christopher soon became Christoph as the official language had been French. De Guerre's doing of course. His mother had been English, but his father had been French. Prince George renamed the Island Chamandia, who knows why. Some think it was the name of his mistress. So de Guerre was exiled, and where he went was a mystery. He was taken aboard a ship sailing to an unknown destination. Since then, the Christoph line has held the monarchy, seceding from British rule back in the late 1800's."

Sam looked over at Sarah, who was standing very still, fully concentrating on what Sam was saying. He smiled and winked at her, trying to get her to react. Just for the fun of it of course. He really was feeling good.

"Well?" Sarah stomped her foot. "Aren't you going to finish?"

"Maybe. Are you ever going to cook that omelet? I'm starving. And starving men don't talk," Sam answered glibly.

"Oh. OH!" Sarah realized both Grace and Sam were waiting on her for breakfast, and she'd totally forgotten. She turned and began furiously chopping the onion and then turned to start cracking the eggs into the bowl.

"Go on. I'm listening, Sam," she said breathlessly. Sam smiled as he watched her move like a whirlwind through the preparation.

"OK then. On to the current situation, or what led up to it. World War II. In 1943, a German ship landed in Chamandia. The crew stayed only a short while, as Chamandia was neutral and they needed the strategically located port too badly to strain relations by overstaying their welcome. Anyway, while there, a German officer named Johann de Guerre introduced himself to a local shopkeeper. Now the shopkeeper knew the island history, all the residents seemed to. And so he asked the man if he was any relation to John de Guerre. Johann suddenly became very tense and left the shop in a hurry. Which led the shopkeeper to believe he was, in fact, a descendant. The shopkeeper sent word up to the palace, as a warning to the royal family. You see Chamandia was neutral, not by choice, but by design. They were an unknown element for the most part, and the Allied forces had been able to convince them to take an officially neutral position. In return, they would be protected. Chamandia would supply valuable information to the Allies about the Germans, gleaned when they were on the island. Everything had gone smoothly till this point."

Sam paused, giving the women time to absorb all of it, then continued.

"The reigning prince, Fidel Christoph, was in no danger from his subjects. Nor from any world powers. The only danger Fidel faced was the unknown descendants of John de Guerre. For John had sworn that someday he, or his heirs, would return and reclaim what was theirs. With Johann de Guerre on the island, things were not so secure anymore." Sam took several more sips of coffee and put the mug down gently. As if what he was about to say was incredibly important and required absolute stillness.

"Three days after the appearance of Johann, Fidel was dead. They said it was a heart attack. Left his widow and young son behind. His widow, Princess Carmen, took control immediately, sending word to London that she needed assistance. A security team was flown down to protect her and the young prince. Things were fine for the next 10 years or so, till Carmen was struck by a hit and run driver while in London. 16-year old Lance became the Prince, and held the throne for 10 years."

Sam paused, getting up to refill his mug.

"Smells good... is it ready?" He leaned over Sarah's shoulder, causing her to shrug him off.

"Just about, sit down, no, get me some plates and then sit down." Sarah smiled sweetly at him. Hoping he was annoyed. Annoyed herself that he took it in stride.

"Here." He handed her the plates. "I'm going to sit now," he said smugly. Seating himself back down, he continued.

"So one day, Prince Lance of Chamandia is found face down in the Oleander, dead. Supposedly fell from the roof, and stinking drunk, they said."

"Who said?" asked Sarah, somewhat politely, knowing that what Sam meant was it was bogus.

"The officials who pronounced it an accident," Sam replied sarcastically.

"And then?" Sarah prompted.

"And then Prince Rolf was crowned. He was only a toddler at the time so his mother remained in charge pretty much until he married. And well, you know what happened to his family. It brings us right up to date, I believe."

"Hmm," was all Sarah said as she brought the plates to the counter for Sam and Grace.

"Eat up," she said to them as she turned to get her own. Joining them at the counter, she looked at Sam.

"It's remarkable how much you know about their history, really. Did you study it for some reason?" Sarah was sounding a bit suspicious.

"I always make sure to bone up on my history when working with anyone, whether it's private industry or government," Sam responded quickly, hoping to quell that curiosity in her.

"Hmm, understandable. There's more, isn't there," she said simply and quietly.

"Yes, but that's enough for now, don't you think?"

"Maybe. Maybe not. In any case, one more question. Are we in real danger right now, at this very moment?"

"No, we're not. Right here, right now, we're safe." Sam replied quickly, wanting to put to rest any doubts Sarah might have. He'd given her plenty to think about. And with that crack brain of hers she would certainly soon put two and two together.

Chapter 11

Sarah was more than bored. She was frustrated. Sam refused to budge on allowing them to go back to the apartment or her to work. Any resistance she put up was warded off by Sam with one word. Addy. Everything was for her protection. Sarah would defend Addy with her life, but this was ridiculous. She couldn't put her entire life on hold like this. But she and Sam had formed an uneasy truce, so to speak. She still had this incredible urge to rattle him, but she knew that urge was symptomatic of something far deeper. She couldn't stand in the same room with him without this intense feeling that swept through her entire body. No man had ever affected her this way. She'd been right up close and personal with some of the best-looking men yet none held the same power over her. She could admire a good-looking guy with the same emotional distance she had when admiring a sculpture.

It was a talent she learned to develop back in school. That old trick she'd learned in debate club, 'imagine them naked' simply didn't work for a hormonal teenage girl facing off against a good-looking guy. So instead she would imagine they were merely statues. Megan had taught her that just before her first competition. Worked like a charm. Men, women, didn't matter. Imagining them as nothing more than lifeless sculptures with no power over her. But not with Sam. She just couldn't seem to do it. His strong, chiseled features reflected not just power and intelligence, but something more. Something intangible. She could see him just as easily in a boardroom as she could envision him standing at the helm of a ship or in her almost daily fantasies, nope, not going there she thought! She couldn't stand to be around him. She couldn't stand to be away from him. She needed something to do, and quickly. No time like the present she thought as she poked her head into his study.

"Busy?" she asked Sam, who was at his desk, his head buried in his tablet.

No response.

"Sam?" She spoke a little louder this time.

He looked up with a sheepish grin, pulling an earbud out of one ear.

"Sorry, hi, just brushing up on my Italian," he replied. "Something you need?"

"Yeah, something to do. I'm sorry Sam, but we've been here over a week and I'm going out of my mind with boredom. Addy's napping, and Grace is knitting up in her room. I could use a diversion," Sarah's voice trailed off.

"Tell you what, maybe you can help me," Sam replied cheerfully. His blue eyes seemed to dance with laughter.

"Sure. What do you need?" Sarah asked cautiously. His reply was a bit too unexpected.

"See those files?" Sam pointed to a stack of folders on the coffee table.

Sarah narrowed her eyes. "You want me to file for you?" Of course, she thought. Should have known better.

"Yup," Sam replied with a grin. He paused a moment, watching the anger swell up. Sarah wasn't good at hiding emotion, he thought. How she got a reputation as a shark in the business world escaped him. He could read her like a book. And he wanted to.

"You want me to file?" Sarah repeated the question, with an incredulous look on her face.

"Yep. But not yet." Sam kept smiling. "First, I'd like you to browse through them."

"What am I looking for?" she asked a bit snidely, knowing full well he probably wanted her to find some paper buried in the wrong file.

"Well, the files deal with Taglio shipping. It's a firm I'm considering buying. I've got a conference call at 1 o'clock with the owner. That's what the Italian is for. Anyway, there's something that doesn't add up. According to the financial reports, their assets total over a billion dollars. My gut tells me something's off. I hope not, but I need to be sure."

Sarah's eyes widened. "You really do want my help, don't you!" She was genuinely surprised. She'd been under the impression that while Sam knew more about her than before, he still didn't consider her to be on the same intellectual or professional level as he was.

"So?" Sam asked. "What do you say? Gonna help me out?"

Sarah smiled and nodded. "I don't suppose you have the data online?"

"Sorry no, seems they literally use manual ledgers over there, though that will change I promise you," Sam chuckled. "How long will it take?"

"Give me an hour," Sarah replied confidently.

"That's my girl!" Sam smiled back. In fact neither moved or spoke for a minute as they just smiled at each other. Each lost in their own moment. The knock at the door snapped them out of it quickly.

A petite, gray haired woman entered the room smiling, not waiting for an invitation. The housekeeper, Emma, Sarah thought. It must be.

"Sam? Sorry to bother you. I just wondered if you wanted me to get dinner together again before I go."

"Actually, Emma, I was just thinking along those lines. Sarah, have you met Emma?"

"No," Sarah replied, smiling warmly at the woman. "I think we've just missed each other every day this week! It's good to meet you." Sarah held her hand out to Emma, who shook it warmly.

"Well it's good to finally meet you as well. Seems Grace and I have gotten to know each other pretty well, and that adorable niece of yours too, but I had to wonder about the mysterious creature who kept disappearing whenever I'd get a glimpse!" Emma laughed. "I've heard enough about you from Sam, though," she went on, chuckling. Sarah turned to look at Sam, who was becoming slightly red in the face.

"Really," Sarah said curiously, turning back to Emma. "And just what has Sam been saying? Anything I should hear?"

Emma replied with another laugh. "Plenty, but you'll not hear it from me, I value my job too much. But I think you'll do," she finished, winking at Sam as she turned to leave.

"I'll do?" Sarah looked at Sam pointedly. "Do for what?"

Sam didn't answer, still counting his blessings that Emma hadn't revealed anything he'd said. She'd been truthful about the way he'd spoken of Sarah, since for the past few days Sam had been following Emma around like a lost puppy. He'd been trying to stay out of Sarah's way, avoid getting any closer. And he'd needed to talk to someone. Emma had worked for the Livingstons for 40 years, and had helped raise Sam. She was more of a mother than a housekeeper. He'd told her that Sarah was beautiful. Smart. Temperamental. A real fireball. And not at all his type. To which Emma had simply replied "humph."

And he could see now that Emma was pleased with Sarah. Well, hell, so was he. He was more determined than ever to keep her in his life. And the first step was getting her comfortable around him. Though maybe the awkwardness emanated from him, not her. He didn't know. He watched Sarah as she made her way over to the sofa and sat down with her legs tucked under.

She was dressed in a pair of jeans, and a t-shirt. It seemed to be her everyday look. She certainly wasn't trying to attract his attention with her choice of outfits. No innuendos there. Yet, she was beautiful as hell in whatever she wore. More beautiful still for not realizing it. He went back to his Italian tutorial, deliberately trying not to watch her as she rifled through the stacks of folders. He was genuinely hoping she'd find something. Though he hadn't thought to ask for her help before, he should have. If he could just get past this physical thing between them, maybe they could find some mutual common ground. Maybe this was it.

They both focused on their tasks. Sam occasionally looking over at Sarah. Sarah occasionally looking over at Sam. It was quiet, with the exception of Sam periodically blurting out some phrase or another in Italian, usually several times to get the pronunciation right, which elicited a smile from Sarah each time. Otherwise it was a companionable silence between them.

It took more than an hour for Sarah to finish but not by much.

"Sam, I think I've found your problem," she said matter of factly.

Sam looked up to find Sarah standing just in front of his desk and pulled out the earbud again.

"And?" was all he said, though it was more out of surprise that she was finished so quickly.

"And," she said as she laid several sheets of paper on his desk, "you'll notice that over 75 million in shipping contracts is for a company called Nordam LTD."

"Yes, well no surprise there," Sam remarked. "I did look through it myself you know."

"Yes, well," Sarah grinned knowing she was in her element now. "Taglio often jobs out portions of the contract if they can't schedule something in, right?"

"Sure. We all do that," Sam replied. "It's good business."

"Exactly!" Sarah jumped in. "Especially if you're jobbing it out to one of your own divisions."

"Standard procedure to give it to your own before going outside for help, Sarah," Sam sounded critical, until he realized where she was going with it. "Sorry, keep going."

"I don't know, you don't sound very impressed," Sarah retorted.

"I said sorry, I know you've got something, so spill it." Sam knew he was acting badly, but he couldn't seem to help it. He wanted this deal to go smoothly and was hoping she'd confirm that the audits were clean.

"Check the balance sheet for Taglio's Mediterranean division. You were right. Something's off. They're reporting the contract revenue as income for both divisions. My gut says that's not the only duplication, either." Sarah smiled smugly and waited for Sam to comment. She knew she shouldn't be so cheerful when a deal might be broken, but she was having fun. She felt alive again. Some would find her work tedious, but she loved the challenge. She started to wonder what it might be like to work for Livingston.

"Sarah?" Sam snapped his fingers to get her attention. Damn that woman was always daydreaming.

"What, I'm right here, in front of you, no need to snap. I'm not a dog," she huffed out.

Sam smirked. "That, I know," he replied. "Can you find the rest?"

"How much time do I have?" she asked. Sam glanced at his watch, looked up at Sarah and shrugged, letting out a small laugh. "About an hour, tops," he said.

"Done," Sarah replied, and turning on her heels strode back to the sofa, picked up the remaining files and began rifling through them.

"Sarah?" Sam tried to get her attention. Hearing her name, she just waved a hand in the air, indicating she didn't want to be disturbed. Sam smiled. He was going to suggest lunch. He figured he was only going to be in the way anyway, so he decided to go fix it himself and bring something back for her.

Sarah looked up as Sam came back in, tray in one hand, and a smile on his face.

"Lunch is served madam," he called out with a very bad British accent, causing Sarah to smile in return.

"What have we got? Did Emma make it?" Sarah narrowed her eyes suspiciously.

"Nope. I did!" Sam beamed. Sarah chuckled. She'd never seen him look more relaxed, and it made her insides turn to jelly. He wore a pair of faded jeans and a white cotton dress shirt, open at the collar, sleeves rolled up. If the food was lousy, she thought suddenly, she could eat him up instead.

"OK, let's see what you've got," she said.

Sam set the tray down and gestured toward it with his hand.

"Voilà!"

Sarah placed one hand over her mouth, stifling an attack of giggles that was certain to erupt. Sam squinted down at her, seeing the laughter in her eyes.

"What? My cooking isn't good enough for you?"

Sarah gave up. Bursting into laughter, she pointed at the tray.

"What. Is. That?" She stopped at each word to breathe. She hadn't laughed this hard since Megan was alive. And it felt so good.

"Eggs and Toast," Sam replied somewhat gruffly, still not seeing what was so funny.

"So which is the egg and which is the toast?" Sarah couldn't help herself.

Sam looked back down at the plates and realized how utterly awful the food looked. Might as well have served canned dog food. Then again, no dog would have touched this he thought.

And just like that, seeing her so completely out of control and carefree, Sam couldn't help but laugh himself. It was a hearty laugh, one that came from deep inside.

Sarah realized right then and there; he was it for her. She was falling truly, madly, deeply and irrevocably in love with the man. He sat down beside her, his shoulders still rumbling from laughter, and casually swinging one arm up behind her shoulders to rest on the back of the couch, he leaned back and closed his eyes. Trying to catch his breath. This was wonderful, he thought. He hadn't felt this good since Greg was alive.

With his eyes still closed, Sam took a few deep breaths to relax, and absently began twirling strands of Sarah's hair between his fingers. Sarah stiffened, eyes wide, and noticing the peaceful look on Sam's face, hesitated to say anything. Hell, she didn't want to stop him. But she knew she had to. If anything started up between them, it was bound to catch fire.

She leaned forward, carefully, not wanting him to realize she was moving away. Grabbing the top file off the pile, she bit back a grin as she swung it just hard enough to swat him on the chest.

Startled, his eyes flew open as he suddenly became aware of the situation.

"You didn't have to whack me, I'm not asleep," he said with a hint of humor.

"I know, it was just too tempting. Guess what I've found?" Sarah's voice was once again morbidly cheerful.

"I'll bite. More duplications?" Sam replied.

"And some other irregular accounting tricks," she continued.

"Bottom line, Sarah, what's it worth?" Sam didn't need the details, and there wasn't time. His gut told him to trust her on this. And he did.

"Not a penny over 650," Sarah replied, her tone was light, but the meaning was clear.

"Lock stock and barrel?" Sam asked, wondering if they were hiding liabilities as well.

"Not sure, but if you let me sit in on the call, I'll be able to help when you draft the offer."

Sam held his hand out. "Shake on it?"

Sarah reached over and clasped his hand. They shook on it, and neither let go. They could have sat there, just like that, for hours. Except at precisely 1 o'clock, the phone on his desk rang. It was time to cut a deal, and have Sarah take the first step towards playing a different role in his life.

Chapter 12

Sam pushed the disconnect button on the speaker phone and looked up at Sarah, now seated directly across from him, one leg tucked up on the chair, making him smile. Sometimes she appeared no more than a teenage girl. No makeup, her loose curls hanging wildly about her face. The small barely visible crinkles around her eyes when she laughed the only clue to her age. The sharpness reflected in her eyes spoke of intelligence. And her relaxed demeanor indicated she was comfortable with herself and those around her. The women Sam encountered, both socially and professionally, were far more rigid. Far more concerned with their appearance. Never concerned with those around them, or how their actions affected them. Sarah, he knew now, was more than capable of going toe to toe in the boardroom. She knew the game. But wouldn't deliberately cause harm to achieve her goals.

It was evident in the way she assisted in the Taglio negotiations. After introducing her to the other calling parties as her associate, he let her do most of the talking. In fluent Italian, no less. He caught most of it, though asked for translations every so often.

When the conversation was directed toward the inconsistencies of the financials, Sarah was smooth and diplomatic. She never implied the erroneous entries were deliberate. Instead, she simply pointed them out as common accounting errors. Sam smiled as he recalled how sweet she'd been, never implying wrong-doing, and empathizing with Franco Taglio regarding this kind of mix-up. She was good. Very good. And the deal went off without a hitch. He could call legal and have them draw up the contracts, with no doubts about the outcome.

"Happy with the deal, Sam?" Sarah queried, noticing the smile on his face.

"You bet. That was fabulous work you did there," Sam replied sincerely.

"Good. You know it felt good to get back in the middle of things again. I really thought I was enjoying the coffee shop. No stress, the socializing, but now that I've had a taste of the wheeling and dealing again, I think maybe I was just trying to be content with whatever I had. But this is better," she grinned as she spoke. "Much better!"

Sam was thoughtful for a moment, and then he snapped his head up suddenly. That's it, he thought. He'd had a brainstorm, now all he had to do was convince Sarah.

"What?" Sarah looked at him curiously. "Something wrong?"

"Not a thing. In fact, Sarah, I've got an idea. A proposal of sorts. Tell me what you think," Sam was drumming his fingers on the desk nervously.

"OK, shoot," said Sarah.

"You don't really want to go back to the coffee shop. We both know that. And you can't go back to Lou because, well, it's too risky, and not convenient. And Addy needs you anyway. But there is a way for you to get back into your career, keep Addy with you, earn a good living, and be safe all at the same time. I mean keep Addy safe, of course," Sam realized he was making a mess of things. Somehow he knew instinctively that Sarah didn't care about her own personal safety, only Addy's.

"And how would I do that?" Sarah asked, very curious. Knowing Sam, it would be some sort of deal that left her in his debt.

"You work for me," Sam answered, and quickly went on to explain. "Look, as I'm sure you're aware, Livingston Industries is parent to over 15 subsidiaries worldwide. From Shipbuilding to Hotels to Shopping Malls. We're very diverse. As Chairman and CEO, I'm responsible for all of it. I can't do it alone. I could use someone like you."

"Go on," Sarah said cautiously. Not letting her excitement show.

"Each subsidiary has its own executive management, who report directly to the board and me. Right now, we meet once a month with each Company President. However, I also like to visit not only the corporate headquarters of each, but the individual properties, including the shipyards, at least every few months. I get quarterly reports, which I then go through with a fine-tooth comb." Sam stood, and began pacing as he talked, arms behind his back.

"The Board of Directors is comprised of myself and 10 other individuals, all independent overseers. The problem is I have no one to help me directly. Outside of the board, there is no one I can trust to view all the financials from all of the companies. We aren't a publicly held corporation. All stock is held by me and a few select individuals. Besides me, only the IRS knows what's going on inside each company. I need someone, Sarah. Someone I can trust to help me. Will you consider it?" Sam paused and watched her face for any clues. She looked thoughtful, as if she was seriously giving it her consideration. Then her eyes took on that familiar gleam. Uh oh, Sam thought, she's gonna give me hell for something, or put me there!

"How long, Sam?" she asked abruptly.

"What do you mean, how long?"

"For how long will I assist you? As you put it. A month? Six months? A year? What are you asking from me?" Sarah sounded awfully suspicious, and Sam had to move carefully.

"I'm talking about a career, Sarah, not a temporary job. Livingston Industries can offer you a stable, long term career. And a great income, by the way."

"Exactly what position are you wanting to fill Sam? Is there a specific title, or just 'Sam's assistant'?" Sarah was a little more relaxed, but not giving anything away.

"Hmm, let me think. Sam's assistant. I like it," he laughed, letting her know he was just messing with her head.

"Really, Sam. Give me some concrete information."

The problem, Sam thought, was this was a spontaneous idea, and he hadn't planned it out.

"Okay. Well for starters, your title would be," he paused and scrunched one eye closed, as if trying to come up with something. He tried to overdo it, so she'd think he was still messing around. He wasn't, but he couldn't let on. He sat back down at his desk, and began jotting notes absently on a scratch pad, scribbling different things.

Sarah said nothing, just waited patiently. She knew he was up to something. And it had mischief written all over it. But it didn't really matter. She had every intention of taking what he offered. If it meant she could take care of Addy, and stay close to him, she'd do it. Whatever it was. She hoped of course it wasn't menial. She hoped he could see how capable she was and offer her something worthy of her abilities. Something to challenge her.

Sam spoke up suddenly.

"Internal Consulting. You'll be President. Your job will be demanding, of course, but necessary." Sam checked to see how she was reacting. Her head was slightly tilted, and her eyes alert. A good sign.

"The division is responsible for establishing and maintaining the relationships and communications between all subsidiaries, as well as investigating and reporting all operational and auditing issues for each. Initially, you'll have a bit of traveling to do, getting some firsthand knowledge of each property, but then everything can be handled from the main office after that. You'll have a staff of course, but the first rule of thumb is no staff member will have access to information for any more than one subsidiary. In fact it's set up with one work group for each subsidiary, ensuring you are the only one with access to all information."

"Interesting concept Sam, kind of like the police have their internal investigators, eh?"

"Exactly," Sam replied. "However in this case your job is not only investigating, but recommending as well. Looking for opportunities between each subsidiary, relationship-building, operational efficiencies. That sort of thing. Look, I know you're young, and under other circumstances I wouldn't consider you for this position for another 10 years at least."

Sarah opened her mouth, ready to object, but he went on.

"But you should know, I have now had the chance to review your background. You've accomplished in 5 years what most don't accomplish their entire careers. It's probably the most impressive resumé I've seen. Ever."

"Oh, well, thank you for that. I appreciate it." She was genuinely surprised and flattered by the compliment. In her world, men didn't generally acknowledge her talents. Whether it was professional jealousy or something much more insidious, like gender bias and misogyny, she'd become accustomed to being almost the invisible player in the room. His attitude buoyed her spirits and exposed another layer to Sam she'd have to consider.

"Truthfully Sam, I'd need help. I'd need one person, an executive assistant, that would be privy to everything. I can't do it alone."

"OK, granted, someone to type up your reports, help research. I'd have to clear them. There are several in our office now who I could let you have. People I trust implicitly."

"And you'd pay how much?" Sarah asked, a hint of a smile appearing on her face. Sam had her now, he knew it.

"$125,000 to start, with profit sharing compensation of 5% on any increased profit margins. Plus all the benefits, the full package, whatever it is we offer." Sam smiled, seeing Sarah had both feet on the floor now, back straight, definitely interested.

"Make that 175 and 8% of the increased margins." Sarah shot back quickly and continued talking so as not to give him any room. "Will my office be in the Rockdale corporate headquarters?" Sarah was two nibbles away now, and Sam knew it.

"Yes. However, you'll divide your time up so that you can spend a few days a week with Addy, home officing, if you will."

"Home officing. From here." Sarah spoke the words slowly, emphatically. "This is your home, not mine, Sam." Sarah sounded a bit peeved. Sam grimaced. Now that had been a slight misstep. He had to think fast.

"Well, that's true. However, since Addy's my niece, and she's welcome to live here and make this her home, which technically it will be someday anyway, as my heir, in fact I've already proceeded to have the house put in trust for her now anyway, and since you are her guardian, your home is with Addy, then this, technically, is your home too." Sam smiled broadly. Checkmate, he thought.

Sarah had to chuckle. She'd been outmaneuvered.

"Touché Sam," she replied. "So I move in here, and work with you on keeping all of Livingston's holdings in one piece."

"That's it. Pretty good, no?" Sam asked.

"Pretty good, yes, Sam, but one more question. Why?" Sarah kept her tone light, but Sam sensed he'd have to tread carefully to answer this one. He drew a deep breath, then exhaled slowly. It was all or nothing. Either he trusted her, or he didn't. If they were to have any future together, he'd have to take the risk. If it backfired, he'd lose everything. But what would it be worth without her anyway?

"Because, Sarah, the last person to hold this job did so because of who he was, and because I trusted and believed in him. Character is everything in this case, and you've got that in spades."

"Who was it Sam?" her voice was gentle and calm. She instinctively braced herself for what was coming.

"Greg." Sarah was truly surprised. It wasn't what she thought. She'd thought he was going to say he did it himself.

"So that whole jet setting freewheeling bachelor gig was a ruse?"

"Yes," Sam replied, and there was sadness in his voice.

"Sam, what really happened to Greg? I was told he was skiing, that there was an avalanche?"

"That's true. We had no rules about his free time. He was in Milan at a factory and decided to take a side trip to the alps for a bit of R&R. Lord knows he deserved it."

"I'm so sorry, Sam. I had no idea he was that involved with your business, and apparently your life. Bill gave me the impression that you two were a bit estranged. You weren't, were you?"

"Actually," Sam smirked, "we were pretty much poster boys for sibling rivalry. And Bill knew about Greg's working with me. But we managed to keep our professional relationship completely separate, who knows how. Our personal lives were another story entirely."

"Why, Sam?" Sarah asked. "I mean Megan and I had issues, but she was my rock. What happened between you?"

Sam smiled. "Girls," he responded. "We discovered girls. And I discovered they preferred Greg. Usually only after they tried me out first. From the time we were in our teens, it seemed if I were to get the first date, Greg would get the next. I resented him stealing my women." He shrugged as if that were perfectly normal. "He resented always getting hand-me-downs. And when he managed to find one first, I'd try to interfere. Wasn't pretty. Bill was right about Megan. Greg never told me. She was quite possibly his first original unused, non-hand-me-down, untouched by Sam, girlfriend." Sam turned away to brush a well-formed tear from his eye. When he turned back, Sarah was absently looking at the ceiling, as if holding back her own tears.

"Will you tell me about her?" Sam asked quietly.

"She radiated kindness, Sam. She was kind, and beautiful and smart and funny and all the things a big sister should be. She wanted to be the next Meryl Streep. I miss her."

Sarah reached for her phone and opened up her photo gallery.

"This is Megan," she handed him the phone. She'd loaded a photo of Megan with Greg. They were standing together, on a covered bridge it looked like, just gazing at each other.

"Where was this? I don't recognize the bridge."

"You've never seen Bridges of Madison County have you," Sarah said softly. "It was their favorite and they decided to act out the scene one day. I went along to document it. It's not the actual bridge from the movie, just one they found upstate."

"They look so happy. So in love." Sam felt a surge of sadness then. That he hadn't ever met Megan. The woman who had stolen Greg's heart. He'd been so busy keeping everyone at a distance, including Greg, he missed out on something big. He could see that.

They sat silent together for a moment, each remembering their loss but feeling a little less alone having spoken about it.

"So how about it, Sarah, will you take the job?" Sam's voice was gentle, and pleading.

"On one condition, Sam," Sarah replied. "The kitchen. You stay out of it," Sarah said wryly. "And one more thing. You need to let me get my stuff from the apartment."

"Done," replied Sam.

Sam stood up and came around to her side of the desk and grabbing her hand, pulled her up out of the chair. Pulling her against him, he meant only to give her a handshake, which seemed to turn into a hug. A kind of welcome to the family or business type of thing. Friendly. But the minute he had her in his arms, he froze. He couldn't let go. And she wasn't fighting it. Not encouraging him, but not resisting. He couldn't know what she was feeling. It was as if they were each holding tight to something, terrified to let go. Her mind was spinning. The scent of his cotton shirt mixed with the musky scent of his skin was intoxicating. He was solid and broad. Being in his arms was in one sense the most calming secure place she could be. And in another, like being caught in a whirlwind. A tornado. Monsoon maybe? Totally out of control. Emotions battled each other. Steeling herself, Sarah let go first and stepped back, her eyes drawn to his automatically. His eyes blazed, reflecting the heat in her own. They stared at each other, breathing rapidly, neither wanting to move. Neither wanting to stay put. Stalemate.

*****

Sarah stood in the slowly darkening room looking around, once again admiring her suite. She loved everything about it. She walked over to the desk and switched on the lamp. It would be dinnertime shortly, and she hadn't gotten herself together yet. She was still recovering from the embrace. Hug. Death defying spiral. He had taken her by surprise. She expected maybe a handshake. Slap on the arm. But being in his arms like that… it was the stuff of dreams. And now she'd be living here, with him, and working with him. Could she manage to keep a professional distance? No way. They were going to be Addy's surrogate parents, and that required far more personal interactions. But that was still a far cry from real intimacy. She wondered too what that bit was about Greg and the women in their lives. Why would any woman dump Sam for Greg? That made little sense. Unless Sam just chose the wrong women. Sarah didn't think so. There had to be something else behind it.

She supposed some women might be put off by Sam's attitudes, his lack of grace in dealing with the subtle nuances of dating. But Sarah could see through all of that. And give as good as she got. The whole thing was baffling. Maybe once she was involved more in his business, and social circle, she'd get a better sense of what the big deal was. In the meantime, she needed to get a list together for what she wanted from the apartment. Tom would drive her into town and they could go through and she'd point out what she needed. Sam didn't want anyone to know she was moving out. So Tom would go back for her stuff without her. She was to keep her apartment leased, and he was arranging to have her calls forwarded to a secure cell phone he'd given her this afternoon. Sam was adamant that she tell no one except Grace and her godparents the actual new number. No one else. All her outgoing calls from the cell phone would be relayed, so that whoever she called couldn't trace her. He said it was safer that way. That until the Chamandian matter was settled, whatever it was, she and Addy were at some risk. Sarah suspected it was far more dangerous than he let on. But she also was getting to know him well enough to tell when he was nervous, or tense. And as it was with Grace, as long as he appeared relaxed, she felt secure. And today's events had pretty much put Chamandia far from her mind. For now, she'd go down and eat, spend some time with Addy, and get a good night's sleep. Well the first two anyway.

*****

Sam sat in the big leather chair in his study, reading one of many trade journals he subscribed to. His mind wasn't on the material though, and he kept rereading the same passages. His mind was on Sarah. The feel of her in his arms. The scent of jasmine in her hair. He hadn't meant to hug her. It was a huge mistake. He'd need to keep a professional distance to make this work, at least for now. He looked toward the foyer as he heard steps coming down the stairs. His heart rate sped up.

"Evening, Grace," he called as he realized it wasn't her, and he breathed deeply while his heart slowed down again.

"Hello, Sam," Graced replied, smiling as she poked her head through the doorway. "Haven't seen you much today. I'm heading in to warm up the dinner, shouldn't take more than 20 minutes or so, according to Emma."

"I can do that, Grace, why don't you take Addy into the parlor, play for a while."

"Sorry, Sam," Grace laughed. "I've already been informed of your skills in the kitchen. According to your agreement with Sarah, I'm told it's off limits to you!"

"I'm not completely useless in there, you know," Sam muttered under his breath.

"I heard that Sam, and I agree. However, why don't you wake Addy up from her nap, and let her play with her uncle for a while instead." Grace's voice faded as she headed back to the kitchen.

Grace was right. This was a far better idea, he thought, as he laid his large frame down on the floor to play with Addy on the mat. She got such a kick out of the little rattles attached to the side, especially when Sam made funny faces at her when he shook them with his own teeth. She'd gurgle and coo, and slobber all over his hand. He never imagined himself as a parent. He'd always known when the time came, he'd marry and have kids, he just never thought about having kids in the real sense. They were merely an idea in his head. And Addy was so very real. The only thing that would make this little playtime better, he thought, was if Sarah were down here on the floor with them. He could see her lying on the opposite side, cooing and smiling at Addy… and at him. Maybe if he played his cards right, it would happen. He'd have to play them carefully. And soon.

Chapter 13

Sam led Sarah into his office suite, with a reception area, several offices to the left, and his corner office to the right. It was walled by windows overlooking the downtown. Furnished in a completely different style than his home office, it was all glass and chrome. The desk was situated against one windowed wall, with a conference table and chairs by the other. The back side featured a bookcase and wet bar. And a separate door led off to a sleeping area and full bath, so late nights he could stay over. "Very impressive Sam," Sarah remarked cheerfully.

"I thought you'd be impressed," Sam replied dryly. They'd just completed a brief tour of the offices, though most of the staff hadn't arrived yet, Sarah at least got the low down on the different players in the building. Her concern would be the 15 analyst teams. The few employees she met seemed to be wonderful people so far, all working in sync. These were the teams handling the East Coast subsidiaries, while those who handled Midwest and Western divisions worked different shifts and wouldn't arrive till later in the day.

They both turned as the intercom buzzed. "Sam, Ms. Barry is here to see you," came the voice over the intercom.

"I'll be out in a moment, Sandy," Sam answered her. Again, it buzzed.

"I'm sorry, sir, she insists on seeing you now."

"Send her in," Sam replied with a sigh.

He didn't look too happy about being interrupted, but she must be an important player for Sam to cave in so easily. Or a girlfriend, Sarah frowned at the thought.

"What?" Sam looked at her oddly. "Interruptions are a part of life, Sarah, get used to it."

"Did I say anything?" She asked somewhat sarcastically.

"No, but your expression speaks volumes," Sam replied, matching her tone.

"Sammy, I'm so sorry to barge in," the smooth voice came filtering in as the door opened. "I know you're very busy, especially with the new capitan arriving today." The woman approached defiantly, sparing little more than a glance at Sarah. And the glance she gave her was more like a pat on the head.

"Hello Lindy," Sam greeted her stiffly, though his tone remained neutral. "What can I do for you?" Again Sam kept his voice polite.

"If we could just have a brief little chat, I promise not to take up more than a few minutes," she smiled seductively and manipulatively as she looked at Sam. Sarah wanted to puke. She knew the type. Well-dressed, aggressive, demanding. The sleek black hair shortly cropped, blood-red lipstick with matching polish on the manicured hands, the custom-tailored suit.

The woman turned to Sarah.

"If you could just excuse us a moment, we need to talk a little business. Do you mind?" The last part was a direct request for Sarah to leave. It was also clearly meant to imply she thought of Sarah as one of Sam's playthings.

Insignificant in the big scheme of things. Sarah didn't know whether to laugh or smack this Ms. Lindy Barry. More like Barracuda.

"I don't mind at all," Sarah replied sweetly, waving her hand out casually as if to indicate she'd leave. Instead, she took a seat on the sofa, threw one leg over the other, leaned back, folded her hands in her lap and looked up expectantly. It was all a game, Sarah knew, one she could play well. She was dressed professionally today, while not flashy. The Black A-line skirt, aqua colored silk blouse with an unstructured black jacket looked good on her. She knew from the look on Sam's face this morning he'd admired her appearance in no small way. A hint of makeup, her hair pulled back in a French twist, a few stray curls here and there... all in all she could hold her own. It was a look that emitted an air of confidence. Which she was going to need.

"I'm sorry, sweetie, but this is a private conversation," Ms. Barry smiled broadly at Sarah, but it didn't quite make it to her eyes. And what was with the sweetie business. She was playing a little game all right. And she'd picked the wrong opponent. Sarah looked directly back at her but didn't smile.

"I'm sorry, Ms. Barry, is it? I was under the impression this was business. If it is, then I'm sure Sam won't mind my being here, would you Sam?" Sarah looked at Sam pointedly. How he handled this would prove once and for all where she stood. Sam caught her gaze and didn't miss the silent communication it bore.

He knew he'd have some explaining to do to Sarah later, but for now, he'd have to take sides. He smiled at Sarah, but she could see the hint of annoyance in his eyes.

"I don't mind at all," he replied. "You can speak in front of her, Lindy," he continued.

Lindy gasped. "Oh!" she uttered involuntarily. "I didn't realize..." she looked from Sam to Sarah and back to Sam. "I suppose congratulations are in order?"

Sam smiled. "Yes, I suppose they are," he replied. "Lindy Barry, meet Sarah Bennett," he continued. He was about to explain who Sarah was, but Lindy jumped right back in.

"I had no idea, I mean really Sam, you've kept this one tucked away." Lindy looked over at Sarah and smiled cynically. "No offense but you just don't seem his type. Are you sure you know what you're doing? I mean you are a bit young, and you may find the lifestyle a bit overwhelming," she went on. "Sam, you really should have told us about this, shame on you," she finished with a pout.

Sarah bit back a grin. Ms. Barry was in for a real shocker. She obviously thought they were engaged. She looked over to see Sam's reaction, wondering what he thought. Sam didn't miss a beat.

"As I was saying, Lindy, meet Sarah Bennett, Livingston Consulting's newest President… and your new boss." Sam glanced at Sarah, then turned his gaze back to Lindy. She was white as a ghost. And her eyes blazed with anger. But ever the professional actress, she tried to bury her reaction.

"I'm so sorry," her voice was cool now. She walked over to the couch; hand outstretched. "Please accept my apologies Ms. Bennett. I really had no idea." Sarah didn't take the offer of a handshake. She nodded her head coolly, accepting the apology, well outwardly anyway. Inside she wanted nothing more than to bash the woman's head against a wall.

"I'll leave you to it now, and I do apologize for the interruption," Lindy spoke abruptly. She spun on her heels, making a speedy exit, closing the door with a slight bang as she left. Sarah looked at Sam, expectantly. She was grateful he'd made it clear where his loyalties were. But she needed more. She needed to know who Lindy was in his life. Not just professionally, but personally. It mattered. Sam smiled at Sarah and shook his head.

"You threw me to the lions you know," he said with a chuckle. "I ought to skin you alive for that."

"You let her insult me, Sam, you deserved it," Sarah replied with a chuckle.

"OK. We're even. I suppose you want to know more about her, don't you?" It was eerie how Sam could suddenly read Sarah's moods. He could anticipate her. And she was beginning to enjoy the same privilege with him.

"Spill it, as you're so fond of saying," Sarah remarked.

"Lindy Barry. VP of the Livingston Hotels Internal Consulting. Sharp as a tack, very aggressive. Runs a tight ship, very efficient. Has a crack team behind her. And no, we've never dated." He grinned at that last part.

"I didn't ask, did I?" Sarah smirked.

"Didn't need to, it was all over your face. If I didn't know better, I'd say you were jealous," Sam chuckled. He didn't know why he had said that, but now that he did he was enjoying her reaction. Her face flushed, and her eyes flashed.

"Jealous?" Sarah said, a little too loudly. "Are you insane?"

"Yes. Professionally speaking, jealous." Sam turned back to his desk at that point, indicating the discussion was over. He'd let her fume for a few minutes, then they could get down to some real business.

"I'm going to find myself an assistant while you're gloating," Sarah threw that out as she stomped toward the door. "You said I could take my pick, right?"

"Sure, whoever you want, but use my list," he called back without turning around. Sarah smiled as she closed the door behind her. So Ms. Barry had a crack team, eh? Well that's the best place to look for a new assistant, she thought. Take the best miss barracuda has right out from under her nose. Smiling smugly, she set off down the hall to the elevator bank. Pushing the button, she realized suddenly that she shouldn't really go off on a personnel hunt until she'd been introduced around. Just as she was about to turn around, the elevator doors opened, and Sarah immediately noticed the young, very pregnant woman in the elevator, obviously frazzled, trying to slip her swollen feet into a pair of pumps that clearly caused her pain. Immediately, Sarah's arm shot out to hold the elevator door. The woman looked up apologetically, and seeing Sarah's amused face, smiled back.

"I'm sorry, it's this humidity. My feet just won't cooperate with my shoes."

"Tell you what," said Sarah. "Come into the hall and we'll get you fixed up." Carrying her shoes in her hand, the woman stepped out into the hall, leaned against the wall and sighed in relief.

"Thanks. I could use some help. My name's Donna Trumble by the way, are you new?" It wasn't 9am yet, so the assumption was that only employees would be in the building.

"Yep. First day. Sarah Bennett," she replied. "Do you happen to have a pair of tennis shoes in your bag, tucked away?"

"Sure," said Donna. "But I'm not allowed to wear them in the office."

"Why not?" Sarah was really curious. Who'd make a pregnant woman wear pumps in this heat.

"The Bar, I mean Ms. Barry, my boss," Donna winced as she realized she'd almost slipped on the name.

"The Barracuda, huh?" Sarah laughed softly.

"I didn't say, I mean, how'd you know?" Donna was sure no one would ever say that to a new employee.

"Just a guess. We've already met. I came up with it myself, at least I thought I did," Sarah mused.

"Well make sure you don't repeat it to the wrong person. She can be pretty nasty," Donna said earnestly.

"What exactly do you do for her?" Sarah asked, feigning innocence.

"I'm her personal assistant," Donna replied somewhat ruefully. "Or personal slave...."

"Well Donna, you just landed yourself a new job." Sarah practically beamed. Her first official task accomplished. She liked Donna; it was an immediate reaction. She had a warm, open face, and if she worked for Lindy, she was more than capable. She understood what Sam meant by a crack team.

And knew Donna must have some pretty strong abilities. Especially in the diplomacy department. Sarah didn't think she herself could work for that witch. And there was no doubt Lindy was a witch.

"So. First thing we're gonna do, is put on your tennis shoes!" Sarah laughed. "Then we'll head down to personnel and rearrange things a bit."

Donna didn't budge, she just stared at Sarah like she'd lost her mind.

"What do you mean, I've got a new job? You're not firing me or anything are you? I mean, what exactly is your job here?" she asked, very nervous now. She wondered if she'd said too much, maybe this woman was a friend of Lindy's. But she didn't think so. She was too damn nice to be her friend.

"Technically, my title is President of Livingston Consulting," Sarah replied, still laughing. "Which means technically, I can hire whomever I please to assist me. You are now my new Executive Assistant. Not Personal Assistant, I want to be clear on that. I never liked that term. I'm guessing you didn't either."

"Ms. Bennett, you're a boss after my own heart!" Donna smiled broadly. "I haven't had such a great day since I've been here. And don't worry, I won't take more than 6 weeks for my maternity leave. I'll even try and keep it to four if it will help."

"Don't be ridiculous," Sarah grinned. "You'll take eight weeks, paid, and then we're going to work out a little arrangement that lets you spend more time with your baby. Deal?"

"Deal!" Donna grabbed Sarah's hand and shook it, dropping her oversized bag in the process. Trying to bend to pick it up, she burst into tears when Sarah reached down and grabbed it for her.

"What's wrong?" she asked, genuinely puzzled. Then it dawned on her. "Aaaah, hormones, right?" Donna wiped her eyes with the back of her hand and sniffed.

"Yeah, sorry, I'm just so happy. And you're just so nice, it made me cry."

"Well, maybe we ought to find a box of tissues before we hit the personnel office and arrange the transfer. I have a feeling there's gonna be more tears," Sarah laughed as she held her arm out for Donna to grab, allowing her to slip her tennis shoes back on. They turned toward the elevator, and she pressed the button to wait for the next one.

"What floor is personnel on anyway?" asked Sarah.

"2," Donna replied quickly. "You haven't been down there yet?"

"No, it's on my to-do list."

"Then I should warn you, the personnel director is a bit different, but very sweet," she added quickly. "And whatever you do, don't laugh when you first see him."

"Uh oh," Sarah replied. "Why would I laugh?"

"His toupee," answered Donna with a smirk.

"Gotcha," Sarah smiled. This was going to be a good first day. She knew it. Things were looking up.

They reached the personnel office door, and Sarah paused for a moment. Turning to Donna, she whispered conspiratorially.

"I need you to introduce me, then follow my lead, okay?"

"You got it, boss," Donna tossed back in the same hushed tone.

They walked in, and Donna led the way down a short corridor towards the Director's door. She knocked firmly, and opened the door just enough to poke her head in.

"Bob, do you have a minute?"

Good, Sarah thought, she's obviously well-liked and respected enough by others to allow her this kind of access. It was a confirmation of what she believed. Donna was a goldmine.

"Sure, Donna, come on in," a voice replied from within. It was a bit high pitched, and a little odd. Donna went in first, followed by Sarah. As soon as she saw Bob, of the infamous bad hair day, she was glad Donna warned her. If she hadn't, she would have been rolling on the floor. His toupee was plastered on his head like a mop. And his clothing didn't help. Suspenders held up a pair of tan polyester slacks, with a pale pink dress shirt to round it all off. Unbelievable. He was nearing 70 if a day, which meant Livingston didn't push employees out the door for early retirement. Another good sign.

"Bob, this is Sarah Bennett, our new President up in Consulting." Donna's introduction was pleasant, with a friendly ring. Bob picked up immediately on the tone. Smiling warmly, he shook Sarah's hand and welcomed her to Livingston.

"Mr. Livingston did say you'd be stopping in, we do have a few papers for you to fill out," he said.

"Yes, I can take care of that now. And I wonder, while I'm signing my life away, if you could do a little favor for me?" Sarah smiled sweetly.

"If I can, I'd be glad to help." His reply was genuine.

"I'd like to have Donna as my new Executive Assistant."

Bob paused as he was gathering the paperwork for her.

"Excuse me, did you just say you want me to transfer Donna?" He looked over at Donna and back to Sarah. "Are you sure about this?"

"Positive, Bob, and don't worry, I'll take the heat." Bob breathed a sigh of relief. As long as she was willing to risk it, he'd do it. He'd love to see Donna in a better spot. Lindy abused the hell out of her, and everyone knew it. They just couldn't change it. Lindy never went far enough to take any action.

"OK. Consider it done," he said with a smile.

"Oh and Bob?"

"Yes, Ms. Bennett," he replied politely, though his eyes danced with amusement.

"Perhaps you could see fit to up her salary 20% while you're at it?" Sarah was still smiling, but Bob clearly saw she meant it.

"20%?" he sputtered.

"Yes. Call it retroactive combat pay, if you will." Sarah laughed, taking the papers from his now shaking hands and pulled a pen from the canister on the desk. Leaning over she began signing, while out of the corner of her eye she watched as Bob went over and sat at his computer, pulling up Donna's records. She couldn't help smirking when she saw he was smiling. He didn't want to seem unprofessional, she understood, but he certainly approved. She glanced back to see how Donna was faring in all this. She'd taken a seat by the door and looked positively stunned.

"Hey, Donna, snap out of it. You're supposed to be having a good day!" Sarah called over to her.

"I'm trying. But do you realize how much of a raise you just gave me? What if Mr. Livingston hears about it, which he undoubtedly will?"

"Hear about what?" They all turned at the sound of Sam's voice. "I was told I'd find you down here, Sarah," Sam remarked. Seeing Donna against the wall, in the waiting chair, he nodded in greeting. "Morning Donna, how's things today?"

"Very good, Mr. Livingston."

"I see you've met our new President."

"I have, yes," Donna replied a bit hesitantly.

Sam looked at each of them, sensing something was up.

"What am I missing here?" he asked cheerfully. Sarah jumped in.

"Nothing much, I've been signing the paperwork. Oh. And I've found my new assistant." Sarah smiled at Sam. He cocked his head to one side and studied her expression. There was a definite gleam of mischief there.

"Well, good." He turned and looked at Donna, noticing the terrified expression on her face. Bingo. He turned back to Sarah.

"I presume you've chosen Donna?"

"But of course!" Sarah grinned. "I think she's perfect for the job. We've been having a nice chat this morning."

Sam looked over at Bob and winced. There was more.

"So what's the problem, aside from Ms. Barry's not being pleased to lose her," he chuckled, knowing Lindy would go ballistic when she learned she'd been trumped.

"Bob? You look a little pale, buddy." Sam had known Bob most of his life. He was a fixture in the company. A bit of a character, but extremely loyal, and did his job well.

Sarah jumped in again, not wanting to put Bob in an awkward position.

"He's just a little uncomfortable with the raise I recommended."

"Well, seems to me it's a promotion, and that does require increased compensation," Sam said thoughtfully.

"Yes, Mr. Livingston, I agree. It's just it seemed a bit, well, much," Bob cautioned.

Sam turned and grinned at Donna, knowing she was worried he'd cut it back down. He turned back to Bob.

"How much is a bit much?"

"20%," Bob said, very quietly, as if the softer he spoke, the less impact it would have. Sam looked at Sarah, one brow raised. It did seem a bit high.

Sarah looked over at Donna.

"How long have you worked for Ms. Barry, Donna?" she asked.

"3 years." She turned back to Sam and narrowed her eyes. Full battle gear on her face.

"Don't you think 3 years working for that woman deserves something substantial?"

Sam laughed outright, his blue eyes crinkling. "Touché Ms. Bennett, touché!" Sam's hearty reply echoed in the room.

"Bob, I've got some things I need to review with Ms. Bennett, if you'll just take care of Donna's transfer, I'll escort these ladies back up to the office." With that said, he helped Donna out of the chair, and taking both women by the arm, led them out to the elevator banks.

Pushing the up button, he spoke quietly.

"Congratulations, Donna. I'm sure you'll enjoy your new position." Donna was a terrific employee, and he'd felt bad that she'd ended up in the claws of Lindy. But it was the highest position available at the time, and he'd let her take it. Lindy treated her horribly, and though she'd never complained, sometimes just hearing the verbal torrents spewing out of Lindy made him wince.

Sam looked over at Sarah and smiled, knowing that she had many reasons for her actions, but this one came from the heart. She was playing guardian angel to someone who, in his eyes, did indeed deserve it. And it proved he was right to put his faith in Sarah, which made him want her even more.

As they headed out of the elevator and towards the executive office suite, Lindy came barreling out looking put out, to say the least. Sarah wondered why, since she couldn't possibly have heard the good news about Donna yet.

"Ms. Trumble," Lindy spewed out in a huff. "Do you have any idea what time it is?"

Well now, Sarah, thought, time to play ball.

"Hello, Ms. Barry, nice to see you again." Sarah looked down at her watch, suppressing a grin. "It's 10:05." Lindy stopped short and opened her mouth to speak, but Sarah just continued on as if she hadn't noticed.

"I'm so glad we ran into you, I wanted to thank you so much for letting Donna come work for me. It really is generous of you. I know how hard it is to find good help," Sarah smiled, waiting for the eruption.

"What?" was all that came out.

"I said I wanted to thank you."

"I heard what you said, but I don't understand. I didn't okay any transfer."

Sam knew it was time to step in. "I'm sorry, Lindy, I'm afraid it's my doing. I told Sarah to take her pick for her new assistant. I suppose she assumed I'd told you." Sam looked apologetic, but Sarah could tell he was enjoying this as much as she was.

"Look, just give personnel a call and have them send you up someone," Sam continued. "I'm afraid we have to get ready for the meeting this morning. I expect you'll be there, right?"

"Yes. I will." Lindy's reply was less than cordial, and she stormed back into the suite and headed towards her office.

"Sam?" Sarah turned to him. "Where exactly is my office?" Sam froze momentarily and winced.

"Next to Lindy's?" It came out a question instead of an answer.

"Uh uh, Sam, no way." Sarah waited for him to come up with something better.

"How about we convert the lounge off my office. It's got plenty of space, and you won't ever encounter anyone you don't want to see. Total privacy. It's got plenty of room for Donna in there as well."

Sarah smiled and nodded. "That's perfect Sam. I believe there's a private bathroom as well?"

"Yes, but it's mine. I mean it was, we'll share..." Sam was stammering now. And even Donna was chuckling. These two were quite a pair, and Donna could sense the electric undercurrents that ran between them. Yep, she thought, this was going to be a hoot.

Chapter 14

The weeks flew by for Sarah. She was thoroughly enjoying her new position. It was challenging, but highly rewarding. Everything had fallen into a routine. Several days a week, she and Sam would travel together to the main office, and work from there. They both discovered through their time together that they shared many common interests, from classical music to the latest BBC miniseries. And they enjoyed each other's company, when they weren't sparring over little petty things. But secretly they both enjoyed that too. The incident with the limo had long been forgotten, and since Grace seemed totally relaxed, and very comfortable in their new lodgings, Sarah felt secure. She used Grace as a barometer of sorts. If Grace was tense, Sarah was on the alert. When she was relaxed, like she was now, Sarah felt more at ease. Grace took care of Addy while Sarah worked at the office, though Sarah always found time to play with her, as did Sam.

The other days, they would work from the house. Tom would drive into Rockdale and bring Donna over in the mornings and return her home at night. Sam had rapidly converted the back parlor into a double office, complete with two workstations, as well as a portable crib. With room for a second one when the time came. Donna was about 6 months into her pregnancy, so there was plenty of time. Sarah and Donna could work undisturbed, and it was convenient to the kitchen for breaks.

Donna was turning out to be a gem but for some reason, she couldn't seem to relax into the job. Finally, one morning, when working from the house, Sarah looked up from her desk and noticed Donna nervously tapping her pencil.

"OK, Donna, time out."

"Huh?" Donna looked up confused. "We need to talk. You're nervous, jumpy and just all-around tense. What gives? Want to talk about it?"

"Um, sorry, everything's fine, really." The hesitancy in her voice betrayed her.

"No, it's not fine. You see I've noticed over the past few weeks that you work really well under pressure, especially if no one is hanging over your shoulder. You're best when you're relaxed. You're self-directed and diligent, which is great. But when you're all tense like this, you can't work. So let's talk about whatever's eating at you, put it aside, and move on." Sarah hoped Donna would confess to whatever was bothering her and hopefully she wasn't afraid to talk with her about it.

Donna took a deep breath and plunged in.

"I'm really sorry, Sarah, it's just, well, I'm waiting for the other shoe to drop. You've never asked about, well, the baby's father. Nothing. And I suppose I should have been up front with it, and I wasn't, and I'm worried when you find out you'll decide not to keep me on." There, it was out. Donna looked nervously at Sarah, waiting.

"Donna, your personal life is your business, not mine. But I hope we can be friends enough that you feel that you can trust me with whatever it is. I'm not here to judge. But I'll listen. OK?"

Sarah was curious, but she meant what she said. She knew the kind of person Donna was, and whatever was bothering her she knew it wouldn't make Donna any less of a good employee. And, admittedly, Sarah really wanted her friendship as well. Ever since Megan's death, her life had been topsy turvy, and her old colleagues were turning out to be fair weather friends. She needed someone to talk to, besides Grace. Someone closer to her own age. She and Karen had a good relationship, but somehow it just wasn't the same.

"OK. Here it is in a nutshell. I had a thing for one of the analysts on our team. It was foolish, I know, and one night we pulled a late one, finishing up a report. I had offered to help, and Lindy was pushing him so hard to make deadlines, he was actually falling behind. Anyway, one thing led to another," Donna smiled sadly. "He was actually really good about it, and things were fine. He even proposed, though I thought we needed more time to be sure about each other. Then, about a month ago, just before you came on board, Lindy suddenly fires Andy, that's his name, for 'misconduct'. He wouldn't take my calls. Wouldn't see me. Wouldn't speak to me. I don't know what happened. It doesn't make sense. I don't even know where he is anymore. He moved, left no forwarding address, no number. Nothing." Donna shook her head sadly. "I don't want you to think badly of Andy. You know he was really nice. I'm just sorry he felt he had to get out of my life like that. He said he was innocent, that he'd done nothing wrong, and I believed him. Maybe I was wrong."

Sarah looked at Donna and shook her head. "Donna, I think you're a good judge of character. If you think he was innocent, he probably was. And when someone takes off like that, there's always something behind it. Something worse." Sarah went on, now tapping her pencil on her desk rapidly as her thoughts gelled. "I think we need to find Andy. Don't worry, I won't ask you to help, especially if it hurts. I'm going to go on a little manhunt, that's all. See if we can't fix this!" Sarah smiled brightly at Donna, letting her know that all was well, and she had an ally. "I'm just gonna poke around a bit, see what I can't learn. Who knew about you and Andy?"

"Actually, no one, well, except Lindy. I had to tell her when I started to show. That was about a month before she fired him," Donna replied.

"Are you saying Lindy was the only one who knew?" Sarah was suspicious.

"Yup," Donna sighed. "And she was actually pretty good about it. Surprisingly."

"What about your family, friends?" Sarah pushed on; something was nagging at her.

"No, I was too embarrassed. I mean they know I'm pregnant, but I basically said it was a brief affair, and it's over."

"Hang on, Donna, I need to do something." Sarah jumped out of her chair and went to the doorway. "Grace," she called up the stairs. "Can you come down for a sec?" Heading back into the room, she went back to her desk and sat down, waiting. Grace arrived a minute later, Addy in her arms, cooing and pulling on a silver chain she wore around her neck. Sarah smiled at the picture they made.

"Grace, I need you to use your little talent for a minute, can you do that? I mean, you know, at will?"

"I don't know, sometimes I can." She looked over at Donna and smiled. "I think this is about you, isn't it?"

Donna looked bewildered. Sarah hadn't mentioned Grace's special gift. As far as Donna knew, Grace was just the sweet older woman who cared for Addy. Hopefully Donna won't be put off by it, Sarah thought.

"Let me see." Grace cocked her head and studied Donna for a moment. She let out a breath suddenly and started talking randomly. Letting her thoughts just ramble.

"The man you worry about. He's a good one. A keeper. But in danger. Everything is linked. Everything. You, Sarah, Addy, the baby, this man, Sam, and there's another, no… several others. There is a secret. It's all jumbled together. You need to find him."

Donna was stunned. As was Sarah.

Donna spoke first. "Grace, are you, well, psychic?"

Grace laughed. "Let's just say I have good instincts, okay? Strong ones."

Sarah looked at Grace with concern. "Is there more, something you're not telling us?"

"No, dear, I just get feelings, that's all. I've told you everything that occurred to me just now."

Sarah looked over at Donna, then tapped the desk nervously again.

"I think it's time we talked to Sam," she said quietly. "Do you mind if we bring him in on this? I don't know why, but I think we need to. Maybe Grace's hunches are contagious," she smiled, hoping to look relaxed. Inside, she was on the verge of panic. Something was terribly wrong in all of this.

"I don't mind, if you think it will help. But maybe we should get these audits finished first. I've got two down, but there's three to go by Friday!"

"Sounds like a plan," Sarah replied, then turned to Grace. "Thanks Grace, I appreciate your help just now. Maybe you and Addy could go for a stroll? It looks like a beautiful day out there, Indian summer, no doubt!" Sarah smiled as she realized she hadn't been outside all day either. "In fact, let's all go. Donna, you can use the fresh air!"

As Grace went to put Addy in the stroller, Donna went to grab a jacket, as the early fall days were getting cooler, leaving Sarah alone in the office. Her cell phone rang suddenly, the new one Sam had given her. Usually she didn't bother to answer, just checked her voicemail once or twice a day. For some reason, she picked up.

"Hello?" At first there was only static. Then the voice on the other end whispered.

"He killed his brother and he'll kill you too. Get out now." Sarah heard a click, and stiffened. The voice had a frightening, chilling quality to it, and as Sarah put the phone down, she stood still for a moment. Frozen in place.

"Sarah?" Donna's voice broke through the spell she'd been under. "Are you OK?" Sarah looked over at Donna, standing in the doorway, and shook her head.

"No." she replied quietly. "Donna, I think we need to bring Sam into this now." She knew maybe it wasn't wise to trust him completely, but she went with her gut. She wanted to believe in him. She needed to. Her heart was already lost to him, but if she didn't have faith in him, it wouldn't matter. Whoever made that call wanted her to distrust him. Maybe she should. But she couldn't.

"What happened?" Donna asked gently.

"I got a strange phone call just now. Donna, how much did you know about Greg?"

"I'd see him at the office every so often, when he was visiting with Mr. Livingston," Donna replied, using the formal Mr. Livingston, as she seemed to be still adjusting to the informality of her new working relationship.

"The call was about him and it scared me," Sarah went on. "I don't like what's happening."

"Who called you, Sarah? What did they say?" Donna approached Sarah as she spoke, and putting an arm around her led her to the sofa and sat her down, taking the seat next to her. Taking Sarah's hands in hers, she spoke calmly.

"Tell me what happened." Sarah looked at Donna gratefully. She was already becoming so maternal. Or maybe for Donna it was instinctive, just her nature. Sarah studied her for a moment before speaking. Her face wore a look of concern. Her short blond hair framed a rounded face, with large green eyes and a smattering of freckles. There was a sweetness about her, as well as an air of trust.

"It was a whisper. I can't tell if it was male or female. They said Sam, well, they said he. They said he killed his brother and he'll kill me too," Sarah shivered, and looked at Donna for her reaction.

"Do you think it's true, Sarah?" Donna's voice didn't hold any hint of what she thought.

"I don't know, no, that's not true. I don't believe it," she said somewhat fiercely. "He loved his brother."

"I agree." Donna was reassuring her. So she trusted him too. That was a good sign.

"I think you're right, Sarah," Donna went on. She squeezed Sarah's hands gently in hers. "We need to tell Sam. Now."

Sarah smiled weakly and sighed. "Just when things were getting so good here. I knew it wouldn't last. I mean I love this job, and having you work with me is wonderful. I knew something had to ruin it. It was too good to be true. I keep telling Grace, I must be cursed."

"I know what you mean," Donna smiled nervously. "But whatever it is, it'll work itself out. At least that's what I tell myself. It has to."

Grace came in at that point, knocking softly on the door, not wanting to interrupt.

"I'm afraid Addy's conked out upstairs, so we'll have to postpone that walk. Besides, I think you have more important things to do right now." Grace gave Sarah a knowing look and headed back up the stairs.

"That's uncanny," Donna said, "and I have to say, a little creepy."

Sarah chuckled. "I know, it creeps me out sometimes too, but she's really very sweet, and wonderful with Addy. And right now, I think we need that little talent of hers more than ever."

"Should we call Sam in here?" Donna asked.

"Yes, I think so. I'll use the intercom, in case he's busy with something." Sarah went over to her desk and hit the intercom button that was linked to Sam's office phone.

"Yes?" Sam's voice was low and husky, and Sarah's heart skipped at the sound of it.

"Sam, can you come in here for a minute? There's something, well… if you could just come in?" Sarah's voice shook a bit, as she recalled the whispered voice on the phone. Just thinking about it gave her the shivers. There was no response from Sam, causing Sarah to frown, till she looked up and saw him in the doorway, his face speaking volumes. His brows knit together, and his facial muscles were tense.

"What is it?" he asked striding into the room, giving Donna a brief glance, but focusing on Sarah. "Something's wrong, I heard it in your voice." Sarah's heart did another skip as she realized his gruffness was out of concern.

Sarah chewed on her lower lip for a minute. "I got a call a few minutes ago, Sam. On my cell phone." Sam's eyes narrowed.

"Who was it?"

"I don't know," Sarah whispered in response. "But they, they," she looked at Donna for support, who nodded to her to go on. "They said you killed Greg. That I should get out. That you'd kill me too."

Sam's hands balled into fists at his sides, anger flashing in his eyes.

"And you believed them?" His voice was dangerously low.

Sarah's eyes widened then narrowed, flashing as brilliantly as Sam's.

"No, I didn't. Or we wouldn't be having this discussion!" She spat out the words. Sam smiled softly, though his body was tense, and he was worried, he couldn't show it. But he'd rather she be angry than scared. He seemed to know just which buttons to push. If she was angry, she'd react using her head. If she was scared, she would make mistakes.

"I'm sure it was just a crank call." Sam went on calmly. It wasn't, he knew it. Someone was going after Sarah. "Let me see your phone, I'll try and trace it if it makes you feel better." Sarah reached out to hand him the phone.

"You can cut the act Sam, both Donna and I know there's something far bigger happening here, and we want some answers. Besides, there's more that you don't know."

"More?" Sam was having difficulty controlling his emotions. "What more?"

"Uh uh, you first," Sarah replied.

"No way, you first," Sam countered as he headed back to his study. "I'm going to see if I can trace this, be right back," he called over his shoulder.

"Idiot." Sarah was miffed. Donna smiled at the term of endearment Sarah had chosen.

Sam came back within minutes. "It's a coffee shop in town, over on third street. Ring a bell, Sarah?"

"What?" Sarah whispered.

"A coffee shop on third street." Sam said again.

"Mine?" she whispered again.

"Yes," Sam answered her gently. "It could be coincidence."

"You know it's not," Sarah spoke quickly. "Somebody I knew there made that call. But who? Who'd want to terrify me like that?"

"I don't know, but maybe if you told me what else is happening, we can sort through it." Sam went and leaned against the desk, arms folded across his chest.

"You first," Sarah was belligerent now.

"No." Sam said tersely.

"Yes."

"No."

"For pete's sake, you two, this isn't the time or the place. Let's all just lay it out on the table." Donna shook her head. "You two are like oil and water sometimes, and we've got some serious things going on. I'm the pregnant one, but you two have the raging hormones of a couple of teenagers!"

Sarah flushed, while Sam appeared contrite. Donna had their number all right.

"Ok," Sam began in his most diplomatic tone. "Tell me what else you're wondering about, and then I'll answer whatever I can."

"What do you know about Andy," Sarah looked over at Donna questioningly. "Andy...?"

"Klapper" Donna realized what Sarah wanted.

"What do you know about Andy Klapper?" Sarah directed her question back to Sam.

"Andy?" He glanced at Donna. "Is he a friend of yours?" Sam needed to know before replying.

Sarah jumped in, after an approving look from Donna.

"He's the baby's father, Sam," she said pointedly. "Apparently, Lindy fired him, and now he's disappeared off the face of the earth. And speaking of Lindy," Sarah went on, "why the hell does she even work for you? I don't care how competent she is… she's a total bitch, who treats her staff like dirt, and you know it. Makes no sense keeping her on, if you ask me."

Sam let out a deep breath. He didn't see that coming. He'd have to give them as much as he could. It wouldn't be right otherwise.

"OK. I think you both have a right to know what's going on at Livingston." Sam paused, and tried to carefully craft his words. There were things they needed to know, and things they couldn't know, for their own safety. But Sam was tired of facing everything alone. He wanted to be able to share some of the burden. If he was wrong about Sarah, and his faith in her was misplaced, then it would all come crashing down.

"We'll start at the beginning. Make yourselves comfortable."

Sarah moved over to the couch to sit by Donna, and they both waited expectantly. Sam began to pace back and forth in front of the window, hands behind his back, his face lost in thought, then went over to the wall and hit the house intercom system.

"Emma? Could you bring us some coffee, and maybe a snack?" Emma's voice came crackling back a minute later.

"Sure thing, be there in a jif."

He pushed the button and spoke again.

"Could you also ask Grace to come down please?" If there was ever a time to believe in extraordinary abilities like Grace's, it was now.

No one spoke as they waited for Grace. Emma popped in with a tray of coffee and muffins, and politely excused herself. When Grace came in, she said nothing. Just went over and squeezed onto the couch between Donna and Sarah, taking one of their hands in each of hers. Sarah and Donna immediately sensed she already knew what was happening.

Sam looked at each of the women in turn, cleared his throat, and began speaking.

CHAPTER 15

"We'll start with Lindy. Obviously I'm aware that she's a bitch and a royal one at that. She's been with us close to 10 years, came to us right out of college. Worked her way up the ranks. She was good at her job. It wasn't until a few years ago, just before you started with us Donna, that she changed. Or maybe she always had that mean streak in her and hid it well. In any case, we let things ride far too long. I also started noticing some discrepancies. Some things that didn't make sense in the reports I was getting. Greg was overseeing our European operations at the time, but I asked him to return and help investigate some things here. We agreed that no one would know, so that he could operate freely. If anyone thought he was involved with corporate, they wouldn't speak openly to him. So we decided he'd take a leave from the company. As far as anyone knew, Greg had decided to go experience life and leave me to run the company alone. It was critical it remained a secret. Which, until now, it has."

He stopped momentarily, drawing a breath and glancing over at the three women. He had their full attention, and they weren't interrupting.

"Greg was my lifeline to the internal workings of the company. Each of the consulting teams would turn the reports into me, and I would hand it all to Greg. He'd cross check and investigate anything that appeared suspicious. And when it came to the hotel group, there was plenty. He and I both believed that Lindy was moving funds around. She had no access of course to be able to embezzle, but she was doing things on paper that made the hotel group appear far more profitable than they were. Greg's last skiing trip was actually investigating a ski resort we own, trying to discover a possible link to management there. In fact, I was going to have you look into this Sarah, see if you could find the link. Greg died before we had any answers."

Sarah couldn't help but interrupt him. "You think the money was being embezzled by individual properties and Lindy was hiding it?"

"Precisely," Sam replied. "I knew you'd figure it out," he smiled at her. Brilliant, he thought. Just one of her many qualities he found fascinating.

"So you keep her on until you have the evidence, is that it?" queried Donna.

"That's it, Donna," he replied, then went on. "And this is where it involves Andy."

"Andy was in on this?" Donna's voice was incredulous.

"Yes, but not how you think. After Greg's death, I needed someone else to keep digging. Andy was the logical choice. He is honest, straightforward, and a whiz with numbers. When Lindy came to me and said he was rigging the reports, I knew it was a lie. But I couldn't confront her yet, not till we finished the investigation. So I agreed she should fire him."

"That seems very unfair to Andy, Sam, to let him think you didn't support him. Maybe that's why he took off. No one backed him up." Sarah's voice didn't hold any condemnation, just sympathy.

"I didn't say I actually let her fire him. I let her think so. Andy still works for Livingston. That's why you haven't heard from him, Donna. And I'm honestly so sorry. He understood the need for complete secrecy and agreed to the conditions. He didn't tell me about the baby. If I had known, I would have let you keep in touch somehow. In fact, I'll see that you can get in touch with him right away. You'll have to be very careful though, and please, let no one know you are in contact. I'll also see he gets back here in time for the birth." Sam smiled at Donna, somewhat sadly. "If I had known about Addy, I would have called Greg home sooner. But he didn't say anything to me. I wish he would have. If only..." his voice trailed off.

"It's not your fault, Sam," Sarah interjected softly. "You can 'if' yourself to kingdom come, and it won't help. It was Greg's responsibility to tell you."

"Yeah, but he didn't. Because he was trying so hard to help me out. He felt obligated. If I had just tried harder in our personal relationship, he might have told me."

"Stop it Sam. Now. It won't bring him back," Sarah's voice was firm, but gentle. "You can honor him now by raising his daughter. That's what counts."

"You're right, I know," Sam replied wistfully. "There's more," he went on. He began pacing again. "Chamandia."

Sarah couldn't help but jump in. "There's a connection, isn't there. Between that limo that followed me and all this mess," Sarah spoke quickly. "I knew it."

"In a sense, yes," Sam replied. He turned to look at her, his gaze locking on hers. Sarah felt herself go weak; she always did when he looked at her that way. She couldn't pinpoint it. It was just as if he was seeing clear into her. That he wanted something from her. She just didn't know what. And now he was doing it again.

"I'm afraid whatever is going on with Lindy is connected to Chamandia as well. I've suspected it for a while. I believe someone, or some entity, is trying to sabotage Livingston. And me."

"What can we do, Mr. Livingston?" Donna chimed in now. Sarah had already noticed how fiercely loyal to the company she was, perhaps since she never expected to move up this far. They'd given her every chance to succeed, and maybe she felt she owed them.

"Could you please just call me Sam, Donna?" Sam was uncomfortable as it was. "Whatever we do, we need to do this as a team." He turned to Grace. "Grace, I'm no big believer in psychic phenomenon, but I do believe you are in touch with instincts that we don't have. I'd appreciate any input from you. I know you have Addy's best interest at heart. And whoever is after me, I think it stands to reason, will be after Addy as well."

"Why Sam?" Sarah put in. "That's what doesn't make sense. I understand stealing, I mean, it's greed. But why would someone go after you, personally and professionally? Unless Lindy is tied in with those in Chamandia who want to see you out of there."

"Bingo," Sam replied ruefully. "I think somehow, somewhere along the way, they recruited Lindy. I'm not sure why, or what it's worth to her. But she's in this with them, I feel it."

"I think you're right, Sam," Sarah said slowly. "And I think we need to hurry and find out what we can. Donna and I will go through the papers, find the links if we can. We'll start with the Chamandian properties. But I also want to know who made that phone call. Because whoever it is, I suspect thinks I'm closing in on discovering them. Not just Lindy, but whoever she's working with. As much as I hate to say it, I think you and Lindy need to have a little quality time together."

"Huh?" Sam turned around to face Sarah, a look of astonishment on his face. "I'm the last person she'll talk to."

"You're wrong Sam, dead wrong." Sarah mused. "From the way she tried to work you that first day at the office, I'd say she was peeved her charms didn't work. And if you let even the slightest hint get out that you found her, say, attractive, she'd use that opportunity in a heartbeat. She doesn't know you suspect her. She thinks I'm the one who poses the risk. She'll try to manipulate you, while you manipulate her. It's a perfect plan." Sarah smiled knowingly, and waited for Sam.

"You think she'll buy it?" Sam still wasn't convinced.

"Donna, please explain to Sam the ways of the world. He's obviously had his head buried in the sand," Sarah laughed.

"She's right Sam," Donna nodded her head in agreement. "Lindy is an exceptionally vain woman. And everyone here knows she's had a thing for you for years. In fact, I wonder if that's why she turned on you so easily, maybe rejection started the whole thing. She never actually, you know, approached you did she?"

Sam appeared embarrassed and thought for a moment before responding.

"Maybe she did indicate an interest, but it was a long time ago, and I made it abundantly clear that our relationship was strictly professional."

"Was that before or after all this funny stuff started happening?" Sarah asked.

"Before, I suppose." Sam pondered that. "You think she was easily swayed to participate in something because I turned her down?"

Donna and Sarah looked at each other knowingly, replying in unison.

"Absolutely!"

"You're kidding, I mean, I'm not that much of a prize," Sam appeared genuinely baffled. "Unless it's my money she wanted." Sam was beginning to suspect he knew exactly what Lindy was after, but that was a conversation for another day. Just the thought of getting close to Lindy made him shudder. Lord he couldn't stand the woman. Then again, it might make Sarah look twice at him.

"So I should romance her, eh?" Sam's eyes twinkled, and Sarah was getting second thoughts. Ridiculous, she scolded herself mentally. He isn't really going to go far with this ruse.

"I suppose I could force myself," Sam continued, grinning. "Some flowers, maybe a candlelit dinner, a few kisses for good measure..."

"Hold on Sam, no one said anything about kissing the Barracuda," Sarah huffed out. "I'm sure you can manage this without physical contact."

"How else am I supposed to show I'm interested?" Sam asked, smirking.

"There are plenty of ways to indicate your interest without that," Sarah said stiffly. "I'm sure we can help you find some."

"I'm sure you can," Sam replied, now with a bit of humor in his voice. "Care to give me some pointers?" Sarah flushed, and decided it would be best not to respond. He was egging her on, she knew it. So she composed herself.

"Sure. Take her to dinner, and stop by her office for no reason, you know, just to say Hi. Give her little token presents, there's lots of ways you can approach this without the other stuff."

"Other stuff," Sam laughed outright. It felt good to reduce the tension that had built up in the room. Not that he was any less worried about what was happening, but a little humor and relief goes a long way.

"Sarah, sometimes you amaze me. OK. I'll do it your way. I'll try and keep my hands off her." Sam grinned. He was sure that was jealousy sparking in Sarah, which could only mean one thing. And he intended to find out if he was right. Not yet, but soon.

He turned to Grace. "You've been very quiet Grace, what's your take on all this. Any hunches we could act on?" Sam kept his tone light, but he was dead serious.

"I think you're all doing fine on your own. Everything feels right. It seems to me that Lindy, whom I haven't had the pleasure of meeting yet, is the key. One other thing. I can't tell you who is doing what. But I sense that whoever is behind all this, is out for more than money. More than power. They want revenge, Sam." Grace and Sam eyed each other carefully, both understanding that this was enough for now. He knew what she meant, and she knew he understood.

Sam cleared his throat and continued.

"Thanks Grace. That helps. So, we're all clear on this. Donna, you and Sarah go through the hotel group financials with a fine-tooth comb. Grace, you mind Addy. And I'll go after Lindy...." Sam couldn't help smiling when he said it.

With that, the women got up off the sofa, Grace leaving to check on Addy, and Donna and Sarah headed for their desks. Sam went to his office, where he picked up the phone to call Lindy and get the ball rolling.

CHAPTER 16

The conference table was stacked high with folders, piles and piles of them. Donna and Sarah sat at their respective desks in their office, their gaze focused on the conference table… staring at the files, neither wanting to be the first to go over there and dive in. While much of the data they needed was normally stored in the cloud, many of the records they needed from the international properties were not.

"You know what we need, Sarah?" Donna asked.

"Hmm. No, what?" Sarah was lost in thought.

"A program that will merge and purge all this stuff, leave us with just the data we need." Donna was smiling smugly.

"You're right, and if you could conjure one up right about now, I'd be grateful," Sarah laughed. What was needed was custom software that as far as she knew, didn't exist yet. It would need to scan, sort, merge and purge using algorithms not yet developed. Donna keyed in a few things on her laptop, and then flipped over the screen to show Sarah.

"Voilà!"

Sarah looked at the screen and then at Donna's face, which bore a self-satisfied smirk.

"No way," she said expectantly.

"Yes way. I've been playing with this for 2 years, trying to make my job easier. It's an app I call Intuition. You just scan and import all the files you need examined, and it will pore through for suspicious entries. I've entered as many possible scenarios as I could into it. I'm quite certain what we want will appear."

"What kinds of scenarios will it look for?" Sarah was really curious. This was too perfect.

"Well, for example, if a purchase is recorded as say, equipment, then it will search the asset and depreciation schedules for the same item. If either doesn't contain the entry, it's red flagged, and appears on a discrepancy list. You can use it to catch the cheaters, too. It can examine an expense log and compare it to a trip log. So if the dates, agenda or expenses themselves don't gel, it'll pull it up."

"What do you mean, don't gel? Give me details here, Donna," Sarah was excited now.

"OK. Say you take a trip to San Francisco, for example. The trip log holds the itinerary. Now, your expense log for the trip will have everything from the airfare to hotel and food, that kind of thing. The program will check all dates and receipts to ensure that the restaurant ticket, for example, matches up precisely with your itinerary. If you're in a meeting, according to the itinerary, but you've got a dinner receipt for the same time, it'll flag it."

Sarah smacked her hand on the table with delight.

"You're a damn genius, Donna, open that baby up and let her rip. If it works I'm raising you another 20!"

Donna grinned as she went to work furiously keying in commands then loading papers into the scanner. She sat back after starting up the app, and putting her hands behind her head for support, she popped her feet up on the desk.

"This may take a while, do you mind if I relax?" She laughed out loud as she spoke, and watched Sarah do the same routine.

Just about to knock, Sam stopped in the doorway and grinned. Seeing the two women in identical poses, feet up and smiling, he wondered what they were up to.

"Don't you two have some work to do?" Sam tried to sound annoyed, but it came out with plenty of humor anyway.

"Actually, Sam, you're just in time to witness Donna's new miracle software in action. She wrote the app herself, and it's a beaut!" Sarah was confident it would work, and if the data appearing so far on their screens was any indication, it would work perfectly. While all the devices in their office were networked, a firewall was put in place allowing them access to the corporate system, while not permitting access from any other workstation. Not even Sam's computer could get in. Sam moved over to stand behind Donna and take a look at what they were doing. Seeing the columns of numbers scrolling, he looked at Donna questioningly.

"What's it doing?" he asked.

"It's finding out where the problems are. Inconsistencies, phony entries, duplicates, you name it." As the scrolling data paused for a moment, Sam suddenly spoke.

"Freeze it would you?"

Donna reached forward and tapped the screen to pause it.

"Look at this! I don't believe it." Sam turned to grab a spare chair and slid it over by Donna and sat down. Pointing at the screen, he said "Do you see this? Do you know what this is?"

Sarah by this time and come around to join them. She looked at the jumble of numbers. "Not me, I don't know all the codes yet. Donna?"

"OK, let's see. 1729, that's a hotel property. I think it's the Ski Resort in Italy."

"I know," Sam rushed the words, "and if it's pulling up something, then maybe Greg found something there. But there's no field headings, I can't tell what it's finding!"

"As I was saying, Mr. Livingston, I mean Sam," Donna grinned. "The sequence after that represents the department codes, purchase order numbers, category, dollar amount and classification." Donna opened another app on her tablet. "I have the decoding system in here, so I can cross reference while it's still going. Let's see, can you read that first line off to me, starting with the 1729?"

Sam rattled the numbers off, while Donna keyed them in.

"Got it!" Donna shouted triumphantly. "I knew this would work... damn!"

"You can celebrate later, Donna," Sam chuckled, "for now, just tell us what it says!"

"According to what I've got here, the Italian property made a major purchase last year for a new heating and cooling system. We're talking $175,000 total. It's not listed on the depreciation schedule or the assets. There's no receipt for the equipment, anywhere. I'm guessing there is no new equipment. We'll have to request a check copy from their bank over there. Find out who the vendor was."

"Don't major purchases come out of the corporate account?" Sarah asked.

"No, each property banks locally, it's always been that way. The funds are transferred to corporate at the end of the fiscal year, if there is any profit. If not, we fund them," Sam responded.

"So whoever has access to the account could have easily manipulated this," Sarah mused.

"That's right. But so could anyone. Basically, maintenance could have requested the funds, but never bought the equipment. Or someone in accounting could have made the entry and stolen the funds. There's endless possibilities." Sam turned to Donna. "Why don't we let that program run some more, see what we get. When it finishes, call me and I'll come back in. We can all do this together."

Sarah looked quizzically at Sam. Did he want to be there to help? Or was he going to try and make sure they didn't discover something. Her sudden mistrust of him gnawed at her. He'd given her no reason to doubt him, yet still.

"Don't you have a date tonight?" Sarah reminded him.

"Oh... yeah," Sam flushed. "I almost forgot. But I can postpone, no problem."

"Yes problem, Sam," Sarah quipped. "You're not going to impress her by cancelling the first time out."

"I suppose you're right." Sam sounded genuinely disappointed. "Well, you guys tend to this stuff, and if you could, Sarah, print it out and bring it home with you." Sarah felt a tingle shoot up her spine. The way Sam said home, well, it was as if he meant it. That it was her home. She knew it was unintentional, but it did seem somewhat intimate. She stole a glance at Sam, just to see if there was any clue to what he was thinking on his face. And he was looking right at her. And smiling. So maybe it wasn't unintended after all, Sarah thought. Or maybe he wanted to charm her, make sure she brought the reports home for him. Why didn't he trust her to figure out this stuff? Why did he need to see it too? Why was she being so paranoid, she wondered. Of course he'd want to see it, that's where Greg was when he died. Naturally it would be important to him.

But she knew what was eating at her. This morning there was a message on her voicemail from Karen. She said she'd been calling all week and why wasn't she returning the calls. Sarah had checked her voicemail daily, and there hadn't been any messages from Karen. She hadn't thought much about it at the time, but suddenly, it was dawning on her. Sam was the only one with access to her cell phone number and voicemail. He'd set it up himself, so he had the password. And he was the only one. So he must be erasing those messages. But why? Why would he try and distance her from Karen? It just made no sense. Then he said the threatening call came from Karen's coffee shop. If that was true, did he think Karen was involved? Was he censoring her calls? She hated doubting Sam, but it couldn't be helped. There was just too much confusion surrounding all of this.

Tom was there to drive her home, alone, since Sam was taking Lindy to dinner, ostensibly to pry information from her. But now Sarah was wondering about that as well. Maybe it was all a ruse, and he and Lindy did have a thing going. But why hide it? Glancing at the stack of paperwork on the seat next to her, she wondered if bringing it home was the right thing to do. She and Donna had found quite a bit of subterfuge, and maybe she was putting herself in danger by letting Sam know she was on to it. She shook her head. Stupid stupid stupid. It's his company, she thought. He's not stealing from himself.

Taking her phone out of her purse, she dialed the coffee shop, hoping Karen was still there. Maybe she knew who had used the phone there. It was a payphone, probably the only one left in Rockdale, so maybe she'd spotted someone. I mean who used payphones anymore? Sarah was sure it wasn't Karen. They were friends, and she had nothing to do with any of this. It wasn't Sam, because he was home at the time. Unless of course it was Sam, and he didn't trace the call to the shop at all. She sighed and leaned back against the seat. She needed Karen.

Karen picked up on the third ring. "Karen? It's Sarah," she spoke quietly, not wanting Tom to hear her, though likely he did.

"Where have you been?" Karen practically screamed into the phone. "I've been calling you for weeks...you never call back," she complained loudly.

"I'm sorry. Something's messed up with my voicemail and I haven't been getting any messages. But I got yours this morning. Everything's fine, I'm staying with someone for a while. I just needed a break." She hesitated to say she was at Sam's, though it was silly not to tell her. But she and Sam agreed no one should know, for now.

"Someone who?" Karen shot back. "Did you meet someone? And didn't tell me? You said you were taking some time off, was that just bullshit?"

"No, certainly not," Sarah replied. "Yes, I met someone, and we're just spending some time getting to know each other. I just got overwhelmed with everything, I'm sorry. I should have told you."

"You damn well should have. Well, water under the bridge. Can you meet me for lunch tomorrow?"

"I think so, shouldn't be a problem. What time and where?" Sarah was looking forward to it.

"Here at the shop, we can close it up for an hour, say 1pm? And just sit and gab, catch up." Karen sounded enthusiastic as well.

"OK. 1 o'clock. Sounds good. I gotta run, but I'll see ya then," Sarah said, relieved. Putting the phone back in her purse, she smiled. It would be great to see Karen again, even if she couldn't reveal too much. Though, maybe if she caught Sam later when he came home she could check with him to see how much she could talk about. She'd really like Karen to know where she was, just in case. If anything should happen to Sarah, Karen was next in line as guardian, well, after Sam. Sarah felt guilty about the last few weeks. Disappearing like that must have driven Karen nuts. Maybe Sam would allow her to bring Addy.... no, not after the phone call.

Sarah sighed. Things were so far out of her control. Trying to be mother to her orphaned niece, while working for her enigmatic uncle, who apparently is the victim of sabotage, for reasons unknown, and linked to a government in alleged turmoil, plus someone is trying to frighten her to boot. When had her life become a damn soap opera. Things like this weren't supposed to happen. Not to her, anyway. Her life was supposed to be about her career. About being a success. About focusing on the goal. She'd barely had time for any more than a date here and there, she'd been so dedicated.

Sarah suddenly laughed outright, causing Tom to glance in his rearview mirror. She just realized she was a single mother who had yet to have a decent relationship. A single mother living with a man, so to speak, who made the GQ cover models look ordinary. Sarah knew by the train of her thoughts that she was losing it; she was going to crack at any moment. What she really needed right now was a slow soak in a tub full of bubbles, with aromatic candles and a glass of wine. No need to wait for a holiday to indulge, she smiled ruefully. Sam Livingston could drive anyone to drink. Even Sarah.

Chapter 17

When Sarah returned home, she had little success getting the security system to unlock the door. Eventually, Tom came walking up from the garage, and without a word, used the voice system to open the door for her. She thanked him, and silently blessed him, as it was dark, and she didn't really feel all that comfortable yet in this secluded area. She watched as Tom headed back down the drive. He used the apartment above the garage, with its own entrance. The only times she saw him were when he drove her and Sam anywhere. And even then, he never spoke much. He was shrouded in mystery, just like Sam. He was big, and bald, but his face belied a gentleness to him. She sensed he was more of the bodyguard type than the chauffeur type. She knew without a doubt he'd come up to the house to assist her, not because he guessed she'd need help, but because he was watching her. But then again, everything aroused her suspicions lately.

The house appeared eerily quiet.

"Hello?" Sarah called out. She figured Grace must be upstairs with Addy. She didn't want to yell too loudly, in case they were napping. When she got no response, she climbed quietly up the stairs. As she approached the landing, she could hear soft whispers from Addy's room. The door was open, and when she peeked in, she saw Grace at the changing table. She was smiling and singing softly as she made quick work of her task. Not wanting to startle her, Sarah spoke quietly.

"Hi," she said, "I'm home."

Grace turned toward the door and smiled at Sarah.

"I'm just finishing up, then we were going to go down and fix some supper. You're hungry, I bet."

Sarah hadn't realized it, but she was famished. She'd been so busy with Donna she hadn't taken time to eat.

"Starved," Sarah grinned. "How about I cook. I'm in the mood for something completely decadent. How does some pasta with a rich creamy Alfredo sauce sound?"

"Sounds wonderful. I'll take Addy and we'll help," she cooed at Addy, "won't we sweetheart?"

Sarah smiled as she saw the look of delight on Addy's face. She was smiling and giggling now, and growing so fast.

"OK. Give me a minute to get comfy, and I'll join you downstairs."

Sarah headed towards her suite, and hummed softly. Without Sam around, she felt so much more relaxed. The minute he was around, it seemed her whole body tensed up, and her nerves were on edge. There was something so secretive about him, and she couldn't quite understand why. On the one hand, he was by any measure, good looking, smart, and at times, appeared incredibly sensitive, even kind. Other times he seemed cold and calculating, even dangerous. And he's hiding something, something big, she thought. But was he hiding it to protect her? Or himself?

The women ate dinner in companionable silence, Grace sensing Sarah's need for quiet. When she was ready, she'd talk about whatever was bothering her. Afterwards, they played with Addy for a while, bringing out some of the toys Emma had stocked up on. At 3 months, Addy was still fairly immobile, but she was making attempts to scoot and roll over. Not yet successful, it didn't seem to bother her. She didn't cry in frustration. She was such a happy baby. Sarah knew that as uncomfortable as she was with what was going on around her, she couldn't disrupt Addy's life anymore. The stability was too important.

Eventually, Grace took Addy up to bed, and Sarah relaxed with a book in the study, waiting for Sam to come home. As the clock struck 11 pm, she closed the book and sighed. She needed some sleep, and obviously the date was going well. Damn, why did she ever suggest that? They could be at Lindy's right now, getting all cozy. It seemed like such a good idea at the time. At least until she started having doubts about Sam. If they were involved, then Sarah had played right into their hands. And if they weren't, then she may be starting something she didn't want to see finish. Deep down, she knew there was more than just fear involved. There was jealousy. From what she'd heard through the office grapevine, Sam's taste in women lent itself to sophisticated, career women. Polished, wealthy, glamorous. Except for the career part, Sarah wasn't his type. And Lindy, who Sam had seemingly agreed was a cold selfish person, could probably turn on the charm when she wanted. Maybe she'd convince Sam somehow that she was just a pawn in all this and then he'd keep seeing her. This was ridiculous. Sarah stood and headed toward the stairway, determined to blank it all out and get some sleep. She would talk to Sam in the morning.

But sleep didn't come easily. Sarah's mind was filled with scenes of Sam and Lindy. In brief periods of sleep, her dreams were repetitive. Sam and Lindy, arm in arm, laughing at Sarah. Mocking her. Playing her for a fool. When dawn finally came, she jumped out of bed and into the shower, determined to somehow rinse away her doubts. And plan. Maybe she shouldn't talk to him about Karen. Maybe she should just go, and make her own decisions about how much to say.

The decision on whether to talk with him first or not was a moot point in the morning. When Sarah went down to the kitchen for coffee, there was a note from Tom saying Sam had spent the night in town. Sarah took a deep breath, feeling a panic attack coming on. Why? How could he have stayed with her? She must have been right about them. They were intimately acquainted, regardless of what he said. Sarah's panic turned swiftly to anger. He'd lied. About Lindy. And about what else? Was all of this some sort of trap she'd fallen into? A way for Sam to somehow gain custody of Addy, and get rid of her in the process? How far would he go? She shuddered. She didn't want to go to the office today. She didn't want to confront him. She'd stay and work at home. Have Donna come over. And what about Donna? Was she involved as well? No. She couldn't be. Sarah's thoughts were all jumbled. She'd have to have Tom drive her in to meet Karen. No, that wouldn't work. Sam would find out. She'd have to cancel. First things first, she'd talk to

Grace though. Get her impressions. But she'd have to keep in mind that that's all they were. Impressions. Intuition. Nothing more.

She picked up the house phone, which connected to the garage apartment as well as the rooms of the house and dialed Tom's extension. She explained that she wasn't feeling up to going into the office, and would work from home, then asked him to pick up Donna. She called her next.

"Donna?"

"Yeah. Sarah?" she replied.

"Yes. Listen, I'd like to work from home today if you don't mind, I'll have Tom pick you up, Okay?"

"Sure, no problem," Donna replied. "Is something wrong? You sound a little, I don't know, off?"

"Yes, but nothing I can talk about now. We'll talk when you get here." Sarah's voice was somewhat breathless, something that happened when she got nervous.

"Then I'll see you in a bit," Donna replied. "And don't worry, whatever it is, we'll fix it!" Sarah smiled as she hung up. Donna's maternal instincts kicking in again. If Donna was somehow involved, Sarah would be devastated, she knew that. Aside from Karen and Grace, she was the only female within 100-mile radius that Sarah could really talk to. Or trust, for that matter. And that included Emma. As sweet as she was, who knew what may lie beneath that exterior. She did work for Sam, practically raised him, which put her right in the thick of things.

The phone rang just as Sarah sat down at her desk. Obviously, it was Sam, as he was the only one other than Donna who knew the number. Sam hadn't liked her giving the number to anyone. But he'd put enough security into it that no one could trace it, so it shouldn't really matter. The phone number was routed a kazillion times before it reached her cell phone anyway. Sam said it would prevent anyone from tracing her phone to a location. Supposedly, for her safety. But Sarah now wondered if it was more a matter of his safety. She picked it up hesitantly, hoping maybe Donna was calling for some unforeseen reason. But no.

"Sarah?" Sam's voice had a worried tone. "Are you OK? Sick? What's wrong?"

"What is this, Sam, the inquisition? I just didn't feel like coming in. Is there a problem?" Sarah tried to keep her voice blasé, but there was an unconscious edge to it.

"No problem, I just thought maybe you were sick, or something." Sam seemed worried.

"No. I'm fine. Donna's coming over and we're sifting through the reports. Is there something you needed?" She was getting testy, and knew it, but couldn't stop it.

"No. I just expected, well, that you'd be here this morning. There are some things I want to go over. From last night." Sam's voice was hushed, and Sarah suspected Lindy was there with him.

"Right. Last night. How'd it go?" Sarah's voice was innocent sounding enough, but Sam detected a hint of anger.

"Great. It went great," Sam replied somewhat hesitantly. If he told her what had really happened there was no telling how she'd react, so he'd let it go for now.

"Great. That's great," Sarah replied. "Well, I hear Donna coming in, so I'll talk to you later."

"Sure, later," Sam replied. Sarah hung up the phone and placed it on her desk. Now she really wished she had gone in and faced him. There's no way to tell over the phone. But if she could see his face when they discussed it, she could read his expressions. Get a handle on what was really happening. For now it would wait.

*****

Sarah's eyes were burning, and her head ached. She and Donna had been staring at numbers all morning. She'd cancelled her lunch, which Karen let her know in no uncertain terms MUST be rescheduled, and soon. She'd also had a tête-à-tête with Grace, who had absolutely nothing to share. Zippo. Sarah suspected Grace knew precisely what Sarah wanted to hear, but just refused to give her the information. Grace was like that. She only shared her feelings when she thought they would be useful. In this case, she seemed to think Sarah needed to figure things out herself.

The morning had flown by, and she and Donna had accomplished quite a bit, in fact, they pretty much had a very clear picture of all the discrepancies and outright theft. But it was slow, tedious work, and she felt the strain. She was about to suggest a break, when Sam's voice came on the intercom.

"Sarah, can you come in the study for a minute?" His voice was brusque, all business. Sarah's head popped up and she rolled her eyes in frustration. She hadn't heard him come in. It was barely after 1pm, and he shouldn't have been home for hours. She gave Donna a knowing look and shook her head.

"I suppose my presence is required by his majesty?" Sarah said with a small smile.

"Sounds that way," Donna replied, her voice bearing the same exhausted ring to it, but an odd expression crossed her face.

"Donna? Something wrong?"

"No no, sorry. Just a thought but it's nothing."

"OK, let me ask you something," Sarah went on, stalling for time.

"Sure," Donna replied curiously. She'd waited all morning for Sarah to bring up whatever was bugging her.

"Do you think Sam is somehow, I don't know, involved in all this. I mean, do you think he and Lindy are somehow together in this?"

"Not a chance." Donna's voice took on a firm tone. "I've worked for them for quite a while now, and I can guarantee Lindy and Sam aren't in anything together. He's never made it a secret how he feels about her, well, at least to anyone with a good pair of eyes. And I'm sure he'd never do anything to jeopardize his company. He lives and breathes for it. Wait till Christmas, at the office party, he'll make this speech and you can almost see the tears in his eyes when he talks about his heritage. The heritage of his family, his company. No, Sam's on the up and up in this, Sarah. Don't worry."

"I hope you're right," Sarah murmured softly. She did actually feel better hearing it come from Donna. It's what she wanted to believe, and all evidence pointed to it as the truth. So maybe it was just the green monster rearing its ugly head. And a vivid imagination. Megan had always said Sarah should write. Plays, movies, whatever. And Megan could star in them. But Sarah avoided anything that smacked of creativity. She'd been a daydreamer most of her life, and by concentrating on business and tangible tasks, she could stay focused. When she let her mind wander, it was a disaster. Like now.

In fact she almost flunked her freshman year at Harvard. She'd gotten it into her head that the mysterious death of a classmate was directly attributed to one of her professors. She was convinced the congenital heart failure story was a cover up. And she spent hours planning her investigation and ultimate success in revealing the culprit. In the process, she completely neglected her schoolwork. And in the end, she learned the young woman did indeed die of natural causes. And now she was at it again, creating murder and mayhem in her mind. She stood up and stretched, breathed deeply and headed for the study. And a much-needed confrontation with Sam. One way or another, she was going to get to the bottom of it all.

Sam was standing by the fireplace, tapping his fingers on the mantle. His thick mane of wavy hair looked as if he'd been running his hand through it repeatedly. His face looked pensive, and Sarah wondered immediately if she should turn and leave.

"Took your time, didn't you?" Sam asked quietly.

"I had to finish up something. What is it?" Sarah replied tersely.

"Relax, would you? You look like you're facing a firing squad." Sam couldn't help but notice the taut expression on her face. And what seemed like fear in her eyes.

"I'm fine. Just say what you need to say," Sarah replied, getting edgier by the minute.

"Don't you want to know what I've learned? Why I came home so early? I certainly want to know what you and Donna have come up with." Her curiosity was getting the best of her.

"OK. Why are you here so early?" Sarah smiled as she repeated the question back to him. "And what did Lindy tell you?" Sarah spoke carefully, knowing she couldn't say the words on the tip of her tongue. Like 'so what did you two do? Did you sleep with her?' No, she couldn't ask those questions. But maybe he'd give a clue if she let him talk. Give a guy enough rope, as the saying goes.

"What I learned is that she has a studio apartment in New York she uses when she's there, on Park Avenue. Pretty pricey neighborhood. I pay well, but not that well. She also seems to know an awful lot about Livingston's holdings, all of them. She was trying to impress me with how much, in fact. She has no clue I'm on to her. That's for certain. Which makes you more of a threat to her."

"What else?" Sarah needed to keep him talking.

"She asked about Addy," Sam said, watching Sarah's face for a reaction. Sarah's head jerked up and her eyes widened.

"You told her about Addy?" They'd sworn not to tell anyone who Addy was. All anyone would be told is that Sarah was Addy's mom. That's it.

"No, I didn't. But I did ask her how she knew about your daughter, to which she replied that she had thought Addy was my niece, but she must have been mistaken. I agreed she was mistaken. She said something about the rumor mill at the office, but I'm not buying it. Someone did tell her. And that's why I'm home early." Sam's voice held a hint of anger. As if Sarah was to blame.

"Don't pin this on me, Sam, I wouldn't have told anyone!" Sarah was surprised at how hurt she was that Sam didn't trust her. Which, considering she didn't trust him either, made no sense.

"And if it was so damn urgent, why didn't you just come home last night?" There. She'd asked, outright. Let's see him squirm out of this one.

"First of all, she didn't ask last night, she asked this morning," Sam replied quickly. "And second of all," he never had a chance to finish.

"Maybe you talked in your sleep," Sarah jumped in. "Or maybe you said something in the heat of the moment," she went on, heedless to Sam's angry expression. "But I can say without a doubt I didn't tell her."

"I'm not accusing you, Sarah," Sam responded, still angry, and a bit rattled by her reaction. She was obviously thinking that he'd slept with Lindy, and she was very unhappy about it. But he didn't have time to dwell on that. He needed to focus. He quickly brought them back on track.

"We need to make a list. A list of everyone who knows Addy's real identity. We'll go from there."

"OK. Easy enough." Sarah, still fuming, crossed over to Sam's desk and grabbed a notepad and pen, and began writing. When she finished, she handed the pad and pen to Sam.

"Your turn," she said. She took a seat on the sofa and waited for him to complete the list.

"I think this does it," Sam said soon after. "Here's what we have. You, me, Grace, Tom, Emma, Donna, Karen, that's your old boss, right?"

"Yes, at the coffee shop," Sarah replied. "And Bill, Carol and Antonio"

"Antonio who?" Sam didn't place it right away.

"Antonio Donofrio, he owns Renaissance?" Sarah answered, a small smile on her lips as she remembered their dinner there.

"Why would he know, Sarah? How well do you know him?" Sam tried to hide his reaction, which was a mixture of anger and fear.

"He was friends with Megan and Greg. It's how I met Karen and got that job."

"He wasn't friends with Greg, Sarah, I know that for a fact. Maybe your sister, but not him." Sam's voice was cold, frigid almost, and Sarah once again felt that nagging fear that Sam was somehow dangerous.

"I saw them quite often together, of course they were friends," Sarah's reaction was one of surprise. "Why would you think they weren't?"

"There are things you don't know, Sarah, things I can't tell you. But I guarantee you Antonio is a problem. Greg was watching him. Maybe it appeared as if they were friends, but he was no friend. It was all a ruse."

"Sam, this makes no sense. You have to tell me what else is going on, or I'm out of here. I will not put Addy or myself, or Grace or Donna for that matter, in harm's way as long as you keep me in the dark. Antonio has been a good friend to me since Megan's death. He's been nothing but kind. So if you've got something you want to share, do so now. Otherwise, I've had enough of all this." Sarah had tensed up and tried unsuccessfully to relax. "Besides, unless Antonio is having some sort of fling with Lindy, which he's not, why would he tell her anything. You obviously think it's him."

"They are, as you put it, having some sort of fling." Sam looked directly at her as he spoke, needing to reassure himself Sarah was totally ignorant of all this.

"That's ridiculous. Even if Antonio was interested in women, which he's not, he'd never go for her." Sam looked startled, and then laughed. It wasn't a joyful laugh, more of a pitiful one.

"You think he's gay? What planet are you on?"

"But I thought..." Sarah was dumbfounded. If Antonio wasn't gay, she'd been taken for a fool. Big time. She was embarrassed, and afraid, and wanted to crawl into a hole.

"Sarah, for a savvy business woman you are the most naive girl I've ever seen. In fact, I'd say you don't have much experience, do you?"

"Experience?" Sarah asked, her eyes narrowing.

"Yes, I mean, from what I can tell, you're not exactly a man-eating tiger like Lindy, are you?"

Sarah suddenly shot off the couch, her eyes blazing, her face flushed.

"How dare you Sam. You want experience, go crawl back into Lindy's bed. Enjoy it while it lasts, because from what I hear, you don't keep them interested for very long, do you?" She shot him a parting look meant to shoot daggers, and started to stalk out of the room, back to her office.

"Touché." Sam replied, dryly. "Just one more thing. Come here for a sec," he spoke slowly, cautiously. Sarah stopped and turned toward him.

"Why?" she asked, unsure whether to obey him or not.

"Because." Sam's voice was bordering on demanding now. She took a few steps toward him. Then hesitated.

"Closer." Sam's face was a stone mask. Sarah took two more steps and stopped.

"Close enough?" she asked dryly.

"No. Closer," he replied. She was within touching distance now and felt a tingle up her spine. Her mind screamed back up, but her body wouldn't move.

It happened so fast. He moved so quickly Sarah had no time to react. Before she could step back, before she could say anything else, he'd pulled her close and kissed her. It was intense, demanding at first, then seemed to relax into something far more dangerous. Something filled with emotions she wasn't yet ready for. She could have pushed him back. She could have protested. But she didn't. She let herself ride the wave of intensity that rushed through her. And then, just as quickly, he let go, stepped back, turned and went over to his desk. He looked back over at her, an unreadable expression on his face, and spoke softly.

"I thought so," was all he said.

Sarah hadn't moved. She just stood staring at him, wide eyed, and stunned. As her heartbeat slowed back down, her shock turned to anger.

Eyes blazing now, she clenched her fists at her side and took a step toward him.

"What the hell do you think you're doing," she said in a rush. "Didn't you get enough last night? Or were you making some comparisons?" Sarah was on a roll now. "I don't know your game, Sam, and maybe I don't want to. But I'm not playing, understood? I won't be some pawn in your grand scheme."

"Are you through?" Sam's voice was neutral, his face a mask.

"For now," Sarah replied in a huff and turned to leave.

"Hold it," Sam said, a little more forcefully.

"What now?" she asked, stopping, but without turning around.

"For the record, I didn't sleep with her. I'm not a monk, Sarah, but I don't jump into bed with just anyone. Give me some credit. Furthermore, stay away from Antonio, he's been in cahoots with Lindy for several years now. He's a clever bastard, Sarah, and for your sake, and Addy's, you need to cut him off, now, do you understand?" Sam's voice was husky, and she imagined she even heard a slight pleading tone in it.

"No, I don't understand, Sam, because you don't tell me everything. You keep me in the dark, and just expect me to have blind faith in you." Sarah turned back to look at him, waited for a response, but Sam said nothing more. Just nodded brusquely at her and sat down.

"Close the door on the way out, please," he said dismissively. He needed to collect his thoughts but needed alone time to do it. He shouldn't have kissed her. But damn, he couldn't help it. And he needed to confirm his suspicion that she was jealous. Well maybe it wasn't necessary, but hell, he had to know if this was all one-sided, or if she felt it too. And now he knew.

Sarah knew they had far more to discuss, especially from the figures she and Donna had put together, but right now she needed to collect herself. This business about Antonio really rattled her. Sam was right about one thing; Sarah had no experience. Not with men like Sam. She had no clue how to react to the kiss, or to him. She was drained. Emotionally, physically, mentally. There was time enough later to hash it all out with him. And though her mind was still having difficulty focusing, Sam seemed to be pretty unaffected by the kiss. Though at the time he seemed to be thoroughly enjoying himself. But maybe it was just her. It had been so long since anyone had kissed her. And never like that. No, never like that. Just one more emotional upheaval to add to the list. A growing list.

CHAPTER 18

Sarah and Donna both looked up when they heard a knock on the door. Sam stood in the doorway, a file folder in his hand. He looked at each of them and smiled. "Can I come in?" They both knew it was a rhetorical question. It was his house. And whether they said yes or no, he'd come in anyway.

Donna looked at Sarah, the question in her eyes. Sarah smiled at her, and nodded at Sam. He came in and pulled a chair up to sit perpendicular to their two facing desks. He looked at Donna first.

"I suppose Sarah's filled you in?" Donna suppressed a smile. She knew he was referring to Lindy and Antonio, but she couldn't help thinking about the rest of it. Sarah had filled her in on everything that happened. Including the small matter of the intimate encounter. Sarah had blushed profusely, but needed to confide in her, and Donna appreciated that.

"Yes, I know about it," she replied, in her most professional tone.

"Good. What have you come up with in here?" Sam asked, all business now.

"Well. For starters, Lindy's in this thing up to her eyeballs," Sarah began. "Over the last 18 months, the hotel group has over 6 million in questionable transactions. In other words, you've got over 6 million in funds out there unaccounted for. The transactions are spread out among all the properties. The interesting thing is that each questionable transaction occurs within 2 weeks of an on-site audit. Which, of course, is headed up by Lindy. None of the red flags are associated with any of the audit team members, however. On the other hand, there are flags relating to every one of Lindy's trips. In essence, every time something funny goes on, Lindy is right in the thick of it."

"Explain," Sam said brusquely.

"OK. Last January, Lindy headed up an audit at the property on St. Thomas. While she was there, she was scheduled in meetings most of the day and the evenings were supposedly to be spent networking with local management. There are no expenses either at the hotel, or from anywhere else, for food, taxis, rental cars, nothing. And the one dining receipt from a nearby restaurant was stamped at 3:45 pm on Tuesday. Her itinerary says she was supposedly in a conference with the comptroller at that time. We were able to confirm she never had that meeting."

"I'm not following, Sarah," Sam said curiously. "I mean, certainly it's suspicious, but nothing we can use," he said thoughtfully.

"Oh, but you're wrong, Sam," Donna interjected. "She was there for four days. And didn't turn in any expenses. But a little checking with the staff down there and we discovered that she'd spent most of that time not at the hotel, but staying elsewhere on the island. We couldn't determine with who, but the point is she was not conducting any official Livingston business down there. And several days after her return, there's a major purchase of 24 new golf carts to the tune of 100,000 dollars."

"Let me guess," said Sam. "The hotel never received any new golf carts."

"Bingo," said Sarah. "And this is the tip of the iceberg. The same scenarios play out across the board. And while it's not proof yet, it is enough to investigate, and I'm not talking about one of us. I'm talking about criminal investigation."

"You're right. But only half so. I've done a little checking of my own this afternoon. Since you didn't quite believe it about Antonio," Sam paused to give Sarah a telltale look. "I wanted you to see for yourself. Take a look at these," Sam continued as he laid the folder of papers on Sarah's desk.

Sarah opened the file folder and began leafing through the documents, a look of concern on her face, which quickly became one of anger.

"Son of a bitch," she whispered softly.

"What is it?" Donna asked quickly.

"Travel itineraries for Antonio," she replied. "Sam, where did you get this stuff?" she asked heatedly.

"Travel agents may be known for their discretion, but believe me, a little green goes a long way. I happen to know who books his stuff for him." Sam was smug.

"Donna, let me see that travel summary for the last quarter for Lindy, would you?" Sarah asked.

"Sure, here," Donna reached over and handed Sarah several pages.

Sarah glanced back and forth from one page to another, marking things with her pencil, cross referencing.

"It all matches," she said, somewhat sadly, shaking her head. "Everywhere Lindy goes, Antonio goes too. I can't believe it."

"Believe it," Sam said gently. "I'm sorry. But it's true. Whatever they're up to, they're in it together."

Sam breathed deeply and sighed. What he had to say next may not go over so well. But it had to be done.

"Look. I know this isn't the best time, especially for you Donna, with only a few months to go, but Lindy's scheduled to go to Chamandia next week, and I need to go with her." He continued quickly, not wanting Sarah to overreact again. "I think that's the source of all this, and this time I can watch her for myself."

"That's fine, Sam, really," Sarah chuckled, though inside she fumed. "We'll get along without you just fine."

"Um, I'm sure you would, but I can't leave you here." Sam's voice was peculiar, to say the least. In fact he turned his head away slightly, as if not wanting them to notice something. "What do you mean?" Sarah asked nervously.

"I mean, we're all going?" Sam tried to sound as if he were asking, but it came off as an order. He knew Sarah would balk at the idea, but the truth was, it was too dangerous to leave them here. If Antonio showed up in Chamandia, he'd get his answers. But if he didn't, and Sarah stayed behind, it could be a disaster. The only way was to take them all with him.

"We're all going? Who's all, Sam?" Sarah asked.

"Well, you two, and Addy, Grace, probably have to bring Tom along as well," Sam started calculating in his head what would be required, which made him smirk.

"Sam, that's ridiculous. You go, take Tom, and find what you need to find. We'll all be fine while you're gone."

"Sorry, no can do, Sarah," Sam's voice was firm now. He shook his head for emphasis. "Do you realize how much danger there is in all this?" His voice became louder and more assertive. "These people are stealing millions, Sarah, and you're the one who's publicly going to put a stop to them. And there's far more underlying this than you know, and I won't for one minute leave you to fend for yourselves. Do you understand? You're coming, that's final." He turned to Donna, his expression still determined. "And you won't mind, because I'm going to make sure you get to spend time with Andy. I know you've only had a few chances to talk to him, and that's unfair."

Sarah's surprised expression was evident. "Donna!" she exclaimed, somewhat angrily. "You never told me you talked with him!"

"Sorry, really I am, Sarah, but Sam made me swear on a bible that I wouldn't tell anyone, even you, he said," Donna sounded sincere and very apologetic.

Sarah turned her wrath on Sam. "How could you Sam?" Sarah thumped her fist on the desk for emphasis. "You know how worried I was for Donna, and all those times I begged you to put them in touch you were just humoring me the whole time. Why? Never mind, I'll answer that myself. You. Don't. Trust. Me!" She spoke each word slowly, for emphasis. "Which is why, I might add, you are forcing us to go with you. You're afraid to leave me here with Addy, aren't you? You don't trust me with her. What are you afraid of? I told you earlier, that I was on the edge Sam, and I wasn't putting up with crap anymore. And here you're at it again. Well. That's it. I'm done." Sarah didn't say another word. She left the room and headed up the stairs, calling for Grace as she went.

Sam stared at her retreating figure, then turned to Donna. She was struck by the look on his face. He looked devastated. And he definitely looked guilty. He hadn't responded to her charges, she realized, and maybe, just maybe they were true. She didn't want to think badly of him, but in this case, Sarah probably was justified in her reaction. It did make quite a mess of things though.

"Do you want me to talk to her?" Donna asked Sam. "Maybe I can calm her down."

"No, thanks, Donna, I got myself into this mess, I'll get myself out," he replied. "I just wish she had a little more faith in me, that's all. It's so damn frustrating."

"Precisely so," Donna replied. "For her as well. If you don't trust her, why should she trust you? Have you given her any reason to?"

"No, I guess not," Sam said with resignation. "But Donna, there is far more to this than simple embezzlement, you know that. I'm stuck between a rock and a hard place."

"Then I suggest you get yourself unstuck." Donna looked at Sam reproachfully. "And quickly."

Grace met Sarah at the top of the stairs, and even without her intuition, one look at Sarah's face was enough.

"You want to leave?" Grace asked her softly.

"Yes," Sarah tried to speak quietly. "Just pack your things and Addy's, and I'll call a cab. We'll be back in town by dinner."

"Are you sure about this?" Grace asked, again, gently.

"Absolutely positively."

"Well, I don't know, Sarah, I'm not feeling good about this. Maybe we should wait until morning?" Grace hoped she'd see reason. Or at least believe in her enough to listen.

"Uh uh, Grace, as much as I respect you and your intuition, he's gone too far. I can't take it anymore."

"All right then, I'll get everything ready," Grace replied, not at all happy about it.

"Thanks. Really, Grace, thanks." Sarah spoke gently as she squeezed Grace's shoulder.

As she threw her stuff into her bags, she thought about it some more. She'd have to provide a formal resignation of course, but all in all, this was best. She'd set up visitation for Addy, but other than that she wanted no part of Sam Livingston in her life. As exciting as her job was, it wasn't enough to hold her. Not when she had to live her life in incredible turmoil. She'd fallen irrevocably in love with a man who may or may not be everything he claimed to be. A man who treats her as a trustworthy employee one minute, potential lover the next, and then turns and acts as if she's under suspicion herself. And while he claims to be telling the truth to her, there are far too many secrets. No, she couldn't stay. While she had the nerve, she would get out.

Sarah held Addy while Grace got into the back of the cab. While the driver held the door, Sarah buckled Addy and her car seat into the middle, and slid in next to her. The driver had loaded their bags already, so they were set to go. Donna had stood silently by, but now reached inside to give Sarah a quick hug.

"Keep in touch, Sarah," she whispered sadly. "Please."

Sarah hugged her back.

"I will, I promise," she replied. "I need to keep track of that precious cargo you're carrying," she smiled softly. "Be careful, Donna, Okay?" Sarah really was worried for her. She didn't want her involved in anything that might bring harm to her or the baby.

"I will." Donna stepped back and let the driver close the door. As the cab pulled away, Sarah looked back towards the house. She could see Sam looking out from the upstairs window. She had just a minute's pang of guilt, then reminded herself this was his doing. She leaned back into the seat, trying to hold on to her anger, for she knew once it subsided, she'd be overwhelmed with sadness. The driver turned and spoke casually.

"Hope you don't mind, but I've got one more fare heading into town. It's just a minute off the road here," his voice trailed as he turned onto a gravel drive. He stopped after only a few hundred yards, however, causing Sarah to get nervous. It was getting dark, and there were no streetlights.

"Why are you stopping here," she asked the driver, trying to sound calm, but frantic inside. He didn't answer. The front passenger door opened suddenly, and someone got in and slammed the door quickly, nodding at the driver.

"Let's go..." It was a woman's voice, and Sarah knew immediately whose it was. Lindy. Her guess was confirmed when she suddenly swung around in her seat, a gun in her hand, aimed right at Sarah.

"Don't move. Don't say a word." Lindy smiled coolly at Sarah. "We're going on a little trip, and if you want to make it round trip, you'll do what I say. When I say." She swerved the gun to her right and aimed it at Addy. "Or you'll have one less baby to worry about."

CHAPTER 19

Sam turned from the window just as the cab left, phone in hand.

"Follow them," he said and hung up. He turned back towards the window, a tightness in his chest making him uncomfortable. He hadn't realized, or maybe he had, how much it would hurt if she left. He needed her. Now more than ever. And he was afraid. For her. For Addy. He couldn't protect them this way. Damnit! He had lost control, made mistakes. He had been raised not to trust. It was ingrained. It was necessary for survival. And while it had cost him in the past, never this much.

He turned and headed toward the door. He was in Sarah's room, and he could still smell her soft, flowery scent lingering. She'd taken most of her things with her, the dresser and vanity were empty now of all her knick knacks. He missed her. Stepping into the hallway, he pulled the door tightly closed behind him, as if to lock in what was left of her. He did the same with Addy's room, after standing for several minutes looking at the abandoned nursery. She had been like a ray of sunshine, and it made him ache to think of her gone. Worse, in danger. If Sarah had just trusted him, this wouldn't have happened. No, he knew he was as much to blame. But if, not if, but when, when he got them back, he wouldn't ever let go again. He shouldn't have let go today. He should have stopped her.

His phone rang, jarring him from his thoughts. He looked at the number. The embassy. Shit! Something's wrong. They never called on this line unless it was urgent.

"Yes." Sam spoke abruptly.

"It's time. You'll have to come in." The voice at the other end was a familiar one, and Sam understood the message immediately.

"How bad?" he asked.

"Matter of time," the voice came back, this time Sam could hear the defeated tone.

"OK. Tom's on an errand, so go ahead and send the car." Sam's voice was firm and decisive. He knew not to say a word more than necessary.

"One hour," the voice commanded, then disconnected. Sam knew it would take at least that long from the embassy. But he had no choice. He couldn't pull Tom now. He had to know, especially now, where they were. It was their only protection. He felt a sudden tingle in the back of his neck. And the phone rang again. Once more, he checked the caller number. Tom.

"Where are they?" Sam practically barked into the phone.

"It's bad Sam," Tom replied quickly. "The cab stopped suddenly and out of nowhere, Lindy appeared."

Sam swore loudly.

"She's armed. I can't get close enough without exposure, but I'm behind 'em now, and it looks like they're headed up past Kingston. I'm guessing the cabin."

"Most likely. I just got the call, Tom, it's time, it's all going down," Sam spoke quietly but with an edge. "Go ahead and bring in the cavalry. It won't matter now."

"Got it," Tom replied, and quickly disconnected.

Sam knew that it was all about to explode. But there was nothing he could do. He'd have to trust the FBI to get Sarah, Addy and Grace back safely. He couldn't do anything more. It was out of his hands. It was too soon. He wasn't ready. But it appeared he had no choice.

*****

Sarah had sat quietly in the cab for hours, it seemed. They were in the Catskills now, and headed who knows where. She'd tried to get Lindy to talk. To find out what this was all about. But Lindy had dismissed her early on, saying only the time had come. So Sarah waited, biding her time, thinking. She'd also noticed a pair of headlights behind them, and it seemed the same car had been there most of the way. Apparently the driver and Lindy hadn't noticed. But Sarah had, and prayed it was Sam or Tom. Someone to help. Grace had said nothing, but periodically would look at Sarah and give her a reassuring smile. Sarah hoped it meant she sensed they'd be rescued.

Without warning, the cab swerved off the highway, onto a barely paved service road, then turned onto a gravel road headed into a heavily wooded area. It came to a stop in front of a cabin, which appeared to be in good condition. The porch light came on, and Sarah was able to see that this was more of a weekend home than a simple cabin after all. Lindy turned then, and still pointing the gun, handed Sarah a phone with her other hand.

"Call him. Tell him he's to get himself 10 million in cash and wait for our instructions. And don't try anything funny," Lindy finished with a snap.

"10 million? Why not go for 20?" Sarah couldn't help being derisive.

"You're really stupid, aren't you," Lindy shot back. "It's not the money, you fool, it's Sam. I don't care if he brings 5 bucks with him. He'll get what's coming either way. And so will you."

So. It was a trap, Sarah thought with a shudder. She'd never been so frightened in her life. And if there was ever a time to put on a show of strength, this was it. Lindy was truly vicious, Sarah thought, perhaps even insane. The look on her face bore such hatred Sarah knew nothing short of a miracle would save them. Her main focus had to be protecting Addy, at all costs. Even her own life. Nothing mattered if Addy was harmed. She focused her gaze on Lindy, though it terrified her. She had to play it cool, keep Lindy off guard.

"Lindy, I have one question. What do you have against me anyway? Did I do something to offend you? If so, I'm sorry." Sarah tried to make her voice sound totally innocent. "I mean I understand that this kidnapping doesn't have anything to do with me per se, but you seem to have it in for me anyway. I'm just wondering why." Keep her talking, Sarah thought, just keep her talking.

"Oh get off the innocent act, will you? We both know the score. Until you came along Sam was mine. Totally. He'd have married me sooner or later. And you come waltzing in with your sweet little Sarah crap and now I'm history. What, you think I should be happy?" Lindy was being snide, and disdainful, and it made her ugly. "Antonio thought you'd be perfect for our plans, but what does he know. He's like all the others. Dumber than a lamp post. Now call!"

Sarah grabbed the cellphone from Lindy, and dialed in Sam's personal, never use unless it's an emergency, number. She had to let him know this was a trap. Somehow.

Sam waited outside the press room at the Chamandian Embassy, his palm size computer device held tightly in one hand, phone in the other. He paced back and forth, waiting for a message from Tom. It was almost time, and he needed to get this settled now. He wouldn't be able to go in there and say a word if he couldn't be assured of their safety. The sudden ring of his phone startled him. He looked down, but the number wasn't recognizable.

"Yes," Sam answered cautiously, but anxiously.

"Sam, it's Sarah," Sarah's voice was high pitched, definitely scared.

"Sarah, where are you? Are you alright?" Sam didn't expect her to answer him, but had to ask anyway, especially if anyone were listening. He had to feign ignorance.

"We're fine, for now, Sam, but..." she trailed off and he heard a muffled voice in the background. "They want 10 million Sam, in cash. They said get the money and wait for instructions." Sarah didn't know if he knew they'd been taken, but hoped he understood.

"You've been kidnapped?" he tried to sound incredulous, as if it was news to him.

"Yes," she answered, her voice trembling. Again he heard the muffled voice in the background, and assumed it was Lindy.

"They want 10 million Sam, please, you've got to come, they'll hurt Addy." Sarah's voice was frenzied now.

"OK. Consider it done. Tell them I'll await their instructions." He wouldn't but it was all part of a game now, one he intended to win.

"And Sam?" Sarah spoke quickly, before Lindy could take the phone back. "I'm sorry about today. Really, I hope you're not still angry. I never meant it you know, about the money. It was never about the money, you understand, don't you?" Sarah prayed Sam understood. They hadn't fought about money. He had to understand!

Sam heard the click and knew she'd been cut off. But her message was loud and clear. They didn't want 10 million. They wanted him. But it was too late. They'd never get what they were after now. Sam had made sure of it. Now all he could do was pray everything came off without a hitch.

His hand device beeped twice and Sam held it up to read the message on the screen. The women were at his mountain cabin. Tom was watching them from a distance, and a team was in place. They should have them out within hours, if all went as planned. The driver of the cab had been identified.

A Chamandian National. He'd taken the cab at gunpoint from the regular driver, who'd had to walk 2 miles to find a phone and call the cops. By the time he did, the assailant had gotten far enough away with Sarah, Addy and Grace that to pull them over would have endangered them.

Sam read the next message. "Mon Dieu" He swore out loud. Antonio was nowhere to be found. That was a problem. He could be already in the cabin or anywhere for that matter. Without him in custody, nobody was safe. He'd go himself and get them out, if he could. But he couldn't. There was no way he was going anywhere but that press room. If he didn't, Sarah and Addy would be in even more danger. As long as they thought there was a chance he'd show up at the cabin, hopefully they'd be unharmed. As he glanced down at his watch, he realized it was almost time. Swearing under his breath, he straightened his shoulders, and adjusted his tie. Running his hand through his hair, he prepared himself for the moment that would change his life forever. And if all went as planned, Sarah's and Addy's as well.

*****

Sarah held Addy tightly in one arm, her other hand in Grace's as Lindy forced them into the cabin at gunpoint. Sarah knew immediately that this place belonged to Sam. From the Livingston portrait on the wall to the model sloop over the fireplace mantel. She felt Lindy push her with the edge of the pistol.

"Over there, on the couch. All of you." She waved the gun toward the couch, and Sarah noticed she looked calmer now. She really was mad, Sarah thought. She could blow them all away in an instant and never think twice. She quickly did as she was told, pulling Grace along with her. Sitting down, she looked at Lindy.

"I need to feed the baby. I don't suppose you've thought about that, have you?"

"What do you think I am, an idiot?" Lindy spat the words out. "I've got baby food here. I've got formula here. I've got diapers, and a crib." She laughed suddenly. "You see, I'm going to take your place, Sarah, didn't you know?" A chill went through Sarah. Lindy was absolutely insane. She wanted to get rid of Sarah and take Addy for herself? Why?

"Why, Lindy? Why do you want Addy? Won't she disrupt your career?" Sarah kept her voice neutral.

"Career? I don't give a damn about a career. You want to know what I care about, Ms. Bennett, I'll tell you what I care about." Lindy suddenly glanced at her watch, and smiled ruthlessly. "Better yet, I'll show you." Grabbing the TV remote from the coffee table, Lindy clicked on the power and flipped through the stations till she hit the news channel.

Sarah gasped out loud as the images appeared on the screen. Sam. Right there on the news. Next to him, according to the scrolling news feed, stood the Chamandian Ambassador. While they sat here in terror, being held by a madwoman, he was obviously paying more attention to some diplomatic situation than them. She didn't know whether to laugh or cry. She said a quick prayer in her head that somehow this involved them, but when the ambassador stepped forward, and made a formal introduction of Sam Livingston, she learned the truth. And the shock was too much. The last thing Sarah remembered before fainting dead away was Lindy's face, an evil twisted smile upon it.

CHAPTER 20

Sarah opened her eyes, dazed, and looked up to see Lindy with Antonio right behind her, holding the gun. Neither was smiling. In fact, they both had looks of pure hatred and revulsion on their faces. She looked over at the TV, but they had cut to another story. Sarah closed her eyes tight and opened them, hoping it had all been some weird dream. The last thing she remembered was the Ambassador to Chamandia, introducing Sam. She gasped, remembering now. He introduced not Sam Livingston, but His Royal Highness, Samuel Christoph Livingston, Prince of Chamandia.

She looked back over at Antonio, her face drawing tight, anger flashing in her eyes. But her look was no match for the anger she saw on his face.

"You!" He yelled at her. "It's your fault. You've ruined it. Everything. You couldn't do a simple thing like lure him here to save you? You're a worthless nothing!" Sarah had no idea what Antonio was saying, her mind stuck on the fact that she was being blamed for something. And she was about to go off the deep end.

"What the hell are you talking about, Antonio?" Sarah stood up suddenly, planting her hands on her hips, screaming at him, gun and all. Somehow, she wasn't afraid any longer. Just plain mad.

"And what is all this about? I don't have any idea what the hell is going on. Your girlfriend here kidnaps me, Sam's a fucking prince, and now you're blaming me for whatever the hell went wrong with whatever you were trying to do. Personally, I don't give a damn about any of it. I've had enough. I told him that today, and I'm telling you now. You want to wave your freaking gun in my face, go ahead. Shoot me. But I'll see you rot in hell if it's the last thing I do."

"Is that what you said to him today? Is that why he isn't here to save you?" Antonio shot back; disgust written on his face. "Maybe if you'd been a little bit nicer, a little bit sexier, he'd be here now!" Sarah looked stricken, and didn't respond. He smiled derisively. "You really don't get it, do you," he said with a sneer. "Well listen up, and I'll explain it. Sam is the official heir to the throne in Chamandia. Only 3 people knew of his existence. Rolf Christoph, his uncle, and up until a few minutes ago, the reigning monarch, the Ambassador to Chamandia, and myself. We took care of Rolf and had plans for Sam too. Then it would be the Ambassador's word against mine."

"Your word about what?"

"About my right to the crown. It belongs to me!"

Sarah laughed; she couldn't help it. Her nerves were frayed, and having Antonio stand there claiming to be a prince was just too much.

"Stupid bitch. Do you know nothing? My name is not Antonio. It's John de Guerre, and I am the legitimate heir to the throne. I would have had it too if you could have seduced Sam into coming after you. But you couldn't. I thought you had it in you, really I did. I chose well, I thought. It was a perfect plan."

"Sorry, Antonio, but I don't get it. What the hell was the plan and what did my seducing Sam have to do with any of it. And furthermore, could you please stop waving that damn gun in my face, I'm not going anywhere. It's cold and windier than hell and we're in the middle of no man's land."

"Sit, dear Sarah, and I'll tell you a tale." Antonio aka John de Guerre smiled sardonically and waved the gun to indicate she should take a seat back on the sofa. He almost looked amused. Sarah was too confused, and too pissed off to care anymore. She just wanted to go home. Her home. With Addy and Grace. Preferably alive.

He cleared his throat, and began speaking in a hypnotic, sing song style, making Sarah shudder.

"You see, it's really quite simple. For years we've known about Sam, though the world was ignorant. I have been raised since birth to appreciate my heritage. To avenge the malicious destruction of my ancestor's kingdom. To rise again and reclaim the Isle de Guerre. And to that end, I had a plan. A wonderful plan. And Lindy, my sweet dear Lindy, has been most helpful. Of course, her motives weren't as pure, but whose are?" he shrugged as if that was insignificant. Lindy shot him a look though, one that said she didn't appreciate the remark.

"All you had to do was cause Sam to become enamored of you. Enough so that when it came down to the wire, he would choose you over his obligations. When Rolf passed away, which we were most certain he would, Sam would have to step in immediately. But if Sam were to say, not show up, then he would be abdicating and I would step in to fill the void. Taking you and Addy was supposed to lure him here, away from the press conference. When no one showed, I would make the call to every major news agency and get things rolling. But Sam didn't come for you, did he?" his voice sneered.

"No, he didn't," Sarah replied quietly. She was on her last thread of composure now. Realizing the truth in all its ugliness hurt like a knife through her heart. He hadn't come for her. He hadn't come for Addy either. He hadn't sent anyone to their rescue. And he'd lied to her big time. Big big time.

"Tell me something," her voice remained soft, hesitant. "How is Sam the heir? What's the connection?"

Antonio laughed.

"You'll have to ask him yourself, if you ever see him again. My guess is he's already on board the royal jet to Chamandia by now. I'm guessing I'll see him before you will." Grabbing Lindy by the arm, he steered her out the door, leaving Sarah, Grace and Addy alone in the cabin. They were alone in an isolated cabin, who knows where. Eventually she knew they'd be found. But nothing would ever ever be the same. And worse, Sarah didn't understand all the connections, but she knew that Addy was no ordinary baby. As Greg's daughter, she obviously must have royal blood. Her niece was a damn princess, and Sarah knew it would mean a complete upheaval for all of them. She closed her eyes and leaned back into the sofa. And Sam was obviously still in danger, especially if he was on his way to Chamandia. For Antonio's implication was clear. They weren't giving up.

"Sarah, dear?" Grace's voice was soothing, and calm. "You rest, I'm going to take Addy and see if I can dig up those supplies that are here somewhere for her."

"Thanks, Grace," Sarah replied, her voice a monotone.

"And Sarah?" Grace went on.

"Yes," she sighed in reply.

"Don't make any snap decisions, or judgements. Sometimes things are not what they seem, and other times they are. I know what you're thinking. That Sam didn't care for you the way you did for him. You feel hurt. You're angry. You've been through a traumatic experience. Just give things time. And give him time. There's still something unsettling left to see to, but it will be fine. In the end, it will be fine." She left the room then, Addy in her arms.

Sarah took a deep breath. Grace was right. She'd been scared shitless, had her heart broken and had her life turned upside down in a matter of hours. This wasn't the time to do anything. Or say anything. But if they were still here in the morning, and no one had come for them, she'd have to make some decisions. First and foremost, how to warn Sam without revealing what she knew. She was going to play dumb for a while. She had to. She was trembling now. She closed her eyes, feeling a panic attack coming. She hadn't had one since her parents' accident. But she vividly remembered how it was, losing control. Unable to breathe. Having the life sucked out of her.

Chapter 21

Sarah could feel the cold air wash over her. But it wasn't registering. Nothing was. She sat, shaking, on the sofa. Her eyes closed, she felt as if she were simply floating. Completely detached from her surroundings. The adrenaline that had kept her functioning for the last several hours was gone. She couldn't think. From somewhere she heard a voice, her name, but she couldn't seem to open her eyes or focus. Sam? No. Not Sam. Someone. She was so very tired. Maybe she could just sleep. She leaned over sideways, resting her head on the arm rest. Yes. Sleep. She needed to drift away. Far away. But the voice was persistent. A hand on her shoulder. Pressing gently. She sensed she was supposed to do something. What? A gentle rocking of her shoulder. Someone was smoothing her hair. Or maybe not. It was cold. So cold. She wrapped her arms around her chest. Blankets. She needed blankets. Why was it so cold? Again, the voice.

"Sarah," it whispered. "Sarah, you need to wake up."

Sarah tried to do what she was asked. She tried to open her eyes. But nothing happened. She felt paralyzed. Weightless.

"She's in shock." A woman's voice. Unfamiliar. The words seemed to echo. "I know," a man's voice answered. Close. Too close. She hugged herself tighter, trying to withdraw further. She felt something over her. A blanket. Yes, warmth. It felt good.

More voices. Jumbled. A cry. A baby. Addy. Her baby. No, Megan's. Megan's dead. She suddenly snapped into focus. Addy! She had to get Addy. Make sure she was okay. Something was wrong. She couldn't move. She tried to talk. Say something, her mind screamed. But her lips wouldn't move. She was so sleepy. And still so cold.

"They're on their way." A man's voice. Another spoke, and another. The words seemed to drift in every direction. "They're in custody" "Not talking" "Plenty of evidence"

Sarah's mind started to try and process the words. They'd been caught. Thank God. Sam was safe. Addy was safe. But there might be others, suddenly she didn't want to think anymore. Someone had her arm. Why were they holding her arm? And a prick. Something in her arm. It hurt. Then there was nothing.

Tom turned to the agent who'd given Sarah the sedative.

"How long will she be out for?" he questioned her.

"Just a few hours, it's a small dose. Her body needs to rest. Shock can play havoc with the body's chemistry. Sleeping it off will allow it to regulate itself back to a normal rhythm," the agent replied quietly.

"They should be here shortly." Tom spoke in the same hushed tones. Though around them, the SWAT team and FBI agents were quickly sweeping the cabin for evidence, and possible explosive devices, they were doing it methodically and quite silently. There was always the chance that the cabin had been booby-trapped. But Tom didn't think so. They'd learn more soon enough. Right now, he focused on Sarah. She was something, he thought to himself. Tom had been with Sam for 15 years and had never thought Sam would find such a treasure. He'd be here soon, Tom thought. Hopefully, she still didn't know. But if she did, would forgive him. Tom knew her anger ran deep. There wasn't much that escaped him. He'd warned Sam early on that if and when Sarah discovered his identity, there would be hell to pay. If Sarah had been like Sam's other women, it wouldn't have been a problem. She'd probably be throwing a party about now. He smiled to himself, watching her expressive face, which even in sleep, spoke volumes. Not Sarah. Too smart. Too independent. Too caring. Perfect for the role destiny was handing her. Things would be so different now, he mused. For years, only a select few knew who Sam was. And luckily, even those that did weren't aware of who else knew. That was key to keeping it secret. And protecting those involved. Including himself.

Suddenly remembering there were others who needed to be reached, he grabbed his phone and hit the speed dial.

"Bill, it's Tom," he spoke quickly into the phone. "I assume you've been briefed?"

"Yes. How's Sarah, and Addy?" he asked in a concerned tone.

"Addy's fine, Grace is with her. Sarah's in shock, but unharmed."

Bill sighed. "Thank goodness for that. Carol and I have packed, and we'll leave with the kids shortly."

"OK, I'll let Sam know as soon as I talk to him," Tom replied.

"Take care of them, Tom." Bill ended the call.

The agents arrived at the FBI offices in Kingston in separate cars. One brought in Lindy. One Antonio. The other the driver of the cab, which had been carjacked just before reaching Sam's house. They had been separated immediately upon their arrest. The team had been in place, ready to move in, when they had come out the door headed towards the waiting cab.

Tom turned as he heard the sound of the chopper. The clearing with the landing pad was hidden away close to 1000 yards behind the cabin, in the woods. It had been designed for emergencies, and this certainly constituted one. Turning to the agent who had sedated Sarah, he spoke with authority.

"Take Grace and the baby out to the chopper please. Just follow the path that leads out back and keep to your right when it splits." The agent nodded and went to Grace to lead her out. As they headed toward the door, Grace stopped suddenly, and looked at Sarah.

"Poor dear," she spoke softly. Looking back at the agent, she smiled. "We've been through the ringer, haven't we? But he'll take good care of her." The agent didn't quite know what Grace meant by the last remark but smiled anyway.

"I'm sure he will," she answered, and taking Grace by the arm led her out back. Grace held Addy tightly in one arm, a blanket wrapped around her, and the carrier in the other. She felt an overwhelming sense of calm wash over her, but in it was a mixture of unease as well. It was conflicting for her. Something was telling her to keep moving, it was okay. But something else was telling her to watch over Sarah. She wrinkled her brow in thought, trying to sort it out.

"Is something wrong?" the agent asked, seeing the expression on her face.

"Yes, and no," Grace replied curiously. "I feel as if Sarah needs something. But I'm not sure what I can do," Grace replied with a soft smile. She shrugged and indicated they should keep moving. It was cold outside, and Addy was her main concern now. She looked into the distance ahead and saw a figure running towards them. But she felt no fear. Ah, she thought, Sam. Good. He stopped short when he reached them.

"You're okay?" he barked out as he glanced from her to Addy. He was breathless, but not from running. "Addy?" he looked down at his sleeping niece. Running a finger along her cheek, which felt cold to his touch, he whispered softly. "You okay sweet pea?" He leaned his head down and kissed her cheek, running his finger once more down her face. He looked at Grace with concern. "They didn't hurt her, did they?"

"No, Sam, we're fine. We're all fine," she added with emphasis. Sam breathed out slowly and nodded, then looked past her shoulder towards the cabin.

"Go, Sam," Grace said softly. "We're doing fine here." Sam looked at her once more, and reassured that all was well, took off at a brisk run towards the house. What was taking so long, he wondered. Sarah and Tom should be right behind Grace. Why weren't they coming out? As he approached, he could see through the open door a multitude of people moving about. He shook his head, when they called in the cavalry, they didn't mess around. But his concern for Sarah was overwhelming. Grace said they were fine, but something told him Sarah wasn't fine. He pushed himself to run faster, he needed to get to her. Now.

Tom stood by the sofa, knowing that Sam would come racing in any second. He could have carried Sarah out to the chopper, but he thought it might be better to let Sam do it. He smiled as he heard footsteps running up the porch steps. Yep. Much better this way.

Sam charged into the room, looking about frantically. Spotting her on the sofa, he quickly made it to her side. Without looking away from her, he spoke to Tom.

"She's okay?"

"Yes, just sleeping. We felt it better this way," Tom replied.

"What way?" Sam asked tensely.

"She was in shock, Sam, we sedated her." Sam hadn't averted his gaze from her once. He noticed her hair curling softly about her face, which was pale. But she was safe. And Addy was safe. He was grateful and relieved. He hadn't had time to deal with the emotions that were playing on him. And they were about to overtake him.

He leaned over carefully, and sliding his arms underneath her, he lifted her up and turned toward the door. Cradling her in his arms, he walked slowly, not saying anything to anyone, just nodding at some of the lingering agents. It was cold, dark and a long way to the chopper pad, but Sarah didn't weigh much, or maybe he just didn't notice. He stumbled once or twice, not paying attention to where he was walking. Only studying her face. What would she do when she awoke? Would she be angry? Sad? Would she hate him? Did she know who he was? Had anyone told her? Whatever she was thinking in that soundless sleep of hers, he wouldn't know. But whatever it was he'd deal with it. Whatever it took, he would keep her with him. He'd finally found what he'd been searching for and wasn't about to let her go. He needed her. Addy needed her. He wouldn't give her a choice.

He leaned down as he approached the chopper to avoid the gusty wind of the whirling blades and handed Sarah up to the young guard in the chopper, climbing up quickly behind. He took his seat and indicated the guard should place Sarah in his lap. He'd hold her, he decided, keep her close. As he drew his arms around to secure her, she moved suddenly, trying to adjust her body to get comfortable. Even in her sleep, Sarah had a way of making her presence known. But when her arms reached around his neck, and her head tucked neatly against his shoulder, Sam had to smile. Now he was sure. If she didn't trust him, didn't want him, even in her sleep she'd have pulled away. Instead she drew closer. As if drawing comfort from him. And giving him some of her own.

The trip was short, just over an hour. When the chopper put down at JFK International, Sam turned to Grace.

"Grace, I know this is last minute," Sam managed a grin as he unbuckled the safety harness he'd placed around Sarah and himself. "But how do you feel about taking a little trip to an exotic island in the Indian Ocean?"

Grace smiled. Sam didn't know how much they'd discovered, she realized that early on. And Grace wasn't about to tell him. Of course, with all the hoopla and FBI and special agents, almost anyone could figure out that

Sam was someone extremely important. But Sam's concern had been over Sarah during the flight, so there'd been no discussion anyway.

"Which island would that be, Sam?"

"Chamandia, of course," Sam grinned. "Whaddya say, you game?"

"I'm game, Sam, but maybe we should check with Sarah when she wakes up?" Grace knew he wasn't going to wait, but felt it was her obligation to speak for her.

"No can do, Grace, she'll be out for a few more hours yet. Don't worry, though, I'm sure she'll love it! It's the perfect place to recover for her, don't you agree?" Sam winked at Grace, and she realized he was almost enjoying this. He had total control at the moment, and Sarah had absolutely no way of countering. But Grace knew if he was enjoying it, it wasn't because he felt this was some sort of power play he was winning, but because he had Sarah where he wanted. Where she couldn't resist. And she knew it was time to back away and let the two of them play it out for themselves.

"OK, Sam, but I hope you know what you're doing. She's got a temper, which I think you've seen way too much of, personally." Grace laughed softly. "It's the Irish in her, you know."

"Don't I though," Sam laughed with her. "By the time she wakes up, we'll be all settled in, and she won't have anything to complain about. That I can guarantee. In fact, she'll be pampered and coddled just like a princess," Sam smirked as he said it, and watched to see if Grace flinched at the remark, or took it as a colloquial phrase, not truth. Grace didn't bat an eyelash. With a perfectly straight face, she countered.

"I'm sure she will be, Sam, and after what she's been through, I'd say she deserves the royal treatment." Their eyes locked momentarily, and the message was clear. Whatever Grace knew, she wasn't going to tell. She probably knew more than she let on, considering her special talent. But Sam wasn't going to offer anything either. Stalemate.

The chopper's illustrious passengers were quickly shuttled over to the private terminal where the Chamandian Royal Jet was waiting. Once again, Sam carried Sarah himself. As they boarded the jet, Grace gasped softly. It was like a movie star's plane. Or the President's. Instead of rows of seats, there were sofas and small tables. A kitchenette and bar, a video screen. Even a small crib for Addy had been set up.

"Sam this is some plane," Grace remarked. "I've only flown a few times in my life, and I'm sure none of those planes were like this. More like cattle cars."

"Well there's a first time for everything, Grace," Sam replied somewhat breathlessly. He'd been holding Sarah for so long he'd managed to get winded without realizing it. Laying her on the soft leather sofa, he sat down next to her and lifted her head up onto his lap. "Why don't you go ahead and put Addy down over in the crib, and then come sit over here. It's a bit of a long flight, but I'll have something prepared to eat, and then we can all sleep for a while."

"Oh, you don't need to worry about me, Sam, I'm not hungry. Go ahead and eat if you are though," Grace quickly added.

"Well you know it's not just us we have to worry about, Grace," Sam chuckled as he heard the sounds coming from outside. "We're not flying solo here." As Sam finished speaking, a sudden burst of children's voices could be heard, with several adult ones as well. Grace turned towards the door and smiled as the parade of passengers embarked. She looked at Sam questioningly.

Sam laughed. "And here I thought you'd have known, Grace. Didn't you sense we'd have company?"

"No," Grace mused. "Guess my intuition battery is running low."

"Well, then allow me to introduce Bill and Carol Abbott, and their 4 little darlings." Grace smiled and held out her free hand. She hadn't yet put Addy down. Carol approached first, shaking Grace's hand and cooing at Addy. Bill came over quickly to do the same. They immediately turned their attention back to their kids, though. Grace looked at Sam puzzled. She'd really had no idea others would be coming along. And their presence, while not disturbing, was a bit odd. But Grace put aside her musings at the sight of the four small children, ranging in age from about 4-10, she guessed. And she could also see the strain in their parents' eyes. Grace knew when she was needed. And it was right now. The kids were running, jumping, pushing, yelling, crying, all the things kids need to do when their lives are topsy turvy. Grace touched Carol on the arm gently.

"Here, Carol, take Addy and put her down, will you? I'll deal with the rest of this." Everyone jumped as Grace put two fingers in her mouth and let out an ear-piercing sound. The kids stared wide eyed, not moving an inch, or making even one sound.

"There, now, that's better, isn't it?" Grace smiled, her eyes twinkling. She took several steps towards the children, and looking from one to the other, said "Hello, there. I'm Grace. Now. Who are all of you?"

The littlest, a tow-headed girl with big blue eyes, smiled shyly and answered first. "I'm Cindy!" The others followed her lead.

"I'm Bill Jr.," said the oldest.

"I'm Timmy, and I'm seven!" said the next.

"And I'm Jill, and I'm 6, and I'm bigger than Cindy," said the last little girl.

"Well," said Grace, "Cindy, Jill, Timmy and Bill Junior, why don't we all go back there to that table and play a game. I know lots of games," she said with a wink.

"I do too," said Bill Jr. quite formally. And he took Grace's hand, declaring himself the leader of the group, and headed towards the rear of the plane. The other children followed behind, and Grace looked back over her shoulder at Bill and Carol, who were fairly dumbstruck at her ability to manage the handful they'd brought on board. Grace nodded at them; the unspoken message clear. She'd take control of the kids and let them talk.

Bill and Carol sat across from Sam on a smaller sofa, and both sighed in unison, making Sam laugh.

"She's something, isn't she?" he said.

"A treasure Sam, a real treasure," Carol replied with another huge sigh. They heard the sound of the plane's door being closed, and the pilot came back to greet Sam, and brief him on the flight plans. As he headed towards the cockpit, the two royal guards on board nodded at the pilot that all was clear. They stood at rigid attention at each of the exit doors, waiting for the engines to kick in before taking their seats right there by each door. Tom was in the back of the plane, seated with two flight attendants, both members of the Chamandian Royal Guard.

Bill spoke up first. "Any news Sam?"

"Yes, my uncle is going to make it. They're still running labs, but from all appearances it was arsenic." Sam's voice revealed his anger in its tone. "A slow, methodical poisoning," he added.

"Do they know who did it?" Bill asked.

"Not yet, but with Antonio and Lindy in custody, maybe we'll get some answers. One thing we do know, it was linked to them somehow." Sam didn't want to think about it right now. Rolf would survive, but no longer be capable of ruling the tiny principality. It was Sam's turn. He'd never wanted this. He'd never as a boy even entertained the possibility. It wouldn't have happened if not for the loss of Rolf's family in the so-called accident. But that was no accident. That was murder. And until they caught the remaining accomplices the danger still permeated his life. Carol spoke then.

"Sam, you can tell me to butt out if you like, that it's none of my business, though I beg to differ, but what about Sarah? What are you planning?" Carol looked down at the sleeping woman with concern.

"You mean what are my intentions, don't you?" Sam smiled; his thoughts now totally focused on Sarah.

"Precisely, Sam," Carol looked at him meaningfully, then looked down again at Sarah, still out light like a light.

"She'll remain with us, of course," Sam replied quickly. Too quickly.

"And how does she feel about all this?" Carol asked, suspicious now.

"Well, actually, um, she doesn't quite know about it all, I don't think," Sam's voice was laced with hesitation.

"What do you mean, she doesn't know?" Carol asked.

"I mean, they had to sedate her, before I arrived, and I'm not sure what she knows."

"You mean she's been out since you found her? She has no idea she's on this plane bound for Chamandia?" Carol was stunned, and a little ticked off at Sam. She truly liked Sarah, even though their one meeting was brief. It had been enough to assure Carol that Addy was in good hands.

"No, she has no idea. I don't even know if she ever learned who I was, or what was happening," Sam replied sheepishly.

"Sam Livingston, you really need your head examined. You're whisking the poor girl off to an island halfway around the world, an island of which I might add, you are now the esteemed ruler, without even asking?"

"Um, yes, I guess so." Sam was cringing now. She was making it sound like a death sentence for Sarah. While he thought he was giving her the moon.

"Do you have any idea how angry she'll be? How you're disrupting her life? Making decisions for her? What in hell are you thinking?" Carol was fuming now, and Sam realized Sarah would be far angrier. They felt the sudden whoosh as the plane lifted off the runway making its ascent into the night sky. Sam looked down at Sarah and realized there was no turning back. Not that he wanted to. But what he wanted and what Sarah wanted may not be the same thing. He'd spent his life selfishly, he knew that. He expected, no demanded, things from people that he probably had no right to. And Sarah was putting all that to the test. If she didn't want to stay, if she didn't want to remain in Chamandia, what would he do? Would he let her go? Or would he use every means at his disposal to keep her there. Watching her eyelids flutter softly he wondered. What was she dreaming about? What did she want? What would she do?

Chapter 22

The hum of the engines was quiet, soothing. Sam looked around the cabin, seeing almost everyone asleep now. His mind was too filled with thoughts to sleep. Though his arm did a good job of staying numb from its hold on Sarah. He should get up and walk about, stretch, but he couldn't let go of her. He did a mental debate back and forth, and decided no, he'd have to get up and move about a bit. So he carefully positioned her so she could continue sleeping uninterrupted, propping a small pillow under her head, and stood up and stretched. Taking the opportunity to go and visit with the flight crew and grab a bite to eat, he went back to where Sarah still slept soundly, and repositioned them both as they were before.

He felt her move, watched her as her eyes slowly opened, just a crack. Then a bit more as she focused on his face. "Sam?" Her voice was sleepy, breathy, and made Sam's heart lurch. Sarah slowly lifted one hand, and realized she couldn't move it very well, as she tried to grab onto him. He was here, she thought, here, with her. But where were they? She felt the soft vibration of the plane's movement but couldn't pinpoint it. "Sam?" she asked again, still watching his face. He seemed exhausted. His face was drawn, and his eyes looked almost tender, none of the flash in them she was accustomed to. She closed her eyes for a moment, trying to recall where they were, what was happening, and suddenly images started flashing. Antonio and Lindy.

The Cabin. Addy. The gun. Her eyes popped open again and she grasped Sam's shirt, bunching it in her fist, trying to lift her upper body, get herself upright. Pulling.

"Addy!" Sarah sputtered. "Sam, we need to get Addy! Where's Addy? And Grace? Sam, they had a gun!" She was frantic now, and Sam calmly pulled her hand from his shirt, and gently eased her back down on his lap.

"Shh, sweetheart, everything's fine, everyone's fine," his tone was gentle, but again Sarah heard the tiredness in it. Studying his face, her own expression was guarded, but hopeful.

"Tell me, Sam, tell me everything. I saw you," she sighed as she collected her thoughts. No easy task, since she felt so tired, and heavy. As if she'd been drugged.

She gathered what strength she had. "You were on TV, Sam, they said you were the Prince, I remember that," she turned her head slightly away. "I remember you didn't come for us," she kept her head turned, as she felt tears well up. She wouldn't let him see her cry. And for some reason, she knew she couldn't stop the tears anyway. Sam placed his hand on her chin and turned her head to face him again.

"I didn't desert you, Sarah, believe me I didn't. I'll explain it all, but we're landing soon, and there's no time now. But I promise, I will." So, she did know about him. He hoped she wouldn't do anything rash till he had a chance to talk with her. But she was in no shape to listen now.

"Mmm," Sarah murmured, still struggling to remain awake. "You, you always say that, Sam, that you'll explain. But you never…. never…. follow through." Her voice was stilted, as it was an effort to keep her thoughts from getting all jumbled. She let the sleepiness overtake her again and closed her eyes. The only thought in her head was a prayer that when she awoke, she'd find out it had all been a dream. She and Addy would be in their little apartment, and nothing would be different. She smiled, picturing her and Addy in the rocker in her room. Then frowned as she realized Sam wouldn't be there. He might not be real. Maybe it would be better if he wasn't. No, she felt a wave of despair suddenly overwhelm her, it wouldn't be better. He had to be real, because she didn't think anyone ever could replace him in her heart. He was stubborn, secretive, mysterious, often domineering, overpowering and she wouldn't have him change for the world. But if he was real, then he was a prince, and she didn't stand a chance. Still frowning, that was the last thought she had as she fell into slumbering again.

Sarah awoke as the landing gear came down, and a flurry of activity began in the plane's cabin. As her eyes opened, she realized she was leaning against something... no, someone. She breathed in slowly through her nose, savoring the musky scent. She felt her hair being stroked softly and heard the low, husky voice. "Sarah," it whispered. "Come on, now, baby, wake up," it crooned to her. She shook her head slightly, still foggy. Looking up at Sam, she sighed. She had no idea where she was, why she was lying there, obviously very cozy with him. And for some reason she didn't care. She had one arm looped across his shoulder, and her head was tucked in the crook of his arm. He was still stroking her head softly, absently. He gazed down at her, and seeing she was awake, maybe even ready to get up, he smiled softly.

"Think you can stand up?" She narrowed her eyes curiously. "Stand?" she asked. Not quite understanding. Not quite caring. Sam chuckled.

"Yeah, as in stand up, walk, talk?"

Pursing her lips, she thought for a minute.

"Of course I can stand up, walk, talk." she replied automatically. Then it seemed to dawn on her suddenly. Where she was. What she was doing. Then the plane hit the ground with a slight lurch, and she bolted upright, smacking him in the jaw with her arm as she did. "Whoaaaa," Sam said softly as he rubbed his chin with one hand, and gently eased her back down with his other arm. "Take it easy," he continued.

"Sorry," Sarah mumbled, still confused. She turned her head to look about, deciding that getting up was a bad idea anyway, considering the way her head was reeling. As her eyes focused, she took in all that was happening. She knew she was on a plane; she recognized the feel of it touching down on the runway. And across from her she saw Bill, Carol and a bunch of kids. Turning to look further down towards the back, she saw Grace. She watched her unbuckling a belt, standing and moving towards a crib. A crib? Addy? And there was Tom walking up from the back towards them. There were others too, but none Sarah recognized. Obviously, they were all safe and sound. Somewhere. She felt more awake now, but somehow, didn't really have any desire to move from the comfort of Sam's arms. She'd wondered what it would feel like to be like this with him. She felt completely at peace, though her heart was beginning to race a bit. She considered feigning sleep again, so she wouldn't have to move, or give up the sensations she was feeling. As she felt Sam move one arm and stretch, she wondered how long they'd been like this. He looked so tired. So drained. No, it wouldn't be fair to him to stay like this. She pushed gently on his chest to help herself get up, and he quickly unbuckled them and placed one arm beneath her back to support and lift her up. He helped her to sit upright, and making sure she was steady, stood up and began to slowly shake out his arms and legs. Sarah smiled, as he really did look quite funny doing it.

"How long were we sitting like that?" she asked, a tinge of sympathy in her voice.

"About 18 hours," he replied with a grin. Sarah was stunned.

"You must be stiff as a board!" she shot out. "Why didn't you wake me?" All thoughts of where they were and what they were doing flew out of her head. The idea that she had slept in his arms for 18 hours consumed her thoughts. "You'll need physical therapy to recover, you know." She really looked worried, Sam mused. No sense telling her he'd taken a few breaks here and there.

"I'll be fine. Now, are you feeling up to standing, do you think you can?" Sam asked.

"I don't know. I feel like a lead weight to be honest, and my head's spinning a bit," she replied. Looking about again, her thoughts were redirected.

"Where are we, anyway?"

"Chamandia," Sam replied with a grin. "An island paradise awaits you...."

"Chamandia?" Sarah was stunned. "We flew all the way to Chamandia, and I slept through it? I'm a very light sleeper, Sam, that's impossible."

"Maybe normally, sweetheart, but you were given a little sedative to help you sleep. Apparently it worked a little too well." Sam looked a bit sheepish. As if it was his fault.

"You gave me drugs? Are you crazy?" Sarah asked, her anger starting to return.

"Calm down, and it wasn't me, the agents who found you did. You were in shock. They were just trying to help," he replied, his voice taking on his infamous dictatorial tone. Sarah sighed.

"Sorry, I can't seem to think straight. I remember now, I do. Well, some things, anyway. Care to fill me in on the rest?" she asked hopefully.

"Later. When you're recovered a bit. Right now, we're going to get off this plane and head to a beautiful place in the hills where we can rest, recuperate and do a little planning." Sarah nodded and smiled softly.

"I'm too tired to argue, and I'm starving. So okay as long as we're going to do some eating too." She stood up and took a step, faltering. Sam quickly grabbed her to steady her.

"Maybe you should hold on to me for support," he suggested.

"It's fine, I'm fine, just give me a sec," Sarah replied stiffly. She hated being out of control. It's why she didn't drink too much. Or take pills of any kind. Feeling steadier, she let go and began to move slowly towards the back, where Grace now had Addy up and was gathering her things together. Seeing

Sarah reaching out with both arms, Grace handed Addy over without comment. She smiled, then, and turned away.

"Grace?" Sarah called softly. Grace turned back around.

"Yes, Sarah, are you feeling better?"

"Mmm hmm, yes, but I just want to say thanks. I don't quite remember everything, but I know you were steady as a rock and we wouldn't have gotten through this without you. Though I'm not clear on what it was all about yet, or exactly what happened. I guess I'm still fuzzy."

"It'll all work itself out, dear," Grace replied turning back to pick up the last of the things she'd left in the back.

"You say that too much, you know that?" Sarah muttered to herself. Looking down at Addy, wriggling in her arms, she smiled though. "Hey, precious, how are you?" she cooed. Addy giggled and her face lit up. "You ready to get off this silly plane, hmm?" Sarah went on. "I know I am!" Turning around, she headed towards the front, where everyone seemed to have gathered. Sam stood, waiting for her, a smile on his face. As she drew near, he took a few steps towards them, his eyes first on Sarah, then on Addy.

"Hey little bit, how's my girl?" He used the same crooning voice Sarah had heard earlier, when he'd spoken to her. A stab of hope went through her. It was a caring voice, reserved for those Sam treasured. Like Addy. Maybe like her? She watched his face as he was busy wiggling Addy's finger back and forth, and making funny faces. He was something, Sarah thought. Perfect. He was perfect. Then it struck her like a bolt of lightning. He was perfect all right, a perfect prince. And he wouldn't have much use for her now, except maybe to stay with Addy. Was this a bloodline thing? Was Addy a true princess? What would that mean for her? For Sarah?

Sam lifted his head to gaze back at Sarah.

"You ready?" She nodded, afraid to speak.

"Good. I need to warn you though, when we get off the plane, there might be a little, let's say, hoopla. I don't want you to be surprised."

"I know, Sam, I remember..." Sarah's voice was disturbingly soft and reserved. Sam could see the look in her eyes, as well. She wasn't angry, no, but she looked sad. Most women, he thought, would be ecstatic. They'd be thinking they'd landed a gold mine. So why did she look so unhappy. Maybe after they'd talked, later, she'd feel better.

"Shall we go?" he took her arm gently.

"Don't you need to go out first, or is it last?" Sarah asked. "You probably don't want to be walking down the steps with me on your arm," Sarah went on, not waiting for his reply. "There's probably paparazzi out there, and TV cameras too. You might give them the wrong impression." Sarah was talking so fast Sam was afraid to interrupt. He grinned slowly.

"My problem, not yours. I don't want you falling head first on the tarmac. In fact, why don't you let me hold Addy, just to be safe." Something in his voice, and the grin on his face, was suspicious. Sarah knew he was up to something. After the last few months, she'd gotten pretty damn good at reading him.

"What are you up to?" Sarah asked pointedly.

Sam put on his most innocent look.

"Up to? Not a thing," he replied haughtily. "Time's wasting, hand her to me and we'll deplane."

Sarah did as he asked, though with reservations, and turned to see everyone had already left the plane. They'd be last off. She knew if she got off the plane with him, and he was holding Addy, not her, the impression would be clear. The whole world would assume she and Sam were an item, more than an item. She wasn't sure how she'd feel about that, but Sam certainly didn't care. He couldn't be that oblivious not to realize the consequences. In fact, she was sure he knew just what he was doing. Of course! Now that he was officially a prince, every single woman in the world would be after him. Self-preservation, that was it. Sam was using her to keep the wolves at bay. Of all the nerve, she thought. But she wasn't going to make a scene here, now, in public. She'd wait until later, then give it to him with both barrels.

She was right of course, the minute they exited the plane and came down the steps, she was blinded by the flashes of photographers' bulbs. Two facing rows of royal guards were lining the tarmac, and music was being played in the background. Must be the national anthem, thought Sarah as she kept her eyes focused straight ahead, her arm linked with Sam's as they walked through the aisle between the guards, and headed for one of the limos waiting in front of a small terminal. Obviously this was not the main airport, but an airstrip reserved for the monarchy. As Sam buckled Addy into a waiting car seat, Sarah was ushered around to the other side and slid into her seat. Not even given time to look about, she felt like she was being whisked away to another world. She tried to peer out the window, but the crowd of people there blocked any view she might have. She turned away as she heard Sam slip into the other side and buckle his seatbelt. He smiled reassuringly at her and reached over to touch her cheek gently.

"We'll be there soon. Stop worrying, you'll get permanent wrinkles," he chuckled, and withdrew his hand. Sarah looked back out the window and felt the tears coming back. So he thought she was too old? Was she getting wrinkles all ready? She chided herself mentally. He was joking. She knew that. Her mom used to say that. But why was she so bothered. This was silly. No, it wasn't. It bothered her simply because she had no idea what came next. Did Sam care for her? Or were his feelings more wrapped up with her as Addy's guardian. Did he only care because of that? Did she mean anything to him at all? She gazed out the window, trying to see what she could through the watery tears. An ocean. Blue, crystalline, palm trees, small villas dotting the landscape. Beautiful. She imagined herself down on the white sandy beach, dipping her toes in the water. And Sam, with her. Suddenly a blazing image appeared in her mind. The kiss. That day in his study. She'd never had a real chance to analyze it. Sure, she'd spoken to Donna. Donna! Oh lord. She turned her head quickly around to see Sam watching her. But she didn't have time to react.

"Sam, where's Donna. I haven't even thought. What happened to her? Shouldn't she be here?" her voice was panicked, and she tried hard to control her breathing. Through all of this she hadn't given a single thought to the one person she considered a true friend. She felt guilty, and ashamed, and frightened that something had happened.

"She's fine, Sarah, in fact more than fine. She's probably sitting at her desk, in the office, trying to adjust to her new position."

"New position?" Sarah asked, again, suspicion in her voice.

"Yes. President of Livingston Consulting," Sam smiled smugly.

"But... but that's my job! Sam, you gave her my job?" Her voice was high pitched, incredulous. Not because she was angry at Donna. She knew her to be quite capable, and highly intelligent. She remembered being surprised to learn that Donna had settled for an EA job when she had an MBA from Brown, and had taken only 4 years to complete her education. But it was Sarah's job. How could he just replace her with no warning?

"You quit, remember?" Sam replied calmly. Sarah realized with sudden clarity she had. She had quit. And now she was riding in the back of a limo with a prince. Unemployed. Basically homeless. And not a clue as to what would happen to her.

CHAPTER 23

Sarah stood on the balcony, overlooking the water. It was stunning. The whole island was. She'd never seen such a beautiful place. The soft palms swayed in the gentle breeze, the waves lapping at the shore. So this was Chamandia she mused. Tropical paradise. She knew she could learn to love it here. She gnawed gently on her bottom lip as she realized once more, she had no idea whether she'd be staying or going. She hadn't seen Sam since they'd arrived, and he'd sent a young woman to assist her. Her very own ladies' maid. Her name was Chara, and she'd lived here in the royal residence her entire life. Her job was to attend to Sarah's needs. Whatever they may be. So far, she'd brought her here to her room, which was not in the guest wing, as she'd originally thought. After Chara had begun unpacking, she began chatting. The room she was in was part of the royal family's private suite. The royal compound, which she learned was never to be referred to as a palace, consisted of 4 complete wings, adjoined at the corners by walkways. They each overlooked a central courtyard, where the family would, in the past, gather for meals or entertain. The courtyard appeared to Sarah to be more of a garden of Eden, however.

Lush with colorful, fragrant tropical plants, it had little stone walkways throughout, and a clearing in the center, to accommodate parties she supposed. Her room had a balcony which overlooked the courtyard on one side, running the span of the entire wing, and a private balcony on the other side, overlooking the ocean. It was perfect. The room had been meant for just her, with Grace and Addy next door, however Sarah had insisted that Addy be with her for the first few nights, to which the staff had agreed and moved the crib into her room. In fact, the staff seemed to be quite agreeable to anything she said. She felt completely welcome, and completely at home.

But she wasn't sure of her purpose here. Would she be allowed to remain as Addy's guardian? Turn into the spinster Aunt? Would Grace be welcome as well? Or would Sam's new obligations force him to send them back to the states, giving him the freedom to choose a wife suitable for his new role. Wife. Sarah's fluent French came in handy in the compound. She heard the staff whispering among themselves about just this subject. Over and over she heard them. He'll be marrying now. He needs an heir. He'll have to marry her. When's the wedding? Sarah didn't know yet who they were talking about, but it rankled her just the same. Perhaps someone had been preselected, perhaps at birth, for him. She felt her eyes water and realized that she was being foolish. She wasn't in the running, anyway. Sam barely seemed to like her, much less have strong feelings. He certainly hadn't thought much of their one brief kiss. While the effect on her had been overwhelming, he seemed totally nonplussed. After all, he seemed to be making a point of one kind or another. He certainly didn't seem to be overly attracted to her.

She wiped the tears away with one hand, while still more built up. She had for those few moments on the plane, thought he'd come to care for her. He'd called her sweetheart. And he'd stroked her hair. Held her in his lap.

But of course, he was an absolute prince, wasn't he? She shook her head sadly and turned as she heard voices drifting out from an open window. She took several steps towards the edge of the balcony, trying to hear them. Sam, she'd know his voice anywhere. The other voice was unrecognizable. It was a deep, male voice, but quiet, as if the volume were deliberately being kept low.

"Next Saturday will be fine, sir," Sam's voice was formal, yet there was warmth in it. He must be talking to Rolf, Sarah thought.

"Good. Good. I'm glad that's settled then, and will Sarah be agreeable do you think?"

"Yes, well, she will be, I'm sure."

"Is everything in place for the wedding ceremony?"

"Yes."

"Do you have your mother's ring?"

"Yes, and I'm thinking since we have her dress maybe she'll wear it."

"We've all been waiting a long time, son, you know that."

"Yes sir, I know."

Son? No, not his father, she knew that. Just an expression. Maybe an older cousin of some sort. How was Sam a prince? She couldn't seem to sort through that one.

"I expect an heir and a spare out of this deal, you realize?" Sarah heard Sam chuckle. "Yes sir, I think we can manage that, at least I'll give it my best try!" Then she heard him laugh. And the other voice laughed too.

Damn him! The rumors were true. He was getting married. And from the sound of it, it's been planned for a long time, she thought. She knew now, this wouldn't work. She'd have to leave. She couldn't stay here, and be near him, day after day, knowing he'd be out of reach to her. There was Addy to consider. She needed a real home. With two parents. And if she wasn't to be part of that family, it would be best for her to go. Home. She'd go home. Come back a few times a year to visit. Sam would surely fly her over when necessary. Maybe that's what Rolf had been talking about, her being agreeable to allowing Addy to stay. Brushing the remaining tears from her eyes, she turned back toward the crib where Addy now slept. Her golden ringlets framed an angelic looking face. She was beautiful. And deserved to be a princess. She deserved more than Sarah could give. She'd do this for Addy.

She heard a tapping at the other door and turned. The courtyard balcony entrance was glass, and with the drapes open she could clearly see who it was. And she wasn't prepared. But she smiled and waved him in. Sam stood in the entry, watching her, noticing the strange expression on her face. Seeing Addy sleeping, he kept his voice low.

"I thought maybe we could talk now, if you're up to it," he said softly.

"Sure, yes, that's fine." Sarah was obviously distracted, but Sam forged on anyway.

"Shall we sit?" he asked.

"I'd rather not, if you don't mind, but you go right ahead," she said waving one hand towards the sofa.

"No, I mean, Sarah please, sit with me." Sam suddenly felt awkward. She sighed and resigned herself to sit as far away from him as possible, seating herself in the corner, tucking her legs under her and crossing her arms. Sam knew enough about body language to get the message.

"OK, where to begin," Sam muttered half to himself as he sat down at the other end of the sofa. Clearly following her signals. "Do you want me to start at the beginning? I suppose I should," he continued without waiting, proceeding to relate the background leading up to the kidnapping. He hoped she'd understand now why the secrecy was so important. He was also leery of her reaction to some of what he would say. She may understand, but she would be furious nonetheless.

"I believe we left off our history lesson with Rolf, right?" Sam couldn't remember how much he'd told her.

"I didn't know it was a history lesson, but yes. His father Lance died and he was crowned as a toddler?"

"Right. Well initially suspicions about his father's death fell on Johann de Guerre, however nothing could be proven. He died about 15 years ago, however, so at least we knew he could not have been involved with the deaths of Rolf's family. Or the latest attempt on Rolf's life." Sam paused, checking to see if Sarah was still following along. Satisfied that he had her undivided attention, he went on.

"Enter Antonio Donofrio. When Greg first met him, he sensed something. Nothing he could pinpoint, just had a hunch, and did a little checking. His real name is John de Guerre. A descendant of the de Guerre line. The last of them, in fact. His meeting Greg and Megan and striking up a friendship was no coincidence. It was all carefully orchestrated. Luckily, we knew early on."

"What attempt?" Sarah jumped in.

"Pardon?" Sam lost his train of thought.

"I said what attempt on Rolf's life?"

"Oh," Sam shrugged as if it were all so obvious. "Sorry, I forgot you were out of it on the plane when we discussed it. Rolf has been slowly being poisoned with arsenic over the last few months. An old buddy of Antonio's it seems, who was hired as a cook last year. There was an arrest two days ago. That's why I couldn't follow you to the cabin. I wasn't deserting you, Sarah, never." He had to get that out. Even if she wasn't quite paying attention.

"Why would he murder Rolf? Or anyone else? And his father a murderer too? For revenge? It seems very odd, I don't get it." Sarah burst in, intensely curious.

"To gain the crown. His father's intent was to wipe out the Christophs, and he'd ingrained that into his son as well. With Rolf gone, Antonio was intending to step in and take over as the only legitimate heir to Chamandia. Except for me, of course. That's why they kidnapped you Sarah. They wanted to draw me out to get rid of me. You see, several years ago, he somehow discovered the American branch of the Christoph family. And began plotting."

"American branch? Could you back up on that one Sam? Or can you fast forward to the part that makes you a prince please? I have vague memories of Antonio yelling and waving a gun around and saying he was next in line, but that's all a bit fuzzy still." As curious as Sarah was, he could see now an utter sadness had overtaken her. Most women would be elated, he thought to himself.

"Sorry," Sam smiled softly and went on. "Where was I, oh yes, the American Branch," Sam said absently. Sarah sat up, unfolding her arms, and looked at Sam suddenly, her eyes shining.

"I've got it!" she burst out. "It all makes sense now," she went on without waiting for a response. "You are a Christoph, somehow, I haven't gotten that part straight yet, but it's your middle name. I saw it on TV, I remember. And you are next in line. And Donna. I get it now. She was always supposed to have my job, wasn't she? You trusted her from the get-go, which means you know her far better than you let on." Sarah suddenly stopped talking, as it became clearer. "I guess I should have known." Her voice trailed off with a sadness in it. "I hope she's not too mad at me, or you, um, you know," she finished.

"I know what?" Sam was intrigued, knowing whatever Sarah was thinking was way off base.

"The kiss. Remember? Of course you don't, meaningless to you. Not to me, though and I told her. But of course I had no idea, oh no, Sam." Sarah's eyes widened. "There is no Andy, is there, I mean you're him. I mean the baby," she was stammering now. It was all so obvious. "I threw a kink in all your plans, didn't I. If I hadn't been around, this would all be settled, wouldn't it?" She covered her mouth with both hands as if trying to absorb all of what she herself was saying.

"Sarah, be quiet." Sam's voice was bemused. "No more talking. No more interruptions. Just listen, for once," he smiled at her, his eyes softening.

"Rolf is my uncle. My mother Adelaide's twin," he paused so that could sink in, watching as her expression went from flustered to curious to finally, the dawn of realization. He had her attention now.

"Addy..." she whispered softly. Sam nodded.

"Yes, I imagine you wondered where the name came from," Sam mused. Sarah started to speak, but Sam held a finger over her lips to silence her.

"Hold that thought. As I was saying, when Rolf and my mother were born, my grandmother knew they were the target of someone's wrath, and understood that to preserve the Principality, they'd have to ensure the Christoph line survived. Only those attending the birth knew of my mother's existence. She was whisked off in secrecy to the U.S. and raised as the adopted daughter of a nice middle-class couple in Westchester. Over the years, they would return, under one pretense or another, to Chamandia so that Rolf could get to know his sister, and my grandmother could spend time with her. My mother told no one except my father of course. We're still not sure how Antonio got the information, but he did. And that's when he hatched his latest plan." Sam stopped for a moment, gathering his strength to continue.

"May I speak now?" Sarah was bursting at the seams and didn't wait for his consent. "I need to ask, what happened to your parents Sam? I mean you never said."

The next part was disturbing, and Sam knew it might shake Sarah up too much.

"They died in a plane crash 10 years ago. Engine failure."

"I'm sorry, Sam. I know what that's like, to lose your parents suddenly like that. I lost mine to a drunk driver. But the plane crash, that wasn't an accident was it, Sam." Sarah knew instinctively there was more.

"No. And Greg's death was no accident either, Sarah." Sam forged ahead, glancing at Sarah's face to see how she was reacting. So far so good.

"I guess I'd somehow known that," Sarah said quietly, the truth adding only to the sadness enveloping her.

"There's more." Sam took a deep breath and went on. "We don't believe Megan's death was an accident Sarah. It's possible her IV contained a blood thinner, which caused her death." He stopped talking and slid over to her and gathered her in his arms. This would be the breaking point, he sensed. He felt her body shudder and knew to give her a few minutes. Sarah didn't know how long they'd sat there in silence, but she had a growing awareness of Sam's arm no longer holding her in comfort, but caressing her now. She jerked away, wanting him desperately, but not wanting him. Because he was already taken.

"What?" Sam looked surprised, and hurt.

"Nothing," Sarah replied, a little too defensively.

"You hate me, don't you. You blame me for all this." Sam's voice was tinged with sadness. "I can't say you're wrong. It is my fault. All of it. I should have handled things better. Maybe if Greg had told me about the baby, I could have been there. Done something."

"No Sam, I don't blame you. Never you. It's not your fault. You had no control over any of it."

"Then why did you just pull away from me like I had the plague?" Sam was baffled. Sarah shook her head and looked at him sadly.

"Because Sam, that didn't feel like comfort you were giving me, and it's wrong. I know about the wedding," she sighed and turned away, waiting for his explanation. Though it made sense now. He'd be marrying Donna. When he didn't say anything, she turned back to look, and found him smiling, as if he were enjoying her discomfort.

"What?" Sarah asked. "You look as if all this is somehow amusing you."

"It is," he replied, smiling still. "So what is it you know about the wedding?"

"That you'll be getting married next Saturday. That your uncle approves. That he's waited for this for a long time." Sarah was close to tears, but couldn't let him see. "Oh. And you have a dress for her. Though I have to say, Sam, I don't think it's going to fit unless it's been sized for someone who's 8 months pregnant," she smiled in spite of her pain. She couldn't help it. Worst of all, she really liked Donna, so she couldn't even hate her for marrying Sam.

"You heard us talking," he said matter of factly.

"Yes."

"And just who am I marrying, Sarah?"

She rolled her eyes at him, half in anger, half in frustration.

"Don't be an ass, it doesn't become you. You're marrying Donna, and I gather you always were intending to marry her. Which of course is why getting married so quickly makes sense. With the baby and all. You'd probably be married already if it weren't for Addy and me." Sarah's voice was wistful. She had to keep going though, had to get it out.

"I've made a decision, Sam," Sarah went on. He hadn't said a word about her last little speech, so now was perfect timing.

"What's that, Sarah," Sam replied, still obviously amused.

"I'm going to leave, go back home. Addy will stay here with you. You and Donna will be good parents to her, I know, and she deserves two parents, a stable home." Her voice was cracking, and tears were escaping down her cheek, but she couldn't help it. And she had to finish this.

"Not to mention she is royal, but I won't fight you on this. It's for the best. But you have to agree to let me come visit her, a few times a year at least. And you have to pay for it." She held her breath, trying to control her shudders, waiting for him to say something. Anything. She could feel her heart breaking into a zillion pieces, and stealing a glance at him, realized he didn't even look fazed. He was just sitting there, smiling, his eyes practically dancing with merriment. Mischief.

Without warning, he lifted a hand and brushed a tear from her cheek.

"Are you through?" he asked, his voice soft, filled with warmth.

"Yes, sorry. Maybe you could just give me a few minutes, Sam," she turned away. She couldn't take another minute of this.

"No." Sam's reply was brief, and he chuckled.

"Please, Sam, I'm not in the mood for your royal dictates."

"Tough. You had your turn, now it's mine."

Sarah looked at him, this time noticing that while he was seemingly cheerful, there was a hint of nervousness in his expression. He was tense about something.

"Donna is my cousin, Sarah, so even if I wanted to, which I don't, I couldn't marry her." Sarah's eyes widened. "Second. Andy is the father of Donna's baby, and," he checked his watch, "should be with Donna right about now!"

Sarah waited, but Sam said nothing more.

"Then who are you marrying? I have a right to know since whoever it is will care for Addy. I want to meet her. Tell me about her!" Sarah was angry, and embarrassed and words were just tumbling out of her mouth.

"I think you'll like her, actually," Sam replied, quite smugly.

"Tell me."

"OK. Let's see. She's about," he raised one hand as if measuring height. "About your height. And weight. Very very smart. But stubborn. Maybe too stubborn. And her temper well, hopefully we can reign that in a bit," he chuckled and lifted a hand to smooth stray curls from her face.

"Is she good in bed?" Sarah clamped her hand over her mouth. She didn't mean to say that out loud. It just came out. Her face flushed as she stammered an apology. "Sorry, that was out of line," she mumbled the words, trying to hide her face.

"Yes, it was, Sarah. As I was saying," he went on with some amusement in his voice. He was beginning to realize that the sedative really hadn't quite worn off all the way and she wasn't quite as sharp as usual. In fact he was certain she wasn't really catching on at all. This was going way better than expected.

"I need a wife who can be my partner in everything. That means not only being the perfect mom for Addy, and the perfect wife for me, but a perfect leader in her own right for the people here. It's quite a demanding list in fact. I just hope she's willing to take it on."

He was looking at her with an odd expression, waiting for her to say something. His blue eyes seemed to pierce her heart. He was so handsome, she thought. And oh so taken. Yet, she had an odd feeling in the pit of her stomach and felt the hair on her neck tingle. Something still wasn't right. She wanted to ask more, but somehow, didn't know what to say. Her name. What was her name? Where was she from? How did Sam know this woman? But she just sat there, staring back. She just couldn't seem to speak. Sam suddenly seemed to look younger, almost boyish, and vulnerable. There was a question in his eyes, but she couldn't figure it out. What on earth did he want from her? Her blessing? Not in this lifetime. She was torn between bolting out of the room and throwing herself in his arms and begging him not to marry this girl. He looked away suddenly and cleared his throat.

"One last thing. In Chamandia, royal proposals are um, public. Not private. And obviously I haven't had a chance yet to do that, so, my bride doesn't actually know she's a bride yet."

"What? I mean Sam, you're telling me you are going to get married in like 2 weeks, to a woman who has no idea she's getting married?"

"Well when you put it that way." Sam looked a bit sheepish.

"What if she says no?" Sarah didn't know what possessed her to push his buttons like this.

"Chance I'll have to take," he replied with a shrug. "I'm, uh, going to go dress for dinner. I'll stop by and get you and Addy in about an hour. We'll eat in the courtyard." He didn't look back at her as he stood and strode toward the door. "And for the record, Sarah, it wasn't meaningless. Not to me," he tossed over his shoulder as he left.

CHAPTER 24

She'd be at dinner. She was probably Chamandian. Probably chosen from birth. Or maybe he met her while he was here on business or visiting his uncle. She was probably wealthy, born to be a princess. She'd be dressed to the nines too. She just knew he was going to propose to someone tonight. That's why he was warning her ahead of time. So she would be prepared. What was she going to do? Pull yourself together, Sarah chided herself. She knew that she hadn't been wrong about the attraction. Sam was attracted to her. Wait. What if Chamandians had some sort of weird customs? What if he assumed she'd simply stay and be some sort of Royal Consort? Well that wasn't going to happen. If he were going to marry someone else, she'd be on the next plane home. And tonight she'd show him just how much he'd be missing without her.

Her spirits revived, Sarah began the slow tedious transformation from desperate, lonely, and dumped to chic, independent and nonchalant. She browsed through the closet and found a beautiful emerald green cocktail dress with an empire waist and low-cut bodice, while noticing once again all the clothes hanging were her size. No tags this time though. Lifestyles of the Rich and Famous she supposed. Perfect for what she had in mind. She arranged her curls to fall loosely around her face, and put only a dab of makeup on. She wanted to appear just as worthy of being chosen to be a princess as Sam's intended bride, whoever the witch was. Sarah wasn't normally vindictive, and if she thought for one moment that Sam was deeply in love with this woman, she'd politely bow out of the scene.

She wouldn't do anything till she saw for herself. She'd know just by how they react to each other. It was a wait and see game. And she was ready. If she didn't like this woman from the get-go, she would do anything and everything to stop the wedding. Or take Addy with her. She wouldn't allow Addy to be raised in a home without love. Not just love for Addy, but love between her parents. Sarah had known a house full of love, and she wanted that for Addy too.

She turned as she heard footsteps approaching, the sound echoing through the open door. Her eyes widened in surprise.

"Donna! I don't believe it! What are you doing here?" Sarah rushed over to the doorway and pulled her friend in for a bear hug. "It's so good to see you. But I thought, no I'm sure Sam said Andy was on his way back to you or with you."

Donna laughed as she disentangled herself from Sarah. "He's right here, don't worry." Sarah looked beyond Donna's shoulder and saw a tall, lanky man with a mop of red hair and a big grin. She automatically grinned back and stepped towards him.

"So you're Andy! I'm really happy to finally meet you!" She gave him a quick hug, and smiled as Donna stepped back towards him, and he laid his arm across her shoulders. They looked perfect, she thought, sighing. Just perfect.

"So why are you here?" she asked again. "Isn't it dangerous for you? I'd think you'd want to stick close to home, in your condition!"

"What and miss the wedding?" Donna smiled, no trace of sympathy.

Sarah narrowed her eyes. Donna knew about her feelings for Sam, or should have, so she should have been more tactful she thought.

"You knew?" Sarah asked, a bit miffed.

"Of course. You've spoken to Sam, right? He told you?"

"Oh, yes, about you being cousins? Does that make you royal too? I didn't even ask!"

Donna laughed and shook her head. "No, afraid not. I'm a Livingston not a Christoph! I know I should have told you, but I simply couldn't. It was tearing me up, believe me."

"No worries, Donna, I get it. I think. There's just so much to unpack in all this, and I'm still a little fuzzy about it all." Sarah sighed, feeling a sense of sadness overtake her.

"Are you okay with all this, Sarah? You don't look too thrilled."

"Why would I be happy about this?" Sarah asked, her voice trembling a bit. "How can you even ask me that?"

Donna pursed her lips and shared a suspicious look with Andy.

"Uh oh. I sense a problem here," she murmured quietly.

"You could say that!" Sarah's spunk seemed to have returned. "I haven't even met this woman. I mean Donna, you realize that whoever she is she's going to be Addy's mom. How could he not tell me about her? How could you not tell me about her?" Sarah looked pointedly at her friend, waiting for answers. "Who is she Donna, you must know, you seem to know just about all of it. Help me out here, as a future mom yourself, you owe me that much!"

Donna sighed deeply, and her expression was now filled with sympathy.

"I'm so sorry, Sarah, I hadn't realized things were this way. Sam assured me everything was fine. I had no idea you were, um, well, that you weren't completely aware of everything. I wish I could explain, but I think it has to come from Sam." Donna squeezed Sarah's shoulder lightly. "Just hang in there, OK? Why don't you get Addy and bring her down for dinner. Grace is down there already. In fact, most of the guests are."

"Sam was supposed to come get me. I guess he forgot, or maybe he has to officially escort the little woman down to dinner." Sarah tried to keep her tone light but the sarcasm bit right through.

Donna tried to smother a laugh at the 'little woman' remark.

"No, he's down there already and he didn't forget, I just wanted to see you first!"

Feeling a bit mollified, Sarah smiled sadly, and turned to get Addy from the crib.

"Come on pumpkin," she said softly, lifting her up and snuggling her against one shoulder. "Let's go face the music, eh? Meet your new mama," her voice broke as she whispered in Addy's ear. "And if I don't like her, we'll run away, k?"

She turned slowly back to Donna and Andy, who'd remained silent the whole time. But he also still wore the silly grin he'd been wearing since she laid eyes on him. Either he'd had too much to drink, or he was a little off in the head, she thought. Shaking her head in wonder, she closed the door to the room and followed them along the balcony to the steps leading to the courtyard. Just as she was trying to contemplate navigating the staircase holding onto Addy she was relieved to see Chara appear, offering to carry her down.

Sarah gazed in awe before heading down. It was still light, but the sun was setting, and tiki lamps were lit along the pathways, and lanterns hung strung up from palm tree to palm tree. The stunning flowers and shrubs scattered about cast off beautiful colors under the glow of the lanterns, and it almost seemed surreal. Once in the courtyard, she saw a few dozen people milling about, none of whom she recognized, except Grace, whom she spotted standing by a table laden with food. She couldn't yet see what was there, but there were platters and bowls overflowing with something. She didn't really have an appetite though the table was beautifully set she realized as she approached. It was long, very long, with seating for at least 15 people on each side. Beautiful floral arrangements placed at intervals that would allow every guest to see each other, and no view would be blocked. The chair at the far end, she noticed, was definitely different than the others. Taller, more ornate, must be Rolf's, or now Sam's, she thought wryly.

Taking Addy back from Chara, she approached the table, noticing many of the guests seemed to be staring at her. Hoping it was Addy they were interested in, she tried to avoid their gazes, her eyes roving, searching for Sam and his intended. She wanted to meet her, and get this over with, before they sat down to eat. She spotted him, over to the side, how she could have missed him earlier she couldn't imagine. He seemed to tower above everyone, his presence overwhelming. She looked away before he noticed her and let her gaze roam over the waiting guests. She frowned as she realized there were very few women who might fit the bill. Most were older and accompanied by someone. Her gaze rested on a younger woman; her head tilted away as she listened attentively to an older man speaking to her. His hand resting lightly on her back. Maybe her. And that's her father, Sarah decided. Wearing a simple ivory cocktail dress, her brown hair neatly falling to her shoulders, she seemed a bit too prim and proper Sarah thought. Librarian? Rocket Scientist? Heiress? Whatever, she was probably just his type. Cold. Unimaginative. Dull. Between being sedated and jet lagged and missing her sister horribly at this point, she couldn't seem to avoid the snarkiness overtaking her. Donna and Andy had drifted away, so she decided to suck it up and to approach the pair, see if she couldn't get a word in. Find out if it was her. Well, she thought, I should at least see what she's like.

She walked towards them, smiling, hoping they'd introduce themselves. She wasn't disappointed. As she approached the woman turned and smiled.

"You must be Sarah, I'm so glad to meet you!" she exclaimed. "I've heard so much about you," she went on. "I'm Genevieve, as I'm sure you've guessed!" Sarah kept the smile plastered on her face and nodded. Nope, she didn't have a clue.

"Oh, isn't she cute," said Genevieve, gazing now at Addy. "Daddy, look at her, she's precious," she went on. Turning her attention back to Sarah, she smiled broadly. "We're all so excited you're here. It's going to be a wonderful evening, don't you think?"

Sarah didn't think so at all. But she smiled graciously, as graciously as she could under the circumstances. And knew she simply had to get away.

"Will you excuse me?" she said suddenly. "I've just remembered something," she turned quickly and hurried over to Grace. Genevieve was actually nice. Too nice. Sarah wanted to hate her but just couldn't. Maybe a palm tree would fall down in the middle of the courtyard and disrupt the evening. Or a tsunami would arrive just in the nick of time to stop Sam from proposing.

"Sarah, what on earth?" Grace gave Sarah a knowing look as she reached out to take Addy and hold her for a bit.

"What?" Sarah really had no clue what Grace was so shocked about.

"Goodness child, you really need to get a grip. I know what you're thinking, and you just perish the thought." Sarah grinned as she realized Grace must have sensed the little mean-spirited idea that had just popped into her head. The little vision she'd conjured up of Sam falling face first into a punch bowl. Maybe having a little help along the way.

"Sorry, Grace, but have you met her? I mean really, I don't stand a chance," she whispered.

"I believe that's the British Ambassador's daughter," Grace chuckled.

Sarah rolled her eyes.

"Oh, fine. Well then who? I mean surely you can sense can't you? I just don't see anyone else who possibly fits the bill," she continued to speak in a hushed tone.

"Don't you worry about it Sarah. You'll find out soon enough. I'm surprised you haven't already, though," Grace mused.

"You know, Grace, I really thought you were on my side, but I begin to suspect you're somehow one of Sam's little secrets too." Sarah was teasing, and Grace knew it.

"No dear, I'm not. And everyone has secrets. Even you." She looked pointedly at Sarah, who was confused by the remark. What secret? Sarah had been honest from day one, hadn't she? There were only a few things Sam didn't know about her, and he really didn't have the right to know anyway.

The sound of children's laughter came drifting over, and Sarah looked over to see the Abbotts with their 4 kids in tow. Smiling, Sarah waved to Carol, hoping to find an ally. Carol waved, and returned the smile, but didn't approach. She was busy with the kids, keeping them in check, and Sarah sighed, wishing she didn't feel so alone.

A chime suddenly rang, signaling the guests should take their seats. She watched the guests drift toward the table. Taking Addy back from Grace, unsure of where they were to sit, she looked around for place cards, but none were there. She jumped as Sam suddenly came up behind her, startling her.

Taking her arm, he murmured softly.

"You'll sit down here at this end." He led her towards the chair at the end, directly to his left. She looked over her shoulder and saw Grace already being seated by one of the staff. Donna and Andy across from her. A high chair with a built-in infant seat had been placed at the corner of the table, between Sam and Sarah, and Sam reached to take Addy from her, seating and buckling her in, brushing his hand over her blond curls and smiling.

"You sit here, little princess," he said softly, making Sarah want to cry. He'd be such a good daddy, she thought. And such a good everything else. Damn, she had to get control. How could he do this to her? Seating her here where she would be under everyone's scrutiny, especially when he made his little announcement. Proposal. Whatever.

When all the guests were seated, there began a slow, steady drumming sound, steel drums, she thought. Looking around, she noticed a lone man off to the side, head bent, using his hands to generate the steady rhythm. She glanced back at Sam, curious.

"Nice, eh? You look beautiful by the way." He smiled warmly at her and took her hand in his. Alarmed, she tried to pull back.

"Steady, sweetheart, relax and enjoy. It's paradise, remember?" Nervously, Sarah began gnawing at her lip. Something was not right here. Was he being brotherly, or something more? Maybe he felt she was family, Addy's aunt after all, and he wanted to keep her near. Or maybe he was a lecherous soul deep down. No way. Sarah knew that much about him. Sam was almost naive when it came to women. She'd no doubt he'd certainly sown his oats, but being good in bed, and being good in a relationship were two entirely different things. Maybe he didn't realize what impression he was giving. Maybe he genuinely thought he was doing the right thing.

Maybe, just maybe, he had no clue how he was tearing her up inside.

She turned her attention away from his penetrating gaze. She was jumpy, and nervous, and the looks he was giving her were not, definitely not, OK. They burned her. If she didn't know better, she'd swear he was ready to jump her. If only.

Without warning, the drums stopped. Sam squeezed her hand gently and nodded towards the entrance to the courtyard. Sam tugged gently on her hand as he stood, indicating she should as well. She did so, as everyone at the table followed suit. A man entered the courtyard, and Sarah knew immediately it was Rolf. Dressed in a tailored suit, he was tall, like Sam, and very similar in looks. Though his hair was grayer, and he seemed thinner, weaker. She realized then that he was still recuperating. How could she have forgotten! He approached the table slowly, though with a regal grace. He had a kind face, she thought, suddenly wishing she'd had the chance to meet him before now. Standing at the other end of the long wooden table, he nodded at Sam, and then waved his hand to allow them to sit down again.

With his hands clasped behind his back, Rolf began to speak. His voice was clear and distinguished. Not quite formal, though, Sarah thought. He sounded almost like a wise man.

"Welcome all," he began. "Bienvenue à tous." He then continued in English, as not everyone at the table was fluent in French. "I am grateful that you could be here for this occasion. Tonight marks a special moment in Chamandian history. Tomorrow, a new Prince will be crowned. My nephew, Samuel Christoph Livingston, son of my sister, Adelaide Magdalena

Christoph." A soft murmur went through the table. Rolf waited a moment, then went on. "And we can mark the end we hope of what has been known as the Christoph Curse." This time the cheers were a bit louder. All those present knew that with the arrest of the last of the de Guerres, the family was safe from further harm. They hoped.

"As many of you are aware, it's also long past time for Samuel to choose himself a wife. With no interference from anyone I might add." Rolf smiled and chuckled softly. "And if he has even one ounce of Christoph blood running through his veins, we can be assured that he has indeed chosen with his heart. Probably the first time he laid eyes on her!"

With that, most of the guests joined him in laughing. For they all knew that Christophs were notorious for falling in love at first sight. The only one who didn't know this was Sarah. But she caught on quickly and realized that whoever it was wasn't even at the table yet. But there were no empty seats either. She looked around at the guests once more, but aside from Genevieve, none fit the bill. She wondered if he had even met her yet. Maybe she's a no-show. That would work.

She turned her gaze back to Rolf, who was about to speak again.

"Here's the sticky part, as my mother liked to say. Here in Chamandia we have one additional tradition. And it's a doozy. The chosen bride is always the last to know, and often in a very public way."

Sarah realized that's what Sam had been referring to. She stiffened as she realized all heads were turned in their direction, and Sam was again squeezing her hand. Rolf looked then at Sarah, and smiled softly, his eyes crinkling with warmth. She suddenly felt lightheaded and flushed. It couldn't be. It just couldn't. Sam let go of her hand suddenly and stood. Sarah kept her gaze down and wished to all the gods of embarrassing situations that she could be anywhere else. She felt like crawling under the table and hiding, but at the same time her heart was racing furiously. Was this it? Was she the one? She didn't want to believe it, because if she wasn't, she'd simply die. A slow torturous death. She was wishing for the moon knowing she'd just end up crashing down to earth.

Sam cleared his throat and nodded at his uncle, who returning the nod, took his seat. Sarah knew Sam was looking down at her bowed head. She stole a glance upward and saw him smiling gently, his big blue eyes dancing. She was too afraid to even move but couldn't take her eyes off him. Was this the point at which she woke up to discover it had all been a dream?

"Thank you my esteemed uncle, for sharing that bit of history with our guests. And yes, I have more than a little Christoph blood, it would seem, as I, like you, and my Grandfather before you, made my choice instantly. In fact, when I first saw her, I was a goner. Beautiful? Yes. Smart? Probably smarter than I am. Funny. Caring. And I don't believe I could ever imagine life without her by my side." He reached out and pulled her hand out from her lap, tugging gently. Looking up at him fully, his gaze nearly knocked her over. She didn't think she could stand up, and he seemed to know it, for he gently pulled her up and placed his arm around her waist to steady her. His eyes never left hers for a moment. "What do you say, Sarah? Are you game? Be my wife? Addy's mother? Be a real-life princess, and stay right here with me the rest of our lives? I mean, you can say no. You're free to live your life as you want to Sarah. But the fact is I love you, and I think you love me…"

Now if this had been a movie, and Sarah playing the leading lady, she would have thrown her arms around him and yelled "Yes!" at the top of her lungs. But it was real life. And Sarah for the first time in her life was speechless. She just stared at Sam, her eyes wide, her voice frozen. Lifting a finger to her chin, he tilted her head up.

"Maybe this will help," he whispered as he leaned down and kissed her. She felt like she was being tossed around in a tilt-a-whirl. Every one of her senses were reeling. She lost herself so completely in his kiss, she didn't hear the laughter and clinking of glasses. She didn't hear the chorus of congratulations. She didn't see the fireworks being set off on the beach, lighting up the sky. She saw and heard nothing, except Sam.

"Is that a yes?" He spoke with laughter in his voice as he pulled away to look at her face. She nodded once.

"That's a yes," she whispered, then threw her arms around his neck and pulled his mouth back down to hers. No way she'd had enough. She could go on like this all night. She could go on like this the rest of her life.

****

About the Author

When she's not making up stories to entertain herself with, MJ Miller can be found looking for ways to beat the southwestern heat. Usually traveling north to just about anywhere. Hobbies include baking chocolate things, eating chocolate things, and using a treadmill to remove the evidence. As the mother of two grown women she loves to write about daughters and sisters and all the tangled-up relationships they tend to have, always believing the road to a happy life is filled with laughter. She and her incredible husband reside in the balmy desert southwest with their Mensa qualifying cat, Darwin.

Other Books by MJ Miller

All About Annie

When Annie dives into a hot new bestseller she suddenly sees her life story come screaming off the pages. Every embarrassing moment memorialized page after page. Add a mysterious author, a ransacked apartment, an attempt on her life and an old flame, and Annie's life is in a free-fall. When fiction meets reality, will Annie finally get her happily ever after?